ISBN: 0-9766231-0-2
Published by Red Raptor Productions, Inc.
<u>BLOOD LEGACY: THE HOUSE OF ALEXANDER</u> Vol 1, 2005. FIRST PRINTING.
Office of Publication: 3250 Julian Avenue, Long Beach, CA 90808.
BLOOD LEGACY it's logo, all related characters and their likenesses are ™ and © 2005 Kerri
Hawkins and Red Raptor Productions, Inc.

What did you think of this book? We love to hear from our readers.

Please email us at: **khawkins@bloodlegacy.net.**

or, write to us at: **Blood Legacy c/o Red Raptor Productions, Inc. 3250 Julian Avenue, Long Beach,
CA 90808**.

BLOOD LEGACY:

THE HOUSE OF ALEXANDER

RED RAPTOR PRODUCTIONS, INC.

Also available from Kerri Hawkins

BLOOD LEGACY: THE STORY OF RYAN
(ISBN: 1-58240-248-5)

visit us on the web at
www.bloodlegacy.com

BLOOD

LEGACY

THE HOUSE OF ALEXANDER

by **KERRI HAWKINS**

CHAPTER 1

THE BAND OF MEN WERE AFRAID. Rough-hewn, dirty and tired, they nevertheless stayed close behind their young master. Many of them kept looking ahead, seeking out his fair hair in the shadow of the hill, seeking reassurance by his presence. This was odd because he appeared one of the youngest of the lot, and although as tall as any of the men, far more slender. The size of the sword he held in his hand offered some degree of explanation for the trust. It seemed nearly as large as the youth himself. He swung it easily, planting it in the dirt in front of him as he paused. The men stopped abruptly in response.

The boy, for he was little more than that, cocked his head to the side as if listening to something. The men strained, but could hear nothing. He turned back to gaze at his second-in-command, nodding grimly. Although the boy's face was startlingly beautiful, the eyes within that face were both ancient and frightening. He motioned to close ranks, and they began moving up the hill.

The band stopped on the rise, and although the men had been hardened by the last few days of horror, a few still vomited. The fair-haired one looked down on the valley below, his expression indecipherable.

There were bodies strewn everywhere, men, women, children, even animals. Some had been cut open, some had been strung up by their heels, some apparently had been beaten to death. Many were nearly unrecognizable as human, so badly mutilated were their features. The smell of death and decay wafted towards the band as the breeze shifted.

The youth glanced over at a nearby cow, who had been gutted and whose entrails were strewn about the ground, now attracting flies.

"I did not realize that cattle were Protestant."

The voice was smooth, melodious, and far too old for the youthful figure from which it came. The comment was incongruous and caused startled, nervous laughter from a few of the men nearby.

The second-in-command glanced over at his master. The grizzled man knew him better than perhaps anyone else in the band, but that was not saying much. "I think we should continue moving."

The boy nodded. "I agree. We are far from home, and in a country that has lost all sanity."

Days passed and the troop continued on. The scenes of carnage repeated themselves throughout the countryside. The band would occasionally get word from frightened peasants who relayed that the Church had declared war on all Huguenots. Some would zealously profess their loyalty to the Catholic Church, at least until they realized the band was not there to bring the Lord's justice, but was simply passing through.

The band would less frequently run into those perpetrating the carnage, but the zealots generally would give the well-armed troop of men a wide berth. Those who did not regretted their lack of judgment.

"You there, what is your business here and where do you stand in the eyes of God?"

The gray-haired man stopped at the voice behind him. He had been unaware of the horses as they approached, but knew that his master had not. That was evident by the fact the youth was nowhere to be seen.

The men in the band all turned towards the horses, eyeing the arms the mounted men carried.

"We are but friends passing through. We mean no harm and take no sides in matters of religion."

Even as the second-in-command finished the sentence, he winced, noticing the priestly garments the man on the horse wore.

"Everyone chooses sides. Either you are with the Church of Christ and the Blessed Virgin Mary, or you are a heathen and a traitor to God, worthy only of death."

"I am probably more worthy of death than anyone here," came a voice from the trees. "But that will not happen today."

The youth strolled from the forest, causing the men to turn upon their horses to see him. His presence caused the horses to stir, and a strange and alien fear stirred in the men as well.

The lead priest gazed down at the youth, feeling icy fingers along his spine. Something was not right. The boy possessed an unnatural beauty and moved with grace to match. He showed no fear, and if anything, displayed indifference to the heavily armed men. To the priest himself the boy was nearly contemptuous.

"Do you intend to butcher us as you have so many idolatrous cattle? I had no idea that heresy among farm animals was such a threat to the Catholic Church." The boy's voice hardened. "Not to mention the women and children that were tending those animals."

The priest's fear disappeared in apoplectic rage. "How dare you mock the Church and those who carry out God's will. You will pay for your insolence and your heresy."

The fair-haired youth bowed disdainfully. "Then by all means, follow your god's edict and strike me down."

The priest could barely contain the sputum frothing from his lips, so angry was he. He spurred his horse forward and it whinnied in protest as he brutally slapped its flanks.

What happened next would be repeated endlessly, the details changing with every retelling. But certain events would be consistent throughout. The priest rode forward at top speed, but did not ride very far. The youth, completely unafraid, languidly raised his hand and the horse responded by sliding to an abrupt halt. This vaulted the priest forward over the horse's head and into the air. In a seemingly impossible move and without apparent haste, the boy drew his sword and leveled it at the careening, airborne priest. In the ultimate irony, the priest's arms were thrown outward so that his body impaled itself upon the sword in the outline of a cross. Although the full weight of the priest was thrown forward into the youth, the youth did not budge and it appeared almost as if the flailing man had struck a wall.

The priest gazed into the youth's eyes in horror and disbelief. In a casual gesture, the boy reached up to fleck a speck of dust from the priest's collar. He then grasped the collar firmly, and pulled his sword from the cleric's torso. He dropped the dead man to the ground.

The boy turned to the men still on horseback. He lightly flipped the sword, then threw it with blinding speed at the man nearest him. It appeared to pass right through him and slice through a fair-sized tree, felling it to the ground. It was only after the sword came to rest with a "thunk" into a second tree that the man realized he had been cut in two.

The mounted men stared at the creature before them as their fatally wounded comrade fell from his horse. It was obvious that they were dealing with something far worse than a Protestant. When the boy genuflected towards them with an intense degree of sarcasm, the entire band turned their horses and fled.

The fair-haired one watched the dust cloud disappear. He was aware of the fear of his own men. It was finally his faithful second who approached.

"My lord, we should probably leave. Those men have fled in the direction that we must go and word will spread, making our passage difficult."

The youth turned his impenetrable gaze on the older man. "If I am a danger to the men, I can always leave."

Only the lieutenant would have dared rebuke the young lord, and even he proceeded gently. "You know we will be safer with you."

The young man relaxed, unaware he had been holding so much tension. "I am sorry, Galois. I just had bad experiences with priests when I was a child."

CHAPTER 2

THE SWORDS FLASHED BRIGHTLY in the daylight streaming through the trees. The two combatants were a contrast in both appearance and style. The man was taller, broad through the shoulders, dark-haired and wickedly handsome. He fought with amazing skill and strength, the power of his blows creating sparks with every contact.

The more slender of the pair was fair-haired and beautiful, with fine features and eyes of indeterminate color. He fought with impossible speed and ferocity to match that of his opponent. Although it appeared he should have been easily overpowered, he was instead easily holding his own.

Neither of the two appeared to be exerting any effort, their battle so equally matched it appeared a dance. It was only the din caused by the clashing metal and the occasional severed tree trunk that indicated the power of the match.

Perhaps it was this great noise that drowned out the approaching roar, but so engrossed were both participants in the battle, they failed to notice the low rumble heading towards them. It was with some surprise, then, that both turned to observe the rather incongruent sight of a BMW 740i careening around the corner and then coming straight at them.

The dark-haired one was not in the path of the racing vehicle, but his young companion was dead aim of the hood ornament. The car struck him at the knees, sending him toppling over the hood and smashing into the windshield, then vaulting up over the roof. The brake lights of the BMW came on and the tires squealed as the car skid to a stop.

The smoke settled and the dark-haired one thrust his sword into the ground. There was no horror or concern on his face, but rather a look of mild exasperation as he made his way to the crumpled body in the roadway. The boy groaned and turned over, and it was apparent for the first time that it was not a boy, but rather a striking young woman. The man helped the girl to her feet as she brushed herself off, seemingly untouched by the violent collision. They both turned as the driver of the BMW stepped out into the sunlight.

True to the oddity of the situation, the woman did not appear the least remorseful for running down the girl, although she did appear a bit amused. The woman, as stunning as the pair, was uniquely beautiful in her own way.

"That wasn't very funny, Marilyn," Victor said dryly, releasing his companion.

"You know," the raven-haired woman replied, "you two really should stop playing in the roadway." She peered closer at the young woman. "No cuts, how unfortunate."

Ryan smiled without humor. "Always looking out for my welfare, I see."

"Hmmm, yes," Marilyn said, her eyes lingering on the girl, then turning to her father. "That is in fact why I am here."

Victor gave one last look at Ryan, belying his studied lack of concern. "Then let us go inside."

Victor handed Marilyn a glass of port.

"There was a time when you would serve me more than wine, my lord," Marilyn said, settling into one of the study's overstuffed chairs.

Ryan cleared her throat from the doorway, and Marilyn did not miss a beat. "Or allow me other, unauthorized pleasures."

Ryan, after nearly six hundred years, still could not control an involuntary blush. How this woman could continue to affect her was beyond her understanding.

"The port is A. A. Ferreira Garrafeira, 1863," Ryan said. "I purchased it in Portugal when it was new."

"You always were one to defer your pleasure," Marilyn said.

Victor settled opposite Marilyn while Ryan chose to stand a safe distance away near the mantle of the fireplace. "So what brings you to our humble castle?" Victor asked, his tone of voice indicating he already knew at least some of what she was to say.

"Ancient enemies and new alliances, my lord," Marilyn said. "I don't believe that you and your offspring," she said with a pointed look at Ryan, "can settle into obscurity once again."

Victor nodded. That was one consequence of the trial he fully expected, but did not welcome. He gazed into the fire. Ryan had been tried and convicted, ironically enough, of his own murder. It had been by his design that the tribunal had been assembled, and it had served its purpose in reuniting him with his wayward child. But it had also brought to light issues that were not going to go away.

Victor turned his attention to the young woman standing by the mantle, who was young in appearance only. Ryan, as his sole progeny, had vaulted in status through their hierarchy, but not simply because Victor was the very Oldest of their Kind.

Ryan was uniquely powerful among them because she was the only one who had been born Changed. Although their Kind had all once been human, they had been Changed by the sharing of blood and were no longer capable of reproducing. They could Change other humans through the sharing of blood, but could no longer have children as their anatomy was radically altered by the transition.

Ryan was the exception, born to Victor and a human woman in the 14th century, Victor had accomplished the impossible. No one had known that Victor had a prodigy for the first 100 years of her life. He had kept her apart from the Others. And no one certainly knew the secret of Ryan's origin until six centuries later. Ryan herself had been oblivious to the circumstances of her birth until she began to sense it through Victor's Memories as they shared blood.

"I knew I shouldn't have killed you," Ryan said casually.

Victor's response was equally understated. "Tried, my dear. Only tried." He crossed one long leg over the other. "But I agree that the trial has stirred up issues that will not easily go away."

Marilyn was not finished with her news. "They have reassembled the Grand Council."

"What for now?" Ryan asked sarcastically, "Have they found something new to charge me with?"

Her father's response was calm. "I know they have reassembled."

Ryan turned to him. "Without your permission?"

"Without my permission, but not without my knowledge." Victor said.

Ryan frowned. "I have little interest in the affairs of the Others, and I have a feeling this conversation is going to do nothing but anger me. I will bid both of you adieu for the moment."

Ryan turned to leave, but out of the corner of her eye caught a movement that gave her pause. Victor ever-so-slightly winced, almost as if he were in pain. So imperceptible was his flinch that Marilyn did not notice even with preternatural senses.

But not only did Ryan see the flinch, she felt it as it went through her like a shock of electricity. So quickly did Victor recover, however, that Ryan thought she had imagined it. Marilyn noticed nothing and Victor continued their conversation, aware that Ryan was regarding him thoughtfully from the doorway. She finally turned away, walking down the hallway

With Ryan gone, Marilyn cut to the chase. "You know it is time."

Victor was calm. "Yes, I know."

"They *will* choose her," Marilyn said.

Victor gazed off after his departing child. "If they are so foolish to do so," he turned to Marilyn, "then so be it. I cannot save them from a catastrophe they wish to unleash upon themselves."

CHAPTER 3

THE SMALL BAND OF MEN CONTINUED through the wasted land, led by their young master. The boy drove them mercilessly, but they understood they needed to move quickly to stay ahead of the wave of destruction behind them. Night fell, however, and the men were exhausted. They would not reach the sea tonight.

"My liege, we need to stop."

The boy turned to Galois, glancing at the tired and dirty men behind him. They hung their heads, ashamed of their fatigue. The boy reluctantly agreed.

"Very well. We will camp here."

Fires were lit, and the men quickly stuffed moldy bread and cheese in their mouths. There was little conversation and without preamble, most fell into an exhausted sleep.

Galois, however, was still awake and gazed across the fire at the boy. The fair-haired one stared into the flames, the light reflecting in his eyes like some creature of the night. He glanced up at the grizzled man.

"Go to sleep, Galois. I will keep watch."

Galois nodded. He knew the boy would keep watch. He knew the boy could hear everything that moved in the forest, and had no need of food or rest. He knew that the boy would already be home if it were not for them.

Galois settled by the fire, pulling his rough blanket over him. The boy returned his gaze to the flames, and Galois took comfort in the strange glow in his eyes.

Galois' dreams were monstrous, full of gory battles and severed limbs, of tortured and maimed women and children, of pus-filled wounds and rivers of blood. He awoke with a start, reaching for his sword. His hand was stayed by a firm grasp, and he looked up to see the boy kneeling over him.

"What is it, my lord?"

"There is something in the forest," the boy whispered, gazing off at something Galois could not possibly see. "I must go."

The boy's words struck terror in the old man's heart. They were softly spoken, with no hint of fear. But there was an edge to them that Galois rarely if ever heard.

The boy stood, still whispering. "You must keep watch. If I have not returned by dawn, continue without me."

Marilyn found Ryan in the courtyard, chopping wood. Although wealthy beyond reason, Ryan split firewood because she enjoyed the pure physicality of the act. She set each piece solidly on the stump, then cleanly split it in two without effort. Marilyn watched the girl for a moment, admiring both the rhythm and her form. Movement itself could be an art when it came to Ryan.

Ryan was so immersed in her task that she was oblivious to her surroundings, including Marilyn. She appeared to be in a dreamlike state, so lost in thought was she. Her rhythm quickened and the strength of her blows increased. Her face was expressionless, but somehow it was apparent that whatever world she was in at the moment was not pleasant. In a final, immense blow, Ryan split a piece of wood and the stump beneath it, clear to the earth below.

Ryan stared at the ax for a long moment and the stump. She seemed surprised by her actions, not only that she had split the stump, but that she had been chopping wood at all.

"You seem a bit distracted."

Ryan glanced up at the dark-haired woman. She had instantly become aware of Marilyn's presence, once shaken from her reverie. She opened her mouth to speak, then closed it, saying nothing.

Marilyn was surprised. Ryan almost always had a ready and sarcastic reply.

Ryan set the ax down, brushing her hands on her pants. She was hesitant, then spoke quietly. "I have been dreaming a lot lately, and I am not certain why."

Marilyn restrained her own, normal banter, mindful of the girl's mood. "You always did sleep much more than any of our Kind," Marilyn said thoughtfully. "Victor once told me it is because you bear much more than any of the Others."

"I don't know what it is that I bear these days," Ryan said somberly, gazing off into the distance. "It seems that my life is a waking dream, that I no longer need to sleep to see that world. But many things from the past are weighing heavily."

Ryan quickly shook her head as if to dispel her own thoughts. "It is of no matter. I will show you to your quarters." She glanced back at the woman following her, a trace of mischief returning. "They are as far from mine as possible."

The boy moved through the forest. It was dark, even for his preternatural sight. As he progressed, it seemed almost to grow darker. The trees here were twisted, grotesquely formed. It was all very odd.

The boy stopped, cocking his head to the side. He was trying to get a fix on whatever was ahead of him. His senses strained the blackness before him, although it was neither his sight nor his hearing that he was relying on.

When he first sensed the presence at the campsite, he thought that it was near. But he realized that the strength of the presence was not a function of its proximity, but rather of its power.

The boy knew he was sensing one of his Kind, someone who was extremely powerful. He tried to compare it to those he knew, but it was different somehow, more malevolent. It was at least as powerful as many of the Old Ones.

The boy started forward once more, his misgivings growing, but unfortunately not as quickly as his curiosity.

Once Marilyn was away, Ryan found Victor seated in his study once more. Ryan stared at him a long moment until he looked up.

"Yes?"

"How are you feeling?"

Victor laughed. "You mean now that I'm back in one piece?"

Ryan had the grace to appear embarrassed. "Uh, yes, now that you have pulled yourself back together."

Victor gazed at his child a long moment. Their Kind were notoriously difficult to kill, and grew more so as they aged, passing into immortality. As he was the most ancient of their Kind, he should have been invulnerable to any attempt. But none of their Kind had ever faced anyone like his offspring. When Ryan tried to kill him, she finished the job, or nearly so, by eating his remains.

Consistent with the extreme predatory nature of their Kind, Victor was rather proud of her ingenuity.

"I feel fine. Your contributions to my welfare have helped immensely."

Ryan gazed at his throat. He was talking about her blood, which he returned in kind. She knew that they both had strengthened from the exchange.

"Don't change the subject. If you are fine, then what did I feel earlier?"

Victor's expression sobered. He attempted to maintain a light tone, but he would not lie to Ryan.

"I am not certain. It is not the first time I have felt it."

Ryan felt a coldness in the pit of her stomach, although she attempted to match Victor's nonchalance.

"Can you describe what you are feeling?"

Victor was thoughtful for a moment. "It is a flash of weakness, a stab of pain. It is brief, then disappears. I thought at first it was still the aftermath from my injuries."

Victor's voice trailed off.

"But you no longer think that," Ryan said quietly.

"No," he admitted, "it has been only recently that the weakness has appeared. I think it would have appeared much earlier in my recovery if it were related, and if so, not persisted to this day."

Outwardly Ryan was calm, but it felt as if a sheet of ice water were flowing down her back. Victor was describing what seemed to be a very mild malady.

But her father was immortal, invulnerable, and not prey to maladies. She was greatly concerned.

She hid her unease, at least from her voice if not from her father.

"Well, one good thing. I know a most excellent doctor."

CHAPTER 4

RYAN STOOD ON THE PRIVATE RUNWAY, the wind whipping her coat around her lithe form. She was again lost in thought, but glanced up when she heard the distant roar of an airplane. It was still far away, and no normal creature could have detected the noise at so great a distance.

The plane was moving fast, and it was only minutes before the sleek jet began its final approach. It lightly touched down in a smooth landing, then taxied toward the lone figure on the field.

The cockpit was blacked out, as were the windows, but Ryan nodded to the pilot, whom she could see. He nodded back deferentially as he brought the jet to a halt in front of her. The door opened and the stairway was extended downward.

A young woman and a small boy stepped from the doorway. The wind caught their red hair, tousling it in the breeze. The boy caught sight of Ryan and sprinted down the stairs.

"Ryan!" he squealed, running full-tilt at her. Ryan caught him in mid-leap and in an astonishing move, tossed him a good ten feet into the air, easily catching him before he hit the ground. He laughed with reckless abandon.

Dr. Susan Ryerson approached with a little more dignity. She glanced at her son, then at Ryan. "You know it scares me when you do that to him."

Ryan gazed down at her, mischief in her eyes. "What's the matter?

You want your turn, too? I'm fairly certain I could toss you into the air, dear doctor, a good deal higher than that."

Susan was a little nervous, never certain when Ryan was joking. "Uh, no thank you. I would be happy with just a hug."

The pilot of the airplane watched the warm greeting with some incredulity. He had never seen his lordship demonstrate that kind of affection with anyone, let alone a human woman and child. He knew that few were invited to this estate, but he had been unaware of the caliber of his passengers. He was glad he had shown the two respect, both for the sake of his employment and the sake of his life.

Ryan glanced up and the pilot had the sudden, frightening thought that she could read his mind. But she merely nodded and he returned the gesture, then began easing the jet toward the sole hangar at the end of the runway.

A black limousine pulled up and Ryan opened the rear door. Jason scrambled inside and Susan moved to settle in beside him. Ryan paused, scanning the horizon, then the sky overhead. Satisfied, she climbed in behind them, and the limousine pulled smoothly away.

Once inside the sleek black car, Jason immediately began pressing every button he could find. Ryan watched him with some amusement, and Susan with much less.

"Jason, cut it out."

"Ah, mom…". He obeyed immediately, however, and began peering through the black window separating them from the driver. "Hey mom, I think the same guy is driving the limo that was flying the plane."

Susan cleared her throat at the observation. Ryan's "help" did have the same kind of eerie, nameless, faceless sort of persona, blending into the background as if they weren't quite real.

Susan glanced over at Ryan. As much as she had been around the woman over the last few years, she still found Ryan's presence overwhelming. Ryan, in typical fashion, was oblivious to the effect she had on those around her.

"Thank you for inviting us to your estate," Susan said.

Ryan turned her attention to the red-head. "You are quite welcome. And you may stay as long as you wish."

Susan glanced out the window, observing Ryan's usual opulent surroundings. "If it weren't for my research, you might not be able to get rid of me."

Ryan smiled. "You know how I am, dear doctor. I don't wish to separate you from your work."

Susan was suspicious. "What are you saying?"

"Ah, there may be 'facilities' available to you during your stay. I hope they meet with your approval."

Susan settled back into her seat, shaking her head in wonderment. She was certain the "facilities" would be more than adequate. The last time she had needed somewhere to work, Ryan had purchased an entire hospital.

Susan and her son had just settled into their suite when there was a knock on the door. A quiet, circumspect servant led them to the dining room, then disappeared. Jason settled into his high-backed chair a little nervously. "Mom, what is all this silverware for?"

Susan glanced down at the formal place setting, the crisp white tablecloth, the spotless crystal. It was as elegant as a five star restaurant.

"Most of it is pretty redundant," Ryan said as she strolled into the room. "Especially for people who do not eat."

Marilyn and Victor entered the room from the opposite side. Her hand was on Victor's arm as he showed her to her place and she settled into her seat. She heard Ryan's comment and now addressed Victor. "Your child is a barbarian."

Victor settled into his own seat at the head of the table. "Yes," he said without the slightest misgiving, "I know."

Ryan sat across from Marilyn on Victor's right, next to Jason. Susan was across from Jason, and now uncomfortably close to Marilyn. Susan toyed with her napkin, smoothing it in her lap. She had not known that Marilyn would be joining them. Victor and Ryan created enough heat and light on their own. The intensity of the three of them together was unbearable. Susan understood how these creatures seduced lesser beings so easily. She glanced over at Jason, feeling strangely protective of her son at the moment.

Marilyn was aware of the doctor's discomfiture, and true to her nature, was enjoying it. She poured Susan a glass of wine. "Here you are, Dr. Ryerson. Perhaps some wine will relax you."

Victor glanced at Marilyn, but said nothing. He nodded to a servant in an alcove and food was quickly brought out for the two human guests. Jason began eating with relish, and as uneasy as Susan was, she realized she was more hungry than nervous. The fact that the food was delicious aided her appetite.

Ryan swirled wine in her glass, gazing deeply into the red liquid. Victor, too, was enjoying his spirit, but was also the perfect host.

"So Dr. Ryerson, how is your research progressing?"

Susan wiped her mouth with a napkin. "Excellent, thank you. Your patronage has been a godsend, and has relieved me of the burden of the public arena. There are few researchers who get to study whatever they want, and none so well-funded as I am. Thank you again."

Victor nodded. "I am sure you are making wonderful progress."

"So what exactly are you studying now?" Marilyn asked, swirling the red liquid in her own glass. "And are you managing to keep our Kind off the cover of Time Magazine?"

Susan folded her napkin. "I am keeping to the agreement. I haven't published anything."

"So what are you studying?" Ryan prompted, giving a sideways glance at Marilyn.

Susan unfolded the napkin, a trace of excitement evident. "I've been examining the cellular process of foreign DNA integration, testing new methods to prevent undesirable genomic alteration from nonhomologous DNA insertion."

The silence at the table was loud, broken only by the clink of Jason's fork on the plate. Marilyn nodded politely as did Victor.

"Yes," Victor said, "sounds interesting."

Ryan was thoughtful. "So you are trying to find a way to insert

DNA that's dissimilar to its host." Both Victor and Marilyn turned to her, eyebrows raised .

Susan nodded excitedly. "I'm actually examining DNA that apparently has mutated from a nonhomologous insertion into the genome, resulting in extremely favorable alteration."

Victor's expression was suddenly impassive and Marilyn cocked her head slightly, also understanding. Ryan, it seemed, was the only one still in the dark.

"Really," she said, puzzled, "how interesting."

Susan leaned across the table slightly. "It's yours, Ryan. It's your DNA. I was waiting for a good time when I could share some of what I've found."

Silence again settled on the table. Marilyn gazed into her glass of wine, twirling the stem in her fingers. The motion caused the liquid to swirl, creating patterns of red light on the crisp tablecloth. She finally spoke. "You realize, Dr. Ryerson, that you continue to cover very dangerous ground. There are many who would go to almost any length to acquire the knowledge you possess. Perhaps it would be wise for you to seek another area of study."

Heat rose in her cheeks and Susan felt the need to defend herself. "I will stop if Ryan wishes me to, or if her father thinks it best I not continue."

Jason sensed his mother's agitation and stopped eating. He glanced at Ryan.

Ryan was watching Victor. He gazed at her impassively, in a way infuriating her. Even possessing his deepest Memories did not give her access to his thoughts when he was shielding them, as he was now. Ryan turned her attention to Marilyn.

"Dr. Ryerson is under my protection. Even now, Edward is covering her tracks from her journey here. If there are those who want knowledge of me, I suggest they come find me themselves."

Marilyn was not dissuaded. "At the risk of stating the obvious," she said, her sarcasm evident, "it will be easier finding Dr. Ryerson."

Ryan felt the heat rise in her own face, and it was certainly warmer than Susan's. But before her anger could peak, something caught her attention that abruptly stayed her reply. It was a slight movement, a motion that she could barely see out of the corner of her eye, but it was enough to send another shock of ice through her veins.

Victor winced, the gesture again nearly imperceptible. But Ryan felt it as clearly as she saw it, and her sense of time and field of vision both expanded. Time slowed to a stop as microsecond events occurred over hours. Ryan saw Susan slowly, painstakingly begin her turn towards Victor, a puzzled look on her face.

Impossibly, the table's human occupant was becoming aware of something that an inhuman occupant was not. Perhaps it was because she was a trained physician, but Susan was definitely noticing Victor's malady when Marilyn had not.

Yet, Ryan thought to herself, not yet. Marilyn would not read it from Victor and would not sense it from her, but she would surely pick it up from Susan. A disaster was in the making.

"Ouch," Ryan said aloud. All attention at the table was suddenly riveted on the thin line of blood that appeared on the knuckle she had apparently cut while brushing a crumb from her mouth. It was quite easy to do. Although her skin was incredibly resilient, her teeth were sharper than cut diamonds.

"Hmmm," Ryan said thoughtfully, "after 700 years you'd think I'd be used to these teeth."

Marilyn was not fooled, knowing the mishap was not accidental. But she mistook Ryan's motives. "You could simply disagree with me, my dear," she said, her eyes drawn to the blood, "you don't have to win an argument unfairly."

Faster than even preternatural eyes could see, Marilyn's hand flashed across the table, snatching Ryan's wrist. She snapped Ryan forward until Ryan was pressed against the edge of the table, instantly reminding her how incredibly fast and strong Marilyn was.

The abrupt action startled both Susan and Jason, and Jason looked fearfully towards his mother. Susan herself could not look away from the unfolding drama. But in the back of her mind, she knew there had been no crumb to brush away.

Victor looked on, still impassive. The drawing of blood had increased the tension at the table a hundredfold, and his internal tension by equal degree. The sight of Ryan's blood created an ache that could be removed in only one way; he knew Marilyn felt the agony as well. But because he fully understood Ryan's deception, he could not intervene.

Marilyn's eyes never left Ryan's, and she held the wrist between them. Very slowly she turned the wrist, putting an obvious strain on Ryan's arm. The cut was now centered over Marilyn's wine glass, and the small stream of blood ran from Ryan's knuckle down her wrist. It was suspended as a droplet for an eternal instance, then gravity overcame it and it plopped into Marilyn's wine glass.

Marilyn released Ryan's arm, and Ryan leaned back rubbing her wrist in a distinctly human gesture. Marilyn raised the glass, swirling the blood into the little wine remaining.

"To you, my dear," she said, raising the glass to Ryan. She held Ryan's gaze as she finished the drink.

Ryan felt the sensation ripple through her and Marilyn smiled. Susan swallowed heavily as Jason sat across from her, his eyes nearly the size of his plate. Ryan glanced down at the wound, which was already healing.

Victor regained his composure, although outwardly it was not apparent he had lost it. He glanced over at Ryan, who was still staring at the healing cut.

"Perhaps I could give you some first aid with that?" he said somewhat sarcastically.

He rose from the table, nodding to Susan. "I know you and your son are tired from your journey." He motioned and a servant materialized. "Please escort Dr. Ryerson to her suite." He turned to Marilyn, "I will discuss more with you later."

Marilyn dabbed her mouth with a napkin, making no attempt to disguise her delight at the situation. "I live to serve you, my lord."

Ryan gave Marilyn a baleful look as she got up from the table and followed her father, feeling as if she were suddenly twelve years old again.

Ryan followed Victor into his chambers. She could sense his exasperation with her.

"Must you always tempt Marilyn so?"

Ryan hid a smile. "You were the one who was nearly falling into your plate. I was hardly tempting her. It was more of a tactical diversion."

"Ah, yes," Victor said, settling into a chair. "But you always seem to utilize a tactic which nearly sends her into a frenzy. It is a good thing she exercises self-control."

Ryan sprawled next to him in an oversized easy chair. "Hmmm… interesting characterization. Self-control is not something I would normally associate with Marilyn. Besides, you were the one who promised me to her in payment."

Victor picked up a nearby newspaper, reading the headline. "Yes," he said absently, "I'm afraid I've created a monster."

Ryan wasn't certain if he was referring to her or Marilyn. "No, dear father," she said, assuming he meant her, "you did that nearly 700 years ago." Ryan grew serious, changing the subject. "What is wrong with you? Are you in pain?"

Victor set the newspaper down. There was a fatigue surrounding him that disturbed Ryan almost as much as his more obvious symptoms.

"I am not certain," he said, "it has been only recently that I have felt…".

His words trailed off. Felt what? he thought to himself. There was no precedent for what he was feeling. Although their Kind could feel pain (and withstand it in great measure) he had never felt it without an immediate discernible cause, such as a knife stuck in his chest.

"I feel almost as if I am getting sick," Victor said finally.

Ryan stared at him. "That's impossible. We do not get sick. We do not fall ill. We do not age, we do not die. You told me that yourself, and nothing in my seven centuries has shown it to be otherwise."

Victor nodded. "I do not disagree."

He fell into a contemplative silence. Ryan fell silent as well, but her restlessness quickly overcame her and she rose to her feet.

"Dr. Ryerson will be rested by the morrow. As soon as Marilyn is on her way, Susan can begin examining you. If anyone can figure out what is going on, it will be her."

Victor glanced up at Ryan. "Where are you going?"

Ryan's eyes were filled with dark humor. "To make certain that Marilyn is quickly on her way."

Susan tiptoed down the long hallway, feeling slightly ridiculous. She was jumping at shadows. All she wanted was something to drink, and she didn't want to bother the servants. They could all probably see her, anyway, in their spooky, ephemeral movement about the castle. It felt as if they were all around her, ghosts from a different time, from a different place, and perhaps a different species.

Susan realized she was holding her breath, frightening herself with her ridiculous thoughts. Nothing would happen to her while she was under Ryan's protection.

A figure materialized out of the shadows directly in front of her, startling her. She barely stifled a scream, struggling to retain her outward composure.

"Hello, Marilyn. I didn't see you there."

Marilyn gazed down at the red-haired woman, and Susan inadvertently took a step back. Marilyn smiled, showing her teeth slightly. She seemed to disappear and simultaneously reappear behind Susan, leaning over her shoulder, so close they were nearly touching.

"So, Dr. Ryerson," she said, whispering in her ear, "while you are so busy revealing the secrets of my Kind, have you given any more thought to becoming one?"

Susan steeled herself, willing herself not to move.

Marilyn continued whispering, now in the other ear. "I understand I have the chosen lineage, that you will become one of my offspring. Perhaps I could accelerate that process, make it happen right now?"

"And instead you would kill her instantly," Ryan said dryly from the shadows. "You know your blood is too powerful to Change her, so unless you have one of your 'children' readily available, I suggest you stand down."

Marilyn smiled and stepped back from Susan. Susan staggered, because although they had not been physically touching, the dark-haired woman had definitely been holding her. Ryan caught Susan's arm and steadied her, guiding her so that she stood behind her.

"I was just looking for the kitchen," Susan said, embarrassed. She tried to shake her feeling of disorientation, knowing it had nothing to do with the layout of the castle.

Ryan nodded her head in the direction opposite that which Susan was heading. "It is down the hall, through the courtyard, and to the right."

Ryan watched Susan move unsteadily down the hall, then turned to Marilyn.

"That wasn't very nice."

Marilyn was amused. "You say that as if it's a characteristic you would normally attribute to me."

"You are right," Ryan replied, "I stand corrected."

Marilyn moved closer to Ryan, and Ryan felt the dark-haired woman's influence settle over her. She, like Susan, had to will herself not to move. Susan was lucky Marilyn had not killed her on the spot. Marilyn's voice again settled into a conspiratorial whisper.

"I am concerned about you, little one."

Ryan tried not to bristle at the nickname. Marilyn had used it against her for almost six centuries and Ryan still could not quell the irritation it aroused.

"And why are you concerned about me?" she replied. "You had no concerns for my welfare when you pulled me from my seclusion and put me on trial."

"Ah, yes. The trial." Marilyn stared off in the distance as if reminiscing about a fond memory. She brought herself back to the present, and her expression darkened. "That will seem a very small thing compared to what you face now."

Ryan's frustration was evident. "Then perhaps you or my dear father could bring yourself to let me in on whatever horrible thing it is that I face. The sooner I meet it and destroy it, the better off I will be."

Marilyn shook her head. "Actually, I am afraid that is exactly what you will do. But it is not my place to tell you things that should come from Victor."

Faster than any human eye could see, Ryan pinned Marilyn against the wall, surprising the other woman completely. Although Marilyn was slightly taller than Ryan, they were now eye-to-eye.

"There are other ways I could find out," Ryan whispered between clenched teeth. "Ways I am sure you would find enjoyable."

Marilyn's gaze traveled down to Ryan's lips, then to her throat. "You should be careful, ma Cherie," she whispered, "you will get the information you seek, but I will get far more than that. And your father will not be happy about either."

Ryan realized immediately that she had made a tactical error. In terms of sheer power, Ryan was probably the superior. But in terms of seduction, Marilyn had few if any equals among their Kind. Ryan became conscious of the fact that Marilyn was now holding her waist as tightly as Ryan was holding her shoulders.

"So what now, little one?" Marilyn asked languidly. "Do you want to finish what you started at dinner?"

Ryan stared at the woman, at a loss. No matter how powerful she had become, Marilyn still seemed to have her at a disadvantage. Marilyn wielded some sort of influence over her that belied understanding.

"Ahem."

The sound of a throat clearing caused Ryan to look over. Susan was standing in the hallway, an uncomfortable look on her face, a diet coke in her hand.

"Um, excuse me. I think my room is that way."

Marilyn gave Ryan one last languid look, then pushed her away. She stood upright, smoothing her clothing, amused.

"Ah, dear doctor. Perfect timing as always. When you are my offspring, we shall have to take steps to remedy that."

Ryan involuntarily shuddered, trying to shake her dazed feeling. Marilyn's lips twitched into a smile. As she moved past Ryan, she brushed a kiss on the throbbing veins in Ryan's neck. She turned again to Susan.

"I will be taking my leave this evening. As much as I have enjoyed this brief stay, I have business to attend to." Marilyn turned to Ryan again, "Please pay my respects to your father."

Before Ryan could frame a response, Marilyn was gone. Susan did not even see her leave, so quickly did the woman vanish. Ryan stood staring down the empty hallway.

"I hate that woman."

Susan took a sip of her diet coke. She raised an eyebrow as she brushed past Ryan.

"Yes, I can see that."

CHAPTER 5

THE WIND WHIPPED AROUND the eaves of the castle. Ryan sat perched on the very edge of the stone turret, oblivious to the cold rain swirling around her.

Marilyn was gone. Dr. Ryerson and her young son were fast asleep. Her father was resting in the far part of the castle. She could sense that he, too, was lost in thought.

Events were accelerating, Ryan could feel it. Pieces were moving about a massive chessboard, pawns that had been positioned centuries before and unmoved since.

The image of the chess game brought a flood of unwelcome memories, thoughts that Ryan had deliberately suppressed for ages. But in her current dark mood, Ryan could not stop the Memories that pulled her into an ancient world that might as well have existed yesterday.

The boy came into a clearing and onto the courtyard of a monstrously large citadel. It seemed a dark and twisted place, so far from any other settlements. Hidden deep in the forest, there didn't seem to be any roads leading to the structure. Odd, because it seemed it would take a large contingency to care for such a castle.

The boy moved closer. And it had been cared for. Although there seemed something unclean about the place, it was actually meticulously maintained. There was dim light streaming from the castle, every room seemed lit by flame.

Whatever the boy felt was in here. Something powerful. And Old. And in a very strange sense, unspeakably evil.

The boy cocked his head to one side. That was odd. It was unlike their Kind to judge things as good or evil, in so ambivalent a state did they live. And yet that was the word that came to his mind in trying to assess what he was feeling. Whatever was in front of him felt evil.

Against his better judgment, he crossed the wooden drawbridge, his footsteps echoing on the planks.

He moved into an empty courtyard. Torches burned brightly in the night, barely flickering in the still air. They seemed almost to welcome him, as if he had been expected. The door to the vestibule stood open. He hesitated briefly, then moved inside.

He moved through shadowy hallways, also lit with torches that flickered as he passed. He could see an opening that led to a great hall that appeared lit by a hundred candles. The light stretched out into the hallway, dancing at his feet, making strange and ominous patterns. He gazed at the light and prepared to step into it. Something caught his eye, however, and he moved to a shadowed alcove.

A chess board was set up, the pieces arranged as if the players had paused in the midst of their battle. The boy ignored the grotesque, demonic renditions of the classical pieces and instead concentrated briefly on the positions on the board. After only a slight pause, he moved a twisted, foam-mouthed horse to a new position. Satisfied with the result, he stepped back into the hallway and stood in the entrance to the lighted room.

The room was filled with a hundred candles, or perhaps a thousand. The flickering light snaked up the walls, writhing with the shadows.

"Hello little one."

The voice was smooth, melodious, mesmerizing, terrifying. It possessed an amused malevolence and sensuality that pulled the boy into the room as if it had wrapped itself about his slender form and lifted him off his feet.

"I've been waiting for you."

The boy stepped into the light, uncertain if he was in fact seeing what was before his eyes.

An Old One sat before the great table. His hair was fair, lighter than the boy's, his features older, aristocratic, handsome. His eyes were striking, an icy pale blue that stole one's breath like a bitterly cold wind. His eyes traveled slowly up and down the boy's frame.

"Now how is it that I have never met you?" he asked languorously.

The boy did not answer. His eyes drifted downward to the table in front of the man.

It was covered in blood, with chunks of flesh spread about the surface in neat patterns. The rib cage was picked bare and several bones were pulled from the carcass. It was nearly unrecognizable, but the beautiful, untouched head attached to the bloody spinal cord gave the disbelieving boy the confirmation he sought. He raised his gaze back to the icy blue eyes.

"Did you know," the man said conversationally, "that you can kill our Kind by eating them?"

The boy's voice was steady, but he moved his hand to the hilt of his sword. "No, I cannot say that I knew that."

The man raised his eyes to the dark hallway and a servant scurried from the shadows. The man raised his foot to the table and kicked the body to the floor. "Take it away," he said in a tone that indicated neither the body nor the situation was of any significance.

The man stood up and the boy inadvertently took a step backward. The man smiled a shark's smile. "Skittish, aren't we? Of course I could make you come to me, so you may as well put yourself at ease since you really have no choice in the matter."

The boy felt light-headed, dizzy from the proximity to so much blood and the proximity to so powerful an Old One. Truly, this man's power rivaled that of most he had met. Still, the boy's voice held steady. "You seem very certain of that fact, having no idea who I am."

The man stopped, as if this puzzled him. "Which leads me to my earlier question. How is it that I have never met you?" He took a few steps toward the boy, assessing him, then turned his back, speaking over his shoulder as he gazed into the fire thoughtfully.

"You are not an Old One, but not a Young One either." He turned to gaze at the boy. "I would guess a few hundred years old, no more."

The boy said nothing, and the man turned to him once more, staring intently. "But there is something about you that I cannot quite place. Something that is not quite right."

The boy felt they were heading toward dangerous ground and began guarding his thoughts. The man felt this, and it intrigued him.

"Come here."

The boy said nothing, simply shook his head.

The man seemed pleasantly surprised at the resistance. Usually, it took but one command.

"I said, come here."

Something flickered deep in the boy's eyes, and again he shook his head. But this time there was a mental rebuke as well: No.

The fair-haired man was amazed and delighted at the voice in his head. The whelp was full of surprises.

"You must know that I find defiance irresistibly attractive." The man's voice hardened. "And utterly futile. I will not say it again. Come here."

The boy's voice hardened as well, and this time he spoke aloud. "It is good you will not say it again, because my answer will not change. I said no."

The man took a step toward the boy and the boy reached for his sword, but both froze as if suddenly locked in time.

Perhaps it was because they now stood but a few feet apart, or perhaps it was because their anger had moved them beyond their defenses, but in that instant, they were totally revealed to one another.

The man gazed down at the boy in astonishment. He had known that the boy was a girl even from a great distance off. It did not surprise him nor did it matter; he dismissed it. What was staggering was the amount of power the "boy" possessed. It ran through the child like a raging torrent, uncontrolled, bottomless, and largely untapped.

Had the boy not been frozen in place, he would have staggered backward from the mental blow of the man's presence. He had grossly underestimated this One's power, sensing a force he had felt in only one other, his mentor.

The man slowly looked the boy up and down, marveling at the

sensations he was now perceiving. His hunger was returning. "Who has made you?" he whispered in wonder.

The boy did not respond, then tried to hide from the sudden invasion of his mind. But the man's power was too great and the boy felt a sharp pain in his head as the man found the name he sought.

The ice-blue eyes shifted through a myriad of emotions: disbelief, amazement, and then slowly dawning delight.

"That is not possible," the man said. "It is not possible that Victor could have Changed you."

The boy spoke with a bravado he did not feel. "And yet here I am."

"Yes," the man said contemplatively. "Here you are." He paused, his perusal of the boy's form continuing. "And what is your name?"

The boy no longer tried to hide his thoughts, knowing it was futile. "My name is Rhian."

The man smiled his shark's smile. "My name is Aeron."

Before the boy was even aware of movement, the man was at his side, his hand covering his own on the hilt of the sword. "You will not need this," he said, removing the sword from the boy's side.

The boy was furious at himself. The anger helped clear some of the stupor that was falling over him. But the man would have none of it, moving closer to him and speaking in his hypnotic voice.

"Won't you come and rest with me for a moment?"

The boy shook his head, but could not resist when the man led him by the arm to a nearby settee. He felt light-headed and slightly nauseous, knowing the man was exerting tremendous power to influence him. His skull felt like it was going to explode.

The man sat, but the boy resisted his attempt to pull him downward. Aeron sat back comfortably, amused at the boy's continued resistance. The boy might not sit, but he was not going anywhere.

"So I see we are at an impasse," he said conversationally, playing with the edge of the boy's leather jerkin. "I am not used to being told no. It is somewhat stimulating."

His voice hardened. "But all games must come to an end."

His ice-blue eyes locked with those of the boy's. "Come here," he said softly.

The boy closed his eyes, as if he could shut the man out. But truly it was too late for that. And although he did not obey, nor did he resist when the man pulled him gently but firmly onto the couch.

He was sitting next to the man, his head on the man's shoulder, the man's arm draped around him. The man toyed with his blond hair, and the sensation made him shudder.

Aeron, for his part, was enamored with the boy. Normally, he would not dally like this, given only to the passion of killing. Nothing satiated him, so there was no anticipation, no expectation of gratification. Only the truly ancient among their Kind could come close to satisfying his desires, and even those rare unions left him unfulfilled.

But glancing down at the boy, he was experiencing a pleasure that was unknown to him. Perhaps it was the thought that he was going to kill Victor's child. Or perhaps it was the thought that the power coursing through the slender body next to him would soon be coursing through his. Or perhaps it was simply the expectation that the boy would fight to the end.

No matter. It would end as all the others.

The boy struggled to concentrate, momentarily regaining lost ground when he pushed the man from his mind. In that instance he steeled himself, focusing all his power on resisting seduction. He realized he most likely would not escape, but he would not go willingly.

Aeron was impressed with the boy's fortitude. His mental discipline was as great as many twice his age, and it was the mental gifts of their Kind that separated those who would otherwise be equals. It separated the mediocre from the extraordinary when all else was the same.

And this One was truly extraordinary. Aeron glanced down at the beautiful creature in his arms. His grip began to slowly tighten.

The boy fought the pressure, holding his arms stiffly. He felt as if he were being crushed. If he had needed to breathe, he would have been unable. Worse, he felt his arms began to weaken, as if they no longer had the will or strength to push this man away.

If that was the case, that was not Aeron's impression at all. He was astonished at the boy's strength, and found himself actually straining to physically overcome him.

"I will not yield to you," the boy whispered defiantly through clenched teeth.

Aeron was now close enough to the boy's throat that his lips brushed the throbbing jugular vein. "You realize that changes nothing," he replied.

And with that, his razor sharp teeth brushed the skin, easily slicing through a surface that was impenetrable to most steel.

The shock was immediate and profound. As the blood flowed into his body, Aeron was stunned to feel his heart stumble within his chest, expanding to accommodate the force that surged through it. The boy's Memories were instantaneous and unbearably intense. They flew at him so quickly he could not place them in any coherent context. He saw Victor, and fire, and a blond woman, and thousands of soldiers, but he could sort none of it. These were not the normal Memories of their Kind, that ebbed and flowed lazily toward him as he Shared, that settled into mediocrity as he killed his prey.

These were the Memories of One whose veins flowed with fire.

Aeron was fascinated.

The boy felt the shock as well as he connected with the man. It was one of his peculiarities, the ability to join with the one who fed upon him, as opposed to merely the one he fed upon. Aeron sensed this and was incredulous. He realized the boy could see his Memories even though none of his blood had passed the boy's lips. He also realized that this amazing creature had never been fed off by anyone other than Victor. And this fact astonished him more than anything that had preceded this moment.

For the boy, the man's Memories were horrifying, and he could make no more sense of Aeron's past than Aeron could make of his. All he saw was blood and flesh, and a hunger that could not be filled by all the death in the world. The man's power was overwhelming, his magnetism devastating, and the boy felt himself drawn to the blackness that always waited just beyond the fire, the blackness from which none of their Kind ever returned.

Aeron felt the boy's heart fight back, and it excited him. He felt himself on the verge of loss of control, careening toward the fire, wanting to waltz the boy into the flames so he could then fling him off the edge into the darkness.

But something else was in play as well. Aeron did not want this feeling to end, he did not want the blood to ever stop surging through his veins. For once he felt himself teetering on the edge of that cliff and contemplating the ultimate pleasure of going over it himself.

The boy felt his heart strain against the quickening pace of the man's hunger. He felt himself begin to weaken, knowing that he was dangerously close to slipping away. The man's hunger was immense, his pace continuing to quicken, and the boy was lost in a blood-red netherworld. The world was on fire, and there was nothing but the boy and the man and the darkness. The boy turned to the blackness and Aeron stood behind him, waiting for him to step off as they all did.

But instead, the boy turned to him. There was no desperation in his eyes, no fear, no drunken desire, no crazed longing, no begging, no pleading, nor any of the thousands of reactions Aeron had seen just prior to killing his prey.

Instead, the boy stood there, balancing playfully on the edge with a knowing look in his eyes and a slight smile on his lips. He gazed into ice-blue eyes with eyes that were now the color of fire.

"Come with me," came the whispered, intoxicating invitation.

And then the world disappeared in flames and Aeron felt his heart explode within his chest. He was no longer in the blood-red netherworld, but back in the great room with the light from a thousand candles flickering on the unconscious boy in his arms. He stared down in stunned disbelief at the pale, prone figure.

No one had ever satisfied his demonic thirst, let alone tempted him with death itself. He searched himself. He had no urge to rip the boy's flesh from his body and consume it, no need to devour him to fill the void that could not be filled.

He glanced down at the boy. He did want to destroy him, but that was the desire of all their Kind. He wanted to kill him in the act of Sharing, because there was no greater pleasure. But, he admitted to himself, that might very well be impossible with this One.

"But I shall enjoy trying," Aeron murmured to himself, stroking the boy's hair. "We did not even complete half the act. I can't imagine what it will be like when my blood passes your lips."

"You will never, ever, have that experience."

Aeron's expression darkened but he did not move. Instead his hand drifted to settle on the boy.

"Why, Victor, what an unexpected pleasure."

Victor Alexander stepped from the shadows, his expression one of barely-contained fury. It was only the vulnerability of his unconscious prodigy that kept him from attacking and utterly destroying this man.

Aeron was wary. He had been caught off guard by Victor's approach, so lost in the act of Sharing had he been. But he was also delighted by the situation. He moved his hand possessively to stroke the boy's hair.

Victor's jaw clenched and Aeron could hear his teeth grinding together. It did not stop him however, and he moved on to stroke the boy's cheek.

"So you must tell me, old friend," Aeron said casually, "how you managed to produce such an amazing offspring." He paused for effect, "Because I really quite enjoyed him."

It was too much for Victor, who leaped toward his enemy. But Aeron had goaded the attack for a reason, and he was on his feet in an instant. He held the unconscious boy between them.

"Do you wish to challenge me?" he said mockingly, in complete control. "You know I live for that day."

Victor was quietly sarcastic. "You would take my place in the hierarchy. Yet you just passed the opportunity to destroy my heir."

Aeron smiled down at the prone figure he held. "I will avail myself of that opportunity some time in the future." Aeron dropped all pretenses and dropped the boy to the ground with a thud. Victor did not glance down. He drew his sword as Aeron drew his.

The two flew into combat, swords throwing sparks as they collided with tremendous force. Aeron was flush with blood, power roaring through his veins, but Victor was fed with an inner fury that had no end. It took but three blows and both swords shattered, and the men were locked shoulder to shoulder.

It was one of the dilemmas of the most powerful of their Kind. If two were evenly-matched, it was difficult to find weapons that could withstand the fight as long as the combatants. And when reflexes were near instantaneous and skill was equal, it would come to a deadlock.

But in this case, although the pair was near evenly-matched, Victor had the slightest edge, and it was all he needed to slowly begin overpowering Aeron. This appeared to cause Aeron little concern.

He stumbled rearward, jostling a table and knocking dozens of candles over. Victor caught the gleam in his adversary's eye, but it was too late. Aeron snatched a now flaming tapestry from the table and flung it toward him.

Victor stepped aside easily and was already moving toward his opponent. But he was half a step off as Aeron knocked more candles to the ground, lighting the woven mats covering the floor.

The room was quickly engulfed in flame and Victor realized Aeron's intent as their eyes met. Aeron smiled a wicked smile. In a flash, he flung a flaming tapestry toward the prone figure on the floor. It was a perfect toss, settling over the crumpled form.

Victor leaped to the boy's side, snatching the tapestry from him. The flames would not kill him, but the wounds would be painful in his weakened state. He gazed up in fury at Aeron, who observed the scene with pleasure.

"One of the downfalls of emotional entanglement," Aeron said with thinly-veiled contempt, flames licking around him. "Unfortunately, as much as I am enjoying this little reunion, I am going to have to bring it to an end."

Aeron slammed his shoulder into one of the weight-bearing pillars of the great room. In an instant, cracks appeared overhead as dust and rocks began to pour from the ceiling above.

Aeron winked, "I have to douse this fire somehow."

Victor did not hesitate. He lifted the boy in his arms, and in one great leap was out the window of the room that was now collapsing behind him. Before he had landed on his feet, the castle caved inward in an explosion of rock and rubble. He moved with blinding speed out of reach of the flying debris.

Once a safe distance away, he stopped and looked down at the boy. He wanted to go back and settle this matter with Aeron, but truly his prodigy's condition was more pressing. He was relieved to feel the boy stir.

The boy opened his eyes, focusing on Victor. He turned away. "I am sorry. I tried to resist him."

Victor's relief was immense, and the boy took comfort in that. Victor shook his head. "There is no need for remorse. You could not have withstood Aeron. Most do not even survive."

Victor's thoughts turned inward. This both puzzled and disturbed him. Aeron was known for destroying their Kind, which in itself was neither immoral nor unjust. What separated Aeron from the Others was his choice to humiliate and desecrate, seducing lesser beings to an ignoble and painful death.

Whether or not Aeron could have destroyed his progeny was debatable. He could, however, have caused injury that would have taken decades to heal.

Victor was distracted from his thoughts as the boy stirred again, fading in and out of consciousness.

"How," the boy began, "how is it that you knew where to find me?"

"It was not so much where," Victor replied. "As when." His next words provided no explanation. "Time and distance are not so very different things."

This made no sense at all to the boy, and Victor shook his head. "You need to rest. We have a long journey home."

The boy settled his head onto Victor's shoulder, and Victor started through the forest, his thoughts returning to Aeron. He had been furious when he felt Aeron begin to bend the boy to his will, and his concern had been great. Aeron's atrocities were well known.

But now, in a way, Victor's concern was even greater. He did not think that Aeron could have killed his offspring.

But it bothered him that Aeron had not even tried.

CHAPTER 6

THE SUN ROSE INTO A BRIGHT RED SKY, telling Ryan the rain from the night before would continue. Storm clouds gathering on the horizon to the west told the same story. It was good the jet was approaching. In an hour the weather would make landing impossible.

Ryan watched from the turret of the castle as the lone figure disembarked and entered a limousine. The car pulled away from the runway and onto the road leading to the gates. Ryan started downstairs.

She exited out onto the upper level of the entry stairs as the long, black car pulled to a stop at the base of the flight of steps. The lone figure stepped out of the car, waved the car off, and started the long climb.

The older man, dressed impeccably in an elegant suit, maneuvered the stairs without effort. He arrived at the landing composed and unruffled despite the fact he had just traveled three thousand miles. He stood before the young woman, then bowed deeply from the waist.

"My lord," he said.

Ryan waited for him to stand upright, then put her hand on his shoulder.

"Edward. Welcome home."

"It is good to be home, my lord. Although there is much that we must discuss."

The two moved into the grand foyer and Edward continued. "I trust Dr. Ryerson reached here safely?"

"Yes, she and her son arrived as scheduled. Thank you for your diligence on that matter."

Edward appeared somber. "It was wise for you to bring her here. I am not certain of her safety outside of your protection."

"And I am not certain she will be safe even within my care if I am distracted by too many matters."

It was a surprising admission and it caused Edward great concern. He glanced at his young liege, who in reality was several centuries older than him. Ryan had chosen an apt word. She did seem distracted, and her next words surprised him even more.

"I did not bring Dr. Ryerson here purely for altruistic reasons." She paused, as if uncertain how to exactly phrase her next comment. "I, or rather my father, has need of her services."

Edward frowned. This did not sound good, in fact, did not even sound possible.

"I trust your father is well?"

Ryan again searched for words, perplexed by the novelty of this situation. "I am not certain. He seems," she paused, at a loss, "well, he seems a bit under the weather."

It was a masterful understatement. For Victor Alexander, the undisputed ruler and sovereign leader of their Kind, to even sneeze would be unthinkable. For him to display the kind of weakness that would cause Ryan concern was dreadfully significant. Edward sought to absorb the ramifications of this impossibility, his mind following every potential twist and turn of the situation. It did not take him long to arrive at his conclusions.

"What do you think is the extent of your father's illness?" he asked quietly.

Ryan shook her head. "I really do not know. There is no precedent for this, no measure by which to judge. Perhaps it is nothing. But I cannot take that chance."

Edwards thoughts continued to sift through every eventuality. "Who else knows of your father's condition?"

Ryan again shook her head. "No one. You. Dr. Ryerson. And myself. That is all. Marilyn was here, but she did not sense it. Of that I am certain."

Edward nodded. "Then Dr. Ryerson cannot leave here with this knowledge." Edward hesitated, always reluctant to question his master. "Are you certain it was wise to involve her?"

Edward was again surprised by her answer. "No. I am not certain of the wisdom of my decision. By placing her in confidence I have placed her in jeopardy. But I have need of her knowledge right now."

Edward was blunt. "I am more concerned that you have placed yourself or your father in jeopardy by involving so delicate a creature."

Ryan smiled wryly. "I do not think Dr. Ryerson is the hothouse rose you believe her to be."

Edward was firm. "And I do not think she could withstand the likes of the Others were they to learn of this development."

"Which is why you will make certain she does not have to."

Edward always had the good grace to know when a conversation was over. He bowed deferentially. "I live to serve you, my lord."

Ryan put her hand on Edward's shoulder. "Then for right now you will protect Dr. Ryerson, and god forbid, my father if he needs it." She turned away, her expression darkening. "I have a feeling I will be otherwise occupied."

Ryan and Edward walked into a fully functioning laboratory. If they had not just walked from a luxuriously furnished hallway, it would appear they were in a major medical research facility.

Victor sat on a table while Dr. Ryerson examined him. He nodded to Edward and Edward bowed low, remaining a respectful distance while Ryan approached.

Susan removed her stethoscope from her ears and draped it around her neck. She turned to Ryan, addressing both her and Victor.

"Well, I am as baffled by his anatomy as I am by yours. I might as well be examining an alien species."

Ryan nodded. "This is to be expected. But I know how creative you can be when you are faced with the unknown."

Susan addressed Victor. "As foreign as your anatomy is to me, I do have one thing to compare it to," she said, nodding at Ryan. "And I have something of a head start because of the research I've been doing."

Victor was gracious. "That is excellent news."

Ryan began thumbing through a stack of papers that Susan had brought with her. "Well, this is all very enlightening," she said in a tone that indicated it was anything but.

Susan took the paperwork from Ryan's hand in a parental gesture that few would have dared. "Let me give you a synopsis."

Ryan sprawled in an office chair. "Please do."

Susan shuffled the papers. "When I originally began studying you I was looking at your immune system, searching for explanations for your accelerated healing. When I realized how old you were, I also began looking for explanations as to why you do not age."

Susan turned on the overhead display, illuminating several charts and graphs. Ryan took one look at the graphs and exchanged glances with her father behind Susan's back. Victor looked down, hiding a smile while Susan continued unaware.

"There are several current theories of aging, and I considered all of them in the context of your physiology. The two foremost theories are that aging is genetically programmed, or that damage to DNA is cumulative and eventually the body is no longer able to repair it."

Ryan was paying attention despite herself.

"If the former is correct," Susan continued, "that aging is genetically programmed, then your Kind may be passing a favorable genetic mutation to one another through the process of the 'Change.' From what I understand, when you first share blood with a human, a physiological transition occurs in which the anatomy is radically altered in a very short time, almost an instant mutation."

"Like the accelerated evolution you've mentioned before," Ryan said.

Susan nodded, then paused. "Are you sure you're not a vampire?"

Ryan had a look of exasperation on her face. "I don't know how to disabuse you of that notion. Vampires are an idiotic myth that I am sure One of my Kind inspired in an insipid moment."

Susan smiled to herself. She knew enough of Ryan to know that although her Kind shared superficial similarities with the fantasy creatures, their reality was far more fantastic. They did not Share blood with humans, other than to reproduce as needed. Their desire was to Share with one another. And they possessed none of the weaknesses of the vampire creature while possessing strengths that Dracula could only dream about.

Susan knew all of these things—she just liked to tease Ryan, which Ryan realized. "Please continue," she said dryly.

"If the second theory is correct, that aging is due to cumulative damage to DNA, then your immune system, which is like nothing I've ever seen, may be healing that damage constantly. Therefore you do not age."

Susan was thoughtful. "There are a few other findings that may be appropriate as well. Certain studies have shown that extreme reduced caloric intake increases longevity. Your Kind exist on little more than the exchange of blood and an occasional glass of wine. I've never known you to consume anything else. I'm not even certain how you generate energy, which I will get to another time."

Susan paused to take a drink of water, then continued. "The other, peripheral finding has to do with cell division. Cells are thought to have a limited reproduction cycle, perhaps as a safety mechanism against uncontrolled cell growth such as cancer. Each time normal cells divide, the DNA at the end of them, telomeres, gets shorter. When it runs out, the cells die."

Victor considered her words. "And ours?"

Susan shook her head. "I haven't really had the opportunity to test your cell replication," she said apologetically. Susan glanced through her paperwork. "Again, this is all speculative, because your anatomy is so different from a human's." She glanced up at Ryan, then over at Victor. "And things are further complicated by the fact that both of your anatomies are significantly different from the others of your Kind that I have examined."

This piqued Victor's curiosity. "Really? In what ways?"

"Well," Susan stopped, almost at a lost for words. "I'm not even sure where to start."

Ryan and Victor were both curious now.

"I have had the opportunity to compare samples that the two of you have graciously provided with samples obtained from Others of your Kind."

Susan paused, thoughtful. "Not all of which were given voluntarily." She resumed, ignoring the ethical implications. "I randomized my collection process so that I could get samples from all age groups, ensuring that I was not identifying something that was age-related as opposed to specific to you."

Susan shuffled some papers. "One of the most fascinating things about the two of you is your genetic makeup. Obviously I have not had time to map your entire sequence. That would take years, even with the advanced computing power I have access to. But I have had time to map the areas of most frequent variation, at least in human beings." She then stopped, at a loss. "To really make you understand how different you two really are, I need to explain what I'm comparing you to."

Susan illuminated another chart. "In a normal human body there are about 50 trillion cells. Every one of those cells has 46 chromosomes, 23 from the mother and 23 from the father. These chromosomes are made up of DNA molecules, which are made up of genes, which are made up of nucleotides."

Ryan turned her head sideways, looking at the illustrations of the chromosomal maps. "I don't think these visual aids are very helpful."

Susan ignored her. "DNA is made of just four nucleotides, adenine, cytosine, guanine and thymine."

"Hmmm, hence the 'A', 'C', 'G', and 'T' on your chart," Ryan said.

"Um, yes," Susan said. Lecturing Ryan was worse than teaching a roomful of graduate students.

"These nucleotides arrange themselves in very particular orders. 'A' pairs with 'T', and 'C' pairs with 'G'. There are about six billion of these pairs that make up about 30,000 genes, which vary in length from a few thousand pairs to two million pairs." Susan paused, "Although with the recent mapping of the human genome, it appears there may be far fewer genes than thought, closer to 20,000."

Susan changed the chart again. "Anyway, genes make proteins, albeit indirectly through a transcription process with messenger RNA. And proteins do all of the heavy lifting in the body. They make organs, handle digestion, circulation, respiration, immune function, etc. Roughly 50% of the dry weight of a cell is made up of these proteins, which number about

100,000 in the human body."

"Okay," Ryan said slowly. "Thank you for the primer. This isn't going to be on the exam, is it?"

Susan rolled her eyes in exasperation. "There isn't going to be an exam." She quickly changed the overhead illustration. "This is a quick mapping of your chromosomal structure."

Both Ryan and Victor perused the diagram silently. "There appear to be a few too many," Victor said finally.

"Exactly," Susan said. "The Others that I tested all have 46 chromosomes, just like humans. You and Ryan have 92."

"And I'm guessing this is a bad thing?" Ryan asked slowly.

"Well," Susan said, her exasperation boiling over, "It's perfectly fine if you're a whitefish or a potato hybrid. But nothing remotely human has that many chromosomes. This type of chromosomal variation, polyploidy, usually occurs only in plants. It is extremely rare in animals, occurring only in certain reptiles and amphibians. It is lethal in mammals, and there is only one known case, which occurred in a rat in Argentina."

Susan glanced at her own diagram, baffled. "In most cases, the addition of a single extra chromosome in humans results in significant birth defects if not stillbirth or neonatal death. I don't even know what to think of an entire extra set."

"Well," Ryan began, "as I don't believe that I am a whitefish or a potato, nor a Red Vizcacha rat, I'm guessing there's some other explanation."

Susan glanced over at her sharply. "I didn't say what type of rat it was."

Ryan smiled an enigmatic smile. "Lucky guess."

Susan stared at her suspiciously. That information had been in her notes, but there was no way that Ryan could have absorbed it by casually thumbing through the papers.

But then again, Susan thought, nothing about Ryan surprised her anymore.

Susan's manner became brisk once more. "That's not even the strangest part about it."

"There's more?" Victor asked mildly.

"I'm not certain about you," Susan said, nodding at Victor, "but Ryan shows significant paternal uniparental disomy."

Ryan looked at Victor. "Okay, I impressed her with the rat. It's your turn."

Victor smiled and waited for Susan to continue.

"Uniparental disomy occurs when an individual inherits two copies of a chromosome pair from one parent and none from the other parent. Either Ryan's mother was genetically identical to you," she turned to look at the diagram, "or most of Ryan's genes come from you. Again, when this condition occurs in normal humans, it causes significant physical problems, skeletal, lung, thyroid defects, dwarfism, and of course, death."

Susan shuffled through some paperwork, talking to herself. "But of course, once again, when it comes to you two, it does nothing of the kind." She held up another chart. "Ah, here it is." She put the transparency on the projector so Ryan and Victor could see it. It was another picture of nucleotides, similar to the "A-T, C-G" pairs previously shown. But this one had an occasional "I" sprinkled in amongst the pairs.

"What does the 'I' stand for?" Ryan asked.

Susan gazed up at the drawing, shaking her head. "It stands for 'I have no idea'," she said slowly. She was silent for a long moment, then shook her head again. "It's like nothing I've ever seen."

She turned back to the Ryan and Victor. "If it is a nucleotide, it has a biochemical structure that is completely unknown to me. I can't even break it down into its constituent parts. It appears to bind with any of the four existing nucleotides, as well as with uracil on RNA. Because I don't know what it is, I don't know what the resulting proteins are that it is creating, or even if they can be considered proteins. I do know this," she said with emphasis, "that the introduction of a single additional nucleotide increases your genetic options on an unimaginable scale."

Susan shrugged, her excitement and frustration both evident. "We don't even know what most of our own DNA does. I can't imagine what yours is doing."

Susan put away her charts and graphs, much to Ryan's relief. Susan's next words did not put her at ease, however.

"I destroyed most of Ryan's medical records, so I will have to do new tests."

"Oh, how awful for you," Ryan said dryly. "I know what an inconvenience that must be."

Susan did not even appear embarrassed. Yes, she was being offered the holy grail of research, but Ryan had asked her this time. "If you would like me to do a less than thorough job…".

"Of course not," Ryan said, sighing, "by all means, feel free to poke and prod my father all you wish."

Victor turned a baleful eye to his offspring. "Yes, of course, right after she does you."

Susan interjected before she lost control of the conversation. "I have a feeling neither one of you is very good in the role of patient."

"Neither one of us has ever been a patient," Victor replied.

"Well, then let us consider this more of a research role."

"Ah yes," Ryan said, "from patient to lab rat."

"Red Vizcacha lab rat," Victor clarified.

Susan was exasperated. "I thought one of you was bad. Two is quite impossible."

Ryan addressed Victor. "She is rather feisty for a human."

Susan was out of patience. "Get on the table."

Ryan raised an eyebrow, but complied, and Susan moved to Victor. She started to put her stethoscope to his chest once more, then stopped, uncertainly. She took a deep breath, started toward him, then stopped again. She stepped back, knocking a metal tray full of instruments onto the floor.

Ryan looked at her curiously. Susan was obviously irritated with herself, as well as a bit ruffled. "Is something wrong?" Ryan asked.

"No, nothing," Susan said brusquely.

Susan glanced up at Victor, who merely smiled knowingly. Both Ryan and Victor heard Susan's heartbeat increase, as did Edward, who cleared his throat. Ryan turned to her manservant.

"Am I missing something?"

Edward made an uncomfortable noise, although he was obviously amused. "Ah," he stopped, then continued. "Many humans, especially female humans, find your father very attractive."

Susan was mortified but did not deny the accuracy of his assessment. Ryan turned to Victor, gazing at him in a sidelong manner, as if trying to process this fact. "Hmmm," she said doubtfully, "I guess so."

It was Victor's turn to look sidelong at his mischievous offspring. "Ryan, stop torturing Dr. Ryerson and allow her to finish her examination."

Ryan shifted on the table. "I could say the same to you," she said under her breath. She glanced at Susan. "Perhaps you should start with me."

Susan took one step toward Ryan, then stopped. Ryan's magnetism was as distracting as that of her devilishly handsome father.

Susan sighed. "I don't think that's going to help," she said.

Many hours later, Ryan revisited Susan in the laboratory. Susan glanced up from her desk, the dim glow of a lamp highlighting her auburn hair.

Ryan raised her hands in mock surrender. "I promise I will behave." She settled into a chair near Susan, her demeanor far more restrained than earlier.

Susan smiled. Ryan was both incorrigible and irresistible. It was difficult for the scientist in Susan to deal with the sensual world in which these people lived. And she was afraid to let the woman in her anywhere near it. She rubbed her eyes tiredly.

"I don't think you're going to unravel the complexities of my Kind in a single evening," Ryan said quietly, noting her fatigue.

"Oh, I know," Susan said. "There are just a few things I wanted to wrap up."

Ryan's tone grew serious. "I appreciate your willingness to help my father."

Susan turned to her. "It would never occur to me to do otherwise."

Ryan settled into silence, a contemplative look on her face.

Susan wasn't completely certain how to ask the question she needed to ask. "Is Victor the oldest of your Kind?"

Ryan turned to her. "Yes, as far as I know. There is no one beyond his Memories, not even the One who Changed him."

Susan was thoughtful. "And he has no Memories of his life before his

Change?"

Ryan shook her head. "No. We have discussed this at length. He remembers only being the way that he is, at his current age. He remembers nothing before that and I have seen nothing in his mind to indicate otherwise."

Susan watched the shadows play across Ryan's face. "Then how is it that the other Old Ones came to exist?"

"I am not completely sure," Ryan said, "and it is my understanding that neither are they."

Ryan realized this was an incomplete explanation.

"I believe most of the truly ancient of our Kind did not survive, but I am not sure why. It is almost as if a generation spontaneously appeared, then were destroyed, possibly through some type of internal warfare." Ryan was thoughtful. "I believe Victor is the only one of his generation to survive." Her eyes narrowed. "Although there might be one more."

Susan glanced over at her. "What about the ones I've met? What about Marilyn?"

Ryan's eyes grew distant as she evoked Marilyn's Memories as if they were her own.

"I-," Ryan stopped, "I mean she, has Memories of her mentor, but it is someone who no longer exists. I believe Marilyn, and Abigail as well, are close to my father in age, but are second or third, perhaps fourth generation."

It was Susan's turn to speculate. "I wonder if there was some large-scale event that triggered some sort of mass genetic mutation, some type of radiation poisoning or something. We've seen drastic mutations in Belarus since Chernobyl."

"Of course," Susan said, continuing her train of thought, "all of those mutations have been horrific." She glanced over at Ryan again. "Yours have all been beneficial, almost by design."

Ryan was quietly sarcastic. "Who knew that God was a vampire?"

Susan glanced down at her hands, smiling. "As you have so often reminded me, you are not a vampire." She looked back up at Ryan, serious once more as she hesitantly approached the question she needed to ask.

"If Victor is the oldest of your Kind, then how do you know that you're immortal? How do you know you're not just extremely long-lived?"

Susan expected some resistance to the question, but Ryan surprised her.

"I have asked that question myself," Ryan said. "And I don't have an answer to it." She reflected on the facts of the moment. "But I would think if my father were suffering from mere aging, his decline would be more gradual as opposed to the sudden, acute onset of his symptoms."

The silence between the two was heavy, and it was Ryan who filled it with what they were both thinking. "Unless, of course," she said quietly, "I have hastened my father's death by injuring him so severely."

Ryan's face was expressionless, but Susan could see the muscles in her jaw tighten. She had the sudden impulse to reach out and hug the preternatural creature, and might have done so had Ryan not dramatically changed the subject.

"So," she said calmly, turning to Susan, "have you considered my father's offer?"

Susan swallowed hard, unable to maintain eye contact. She cleared her throat a few times before she was able to croak out an answer.

"Yes."

Ryan was amused. "Yes you have considered it? Or yes is your answer?"

Susan tried to maintain a semblance of composure. Victor had offered her the opportunity to become one of their Kind. It was an incredible gift, but one fraught with peril.

"Yes I have considered it. And although I don't think now is an appropriate time, I think that I might be willing to undergo the…" Susan's voice broke, "…the possibility sometime in the future."

Ryan smiled a wicked smile, and Susan was reminded of what a complete predator she was.

"Excellent."

Ryan sat in a chair next to Victor's bedside. He was resting comfortably, nothing in his handsome visage indicating anything out of the ordinary. His eyes were closed, but Ryan knew he wasn't sleeping. She took the opportunity to examine his features, the high cheekbones, the perfect mouth, the long, dark eyelashes resting against his smooth, unlined skin.

His eyes opened. "What?" he asked at her brash scrutiny.

Ryan smiled. "Just trying to see what Dr. Ryerson sees in you."

Victor closed his eyes again. "Go look in the mirror."

Ryan smiled further at the irony in his tone. She moved to his side, sitting on the edge of the bed. He again opened his eyes, and this time there was the subtle sensuality in his gaze that always existed between he and Ryan, the desire that Susan Ryerson found both fascinating and disturbing.

He took her hand, turning the wrist and examining the veins beneath the skin. His marked examination began to loosen the coiled spring that always lie tensed just beneath Ryan's skin.

"Is there something I can get you?" Ryan asked mockingly.

"No," Victor said as he brushed his lips across the veins. "But there is something you can give me."

The razor-sharp teeth brushed the skin, splitting it and the vein beneath without effort. Ryan closed her eyes, but not in pain. Victor drew her blood into his body, taking the strength, power, and immense pleasure that came with it.

As always, Ryan was immediately connected to him both physically and mentally. She could feel his pain and see the looming darkness, but was comforted by his lack of fear. He seemed unconcerned with his fate and far more concerned with hers.

She began to feel the lethargy take hold, the wonderful lightness of being that came with being fully bled. It was a precarious state for most of their Kind. At this moment, it was no danger to her whatsoever.

Victor released her arm, sated. Ryan gazed down at him, fighting her predatory instincts.

"You know I will let you," Victor said, gently taunting.

"And you know I want to," Ryan said, "more than life itself." She leaned back from him. "But not more than your life."

Ryan grew somber. "The dark gift is all I can give you right now," she said, "and my helplessness fills me with rage."

Victor nodded, understanding the fire that flowed like molten lava through his child's veins. It flowed through his as well.

"There is one more thing that you can do for me."

Ryan glanced down at him, suspicious at his tone.

"You will receive a summons from the Grand Council, most likely within the next few days."

Victor could feel Ryan's formidable temper rising, and took her hand, forcing calm upon her.

"I know what they want of you."

Ryan exploded. "I don't care what they want of me. I only care what you want of me."

Victor was patient. "Then you will obey their edict."

Ryan started to argue, but Victor cut her short, placing a finger on her lips. "If you wish to do my will, then you will obey the edict of this council."

Ryan's jaw tightened, but Victor simply shook his head.

"I will say no more on this matter."

CHAPTER 7

RYAN SAT BEFORE THE EMPTY TABLE in the great hall. "Sat" was probably too loose a description, for she sprawled in the lone seat that faced the raised dais that held the massive council table. The entire room, from its cathedral ceilings to its elaborate marble columns, was designed to emphasize the pre-eminence of the council seats and the lonely inferiority of the chair beneath them. It failed to affect the chair's current occupant in any such way. Not that it would have under normal circumstances, but Ryan was currently oblivious to almost everything around her. Her thoughts were only of Victor, and of the current distance between them.

She became aware of the presence of the Others approaching her from the rear. She did not turn when they entered the room behind her, filing in to fill a semi-circle arrangement of seats surrounding her back.

These would be the twelve witnesses, Old Ones, but not as powerful as those who would sit as part of the Grand Council. Their duty was to bear witness to the proceedings.

Ryan extended her senses to assess them while blocking their probing. She was surprised to feel a familiar presence. She turned to the twelfth witness, seated to her right at the end of the semi-circle. It was Edward.

She glanced briefly around the room, then turned away disinterested.

The Others gazed at the golden-haired young woman seated in the center of the room. Most had never met her, although all had heard of this strange creature with the extraordinary past. They stared at her, as if trying to square the myth with the reality. It was difficult, because although the girl possessed a startling, androgynous beauty, it was difficult to gain much more from her than that. It was almost as if she shifted before them, ephemerally coming in and out of focus.

In a shocking breach of decorum, Ryan stood and walked over to Edward. All eyes followed the lithe figure.

"I would hardly consider you an impartial witness," Ryan said dryly.

"I do not believe these will be impartial proceedings," Edward said, just as dryly.

Ryan glanced at his robe, required garb of the council members. "I am not certain that red is your color," she said with mock seriousness.

Edward glanced at Ryan's black clothes, elegant and form-fitting, accentuating her athletic build. She wore a cloak on her shoulders that was more cape than coat. "I see that you have worn your favorite color," he said, even more dryly than before.

"You didn't think I would change for this, did you?"

Edward shook his head. "Of course not."

In accordance with protocol, the twelve witnesses wore red, the members of the Grand Council wore ceremonial white, and the head of the Grand Council wore black. The fact that Ryan wore black as well sent a distinct message.

Ryan turned, sensing more familiar presences approaching. Powerful presences. Ryan nodded to Edward and returned to the center of the room. Edward was surprised to see her remain standing, but soon realized why.

Ryan bowed her head and closed her eyes, as if gathering strength. She opened her eyes, and with a flourish removed her cloak, swirling it about her. As the cloak came off, so did the perceptual veil with which she had surrounded herself.

Edward smiled. He could feel, if not hear, the intake of breath from those in the room. The female next to him took an instinctive step back and he graciously caught her elbow to keep her from tumbling over the chair behind her.

Ryan's full presence was crushing, her charisma unmistakable, her influence overpowering. Even those witnesses who had predetermined their aversion to this One were suddenly and emphatically served notice: resistance was futile. And it certainly wouldn't be as enjoyable as giving in to this creature.

Edward smiled again. He could sense that those approaching had received the message as well. Ryan set her coat down casually, as if the entire situation were of no matter. Normally those called before the Council were supposed to stand respectfully at their seat, and to sit once the Council was seated. In another complete breach of protocol, Ryan stepped forward up onto the dais and stood before the opening door.

One-by-one, the members of the Grand Council began to file into the room. Those bearing witness watched expectantly, curious as to how those of the Grand Council would view this breach of etiquette. It was not what they expected.

The first through the door, an exceedingly handsome and distinguished Asian man, stepped forward and stopped in front of Ryan. Clothed in the white robes of the Council, he gazed intently at the black garbed figure in front of him. The two stood eye-to-eye, expressionless. Then, in a gesture that completely surprised Edward, Ryan clasped her hands in front of her and bowed deeply from the waist. In a gesture that completely surprised everyone else in the room, Kusunoki clasped his hands and returned the gesture, bowing just as deeply. He stood for a moment longer, gazing at his former apprentice, then stepped to the right to stand before his seat.

Ryan turned her attention to the next One coming through the door. A gorgeous, earthy, immense woman entered the room, moving with the grace and dignity of a queen. She stopped before Ryan and an exotic sensuality filled the space between them, snaking out with tendrils that seemed to wrap around Ryan's torso and pin her arms to her sides. The woman was overwhelming in every way, with ebony skin and startling green eyes that burned into Ryan. Ryan heard a deep, throaty voice in her head.

My name is Ala.

Ryan shrugged the imaginary tendrils from her arms as the woman extended her hand. In a gesture that again completely surprised Edward, Ryan took the woman's hand in her own and bowed in a chivalrous manner. She brushed her lips lightly on the back of the extended hand, lingering perhaps just a moment.

There was amusement in the green eyes, amusement at the impudence of this One. Ala withdrew her hand slowly, brushing the girl's cheek. Her thoughts were her own as she, too, went to stand before her seat.

Ryan turned her attention to the third member of the Council. Although she had expected Abigail's presence, she still felt the wrench of her magnetism, causing her equal parts pleasure and irritation. It caused Abigail only pleasure. Stunning, elegant, and possessing a motherly sensuality that was both alluring and disturbing, Abigail moved to face the girl. She raised her hand for Ryan's kiss.

But Ryan would have none of the formalities with One she knew so well. As Abigail raised her hand, Ryan stepped forward, taking the hand and resting it lightly on her chest. She leaned forward and Abigail complied with the implied request, brushing her lips on the girl's cheek.

If Ryan was to take liberties, however, then she would take her own. She continued her kiss, moving forward and brushing her lips on the veins on the side of the girl's throat. It was all Ryan could do to suppress a shudder.

Abigail took her place at the table, an enigmatic smile on her face. She sensed Ala's amusement, although Kusunoki was as inscrutable as always.

The fourth member of the council entered, and Ryan inwardly sighed. Marilyn. Of course. The woman conveniently forgot to tell her pertinent details, for example, that she herself was seated on the Grand Council. Marilyn's eyes flashed wickedly, reveling in Ryan's discomfiture. Ryan inwardly sighed again. Clothed so inappropriately in white, Marilyn was as bewitching as ever.

True to form, Marilyn did not bother with a formal greeting but rather grasped the girl by the collar and pulled her firmly forward. There were shocked looks from the gallery as the dark-haired woman kissed the indicted One firmly on the mouth. Even those at the head table cast sideways glances as the kiss lingered. Finally, Marilyn pushed the girl away, unrepentantly pleased. She took her assigned place at the head table.

The twelve witnesses, with the possible exception of Edward, shook themselves as if awakening from a stupor. The commencement of proceedings had been quite unlike any other, the sensual greetings between the Grand Council and the One summoned unheard of. In fact, few had seen anything like this under any circumstances, let alone in such a formal setting.

Ryan turned to step off the dais, and then stopped, as if a thought had suddenly occurred to her. Her back was to the Council Members, and to the entrance from which the Council emerged.

"Only four Council members? And yet there is a place for a fifth." She paused, as if for effect. There was complete silence in the room, as beings who had no need for air held their breath.

"And who will take my father's place?"

There was a long pause, and then a voice emerged from the shadows of the entrance way.

"I guess that would be me."

The voice was smooth, melodious, mesmerizing. It possessed an amused malevolence and sensuality that wrapped itself around every person in the room, but most tightly about Ryan.

Ryan did not turn. "You wish," she said sardonically, under her breath. She turned, and to the amazement of everyone in the room, there was amused recognition in her eyes.

Aeron stepped from the shadows. A pleased smile tugging at the corner of his mouth as well. The other four council members all turned to glance sideways at the dark-robed figure. Abigail's surprise was evident and even Kusunoki uncharacteristically raised an eyebrow. There had been no previous indication that these two had ever met. And yet now it was as if they were old friends, sharing some great private joke.

Perhaps not friends. The intensity between Ryan and the Council Head was not entirely cordial, and there was a predatory aspect to it on both their parts. The proximity of the two created a sudden influx of sensations that swirled through the room, dark, complex, and unfathomable.

Ryan gazed up at the man who had so brutally seduced her centuries before. Even now, she could feel his influence settle over her, his persuasion circling, seeking prey. He had been overwhelming four centuries before; the years had done nothing to diminish that advantage.

Aeron stared down at the creature in front of him, captivated. He knew that the "boy" he had met centuries before would grow more powerful. But he had no idea the child would grow into the being in front of him.

"I've missed you, my dear. I had no idea that you and I would have so much in common."

Ryan knew instantly to what he was referring. "Ah, but you were wrong. Despite my best effort to consume him, Victor lived."

Aeron smiled as if the thought gave him great pleasure. "If I had known you wanted to kill him, I would have joined you for the meal."

There was dark humor in Ryan's reply. "Attempts on my father's life are my privilege." She paused, and there was warning in her voice. "And mine alone."

Aeron did not miss a beat. "Ah yes, your 'father'." His emphasis on the word left little doubt to his meaning. Aeron had not been present at the trial, but the facts of Ryan's birth were now well-known. "Another little impossibility that we shall have to examine in greater detail. Another time."

He took his seat, as did the other four members of the Grand Council. Each of the four was intrigued by the exchange between Aeron and Ryan. None was aware of any previous contact between them, and it was now evident that something substantial had occurred. Abigail and Marilyn, who knew Ryan as well as anyone could, were surprised and fascinated by the dark eroticism between the two.

Aeron raised his hand, indicating the twelve witnesses could be seated.

Or they could try. All but Edward made the attempt. He knew better.

Ryan stared insolently at Aeron as the twelve stood at involuntary attention. She very slowly settled into her seat, smoothing non-existent wrinkles from her clothing. Without breaking eye-contact, she crossed one long leg over the other, then casually raised her hand. The subtle influence she was exerting over the witnesses was withdrawn, and several stumbled as they were released. There were confused murmurings as the twelve took their seats.

Aeron was unsurprised, more amused than insulted by the display of power. The more the girl revealed her strength, the more it excited him.

Ala gazed down at the creature in front of her. She had been curious about this legend, this extraordinary crown prince of their Kind. Thus far, she was not at all disappointed. In fact, she was strangely pleased at the girl's insolence, although none of these thoughts were revealed in her impassive expression.

Kusunoki's expression was also inscrutable, his emotions and thoughts as closed to the room as his body language. His pupil had changed much over the centuries, and he had yet to determine if that change had been good or simply exceedingly dangerous.

Ryan turned her gaze to Abigail, who gazed at her intently.

Be careful Little One.

Ryan inwardly smiled. She was aware of the undercurrents passing through the room. She was rarely in the presence of so many Old Ones, especially at this proximity, and she was enjoying the subtle push and pull of power. But Abigail was correct, this was a very dangerous situation.

Aeron quickly underscored that fact. "So," he said, pausing for effect, "how is your father?"

Ryan did not react, but it was rather the force of her non-reaction that attracted the attention of all members of the Council. It was as if a huge shutter had slammed downward, closing all access to her mind. Where there had been a current and constant flow of emotions, now there was nothing.

"He sends his regards," Ryan said evenly.

Aeron smiled his shark's smile. "I'm surprised he let you come here alone."

The insult was apparent, although whether it struck its intended mark was less so. Ryan's demeanor was tightly controlled.

"It is only due to his insistence that I came at all," she replied.

The implication was obvious; she was not here at the behest of the Council. Lest there be any doubt as to her meaning, she continued. "I am here because my father wishes it."

Aeron gazed at her thoughtfully. There was something there, something he could not quite get a hold of. He turned to Abigail, who had leaned forward slightly. She, too, had felt something. Not so much a glimpse of something hidden, but a glimpse of the act of hiding. He turned back to the girl, intrigued.

"And did your father tell you why you were called before the Council?"

Ryan did not reply, although her jaw clenched.

"Of course not," Aeron said smoothly.

He surprised Ryan by standing, and it was all she could do to keep from standing as well. She felt at a disadvantage in her seated position.

Abigail drew the girl's attention. "Do you remember many years ago when you were a child, you asked me why there were not more of our Kind?"

Ryan nodded. "I remember the conversation."

"And what did I tell you?"

Ryan thought back to the exchange that had occurred centuries before. "You told me that few survived the Change, because it was a difficult and painful transformation."

Abigail nodded, and Ryan continued.

"You told me that our Kind are predators, and that we like to kill our Young, so that few survive."

Abigail again nodded.

"And you said that only those occupying the middle ground were able to reproduce. That Young Ones were not powerful enough to initiate Change and Old Ones were too powerful, their blood was toxic."

Abigail was thoughtful. "Yes, that is correct."

Aeron materialized behind Ryan. "In theory," he amended. "With one quite fascinating exception."

Ryan's hand sought the sword that wasn't at her side. Aeron caught the reflex gesture and smiled.

"That didn't help you before," he whispered in her ear.

Ryan stared solidly forward. Her eyes caught those of Kusunoki. Out of everyone in the room, perhaps only he understood the depths of her current struggle, the itch in her palm to be holding a weapon. He held her gaze and it calmed her.

Abigail watched Ryan, knowing her temper and knowing that Aeron was deliberately provoking her. It was as entertaining as it was dangerous.

"There is one more reason why there are so few of us," Ala proffered, as if to expedite the proceedings. She, too, was entertained, but she looked with some disapproval at Aeron. She turned her attention back to Ryan. "Are you familiar with the Cleansing?"

Edward glanced over sharply. This could not possibly be what this was about.

Ryan frowned. "No, I am not familiar with that."

Abigail was incredulous. She had expected some degree of ignorance since the full extent of the Cleansing was known only to a few. But once again the whelp knew nothing of their Kind.

Marilyn was amused. "It is truly amazing the things your father keeps from you."

Ryan's anger was obvious. "And others, as well. It is not as if you have taken the opportunity to educate me."

Marilyn let her eyes linger on the girl. "You have a standing invitation for instruction, my dear. You have availed yourself of it only once."

This piqued Aeron's interest. Without removing his gaze from Ryan, he addressed Marilyn. "Really," he said in his clipped, aristocratic accent, "we shall have to compare notes sometime."

Marilyn raised an eyebrow, "Indeed."

Ryan raised her eyes to the ceiling in exasperation.

Abigail brought the discussion back to the matter at hand. "In order to keep the strength and purity of our Kind, we conduct periodic purges, a controlled 'hunt' if you will."

Aeron leaned down toward Ryan again, his tone intimate. "Quality control, of course."

"I see a few have slipped through," Ryan replied without missing a beat.

Aeron merely smiled and stepped away.

Kusunoki interjected before the conversation could again degenerate. "A hunter is chosen to cull the weak."

Ryan raised an eyebrow. "A single hunter? And how is this hunter chosen?"

Abigail again took up the thread of conversation. "It depends on the level of the cleansing. There are the short-term, which take place once a decade. And there are the 100-year purges which take place at the century mark. A hunter of suitable ability is chosen each time to fulfill the purpose of each hunt."

Ryan was growing wary. This sounded barbaric even for their Kind.

"And again, that purpose is?"

Aeron settled back into his high-backed chair. "The decade purges are primarily to cull Young Ones, to weed out the weak." He examined his perfect finger nails. "In a century purge, a hunter would perhaps target some of the older of this group, some just prior to the age of reproduction." He raised his eyes and Ryan felt the coldness of his gaze penetrate her, hold her captive. He was pleased that her gaze did not waiver, and more pleased when she queried him in even tones.

"And how does the hunter determine who will survive?"

There was suddenly much shifting in the room behind her. Aeron smiled. "You see, that's the beauty of it," he said, savoring the words. "There is no judgment involved."

Ryan found herself holding her breath, an act that had no physiological significance to her anatomy, but was a carryover from an ancient human existence.

"It is the job of the hunter to kill every One of our Kind that he is capable of."

The words echoed, and then silence filled the great hall. Ryan pondered the meaning, unable to grasp what this had to do with her. They could not possibly be warning her. She would destroy any hunter that came near. She had no offspring to protect, and her father, at least in their minds, needed no protection at all.

Aeron could see that Ryan was still not grasping the intent of the Council and he was enjoying her puzzlement. He spoke quietly, matter-of-factly in his clipped, aristocratic accent.

"This is a millennial purge. There has only been one other in the Memories of our Kind."

Ryan began to comprehend.

"-And Victor was the hunter chosen at that time."

Ryan did not speak. It was all beginning to make sense, pieces falling into place. The eyes of all the Council members were upon her, as well as those of the witnesses. The silence in the room was absolute, broken only when Aeron delivered his final pronouncement.

"And we have chosen you as his successor."

Ryan's reply was as quick as it was abrupt. "Then you are insane."

There was an explosion of murmuring behind her, both at Aeron's unexpected announcement and Ryan's cutting reply. Aeron did not respond, but simply gazed at Ryan with obvious pleasure.

"Why would you choose me?" Ryan demanded, "You know that I would decimate the population of our Kind."

"Exactly our reasoning," Aeron said smoothly, "Quality control, my dear. Remember?"

Ryan did not bend and her words were sharp. "As much as I might enjoy a little killing spree, especially given the opportunity to weed out some of the undesirables amongst our Kind," her emphasis on the last word and her glance at Aeron gave little doubt as to whose offspring she was referring to, "this is not a good time for me."

Aeron did not hesitate. "And why is that, my dear?"

Ryan's jaw clenched and the shutters of her mind slammed downward. She had nearly walked into that trap again. She had the sudden fleeting thought that perhaps that was why she was being sent on this task in the first place. But she could not entertain the thought and withstand the mental onslaught of the five in front of her. She blanked all trace of her father from her mind, and instead responded with her own question.

"And if I refuse?"

Aeron glanced at his perfectly manicured fingernails. "Then you will pay the price for disobeying this Council."

Ryan rolled her eyes and her voice dripped with sarcasm. "Oh no, not that."

This angered Aeron and his eyes flashed as he sat forward in his chair. But before he could address her insolence and dismissive attitude, Abigail interjected.

"What did your father tell you to do?" she asked calmly.

Ryan was silent as Abigail gazed at her intently. Ryan held her gaze, then looked downward. The silence was pronounced

"He told me to obey the edict of this Council."

Abigail sat back, exchanging a significant look with Aeron. Ryan's eyes were cast downward, and she missed the exchange, but Marilyn did not. Marilyn's expression did not change but she filed the piece of information away.

Ryan looked back up, addressing Abigail. "Victor knew why you called me here?"

Abigail was both gentle and not. "Of course. I spoke with him myself. I am surprised he did not make you aware of what you faced." She paused, her voice lowering. "Ah, but I forgot—your father tells you nothing of our Kind, forcing you to learn everything the hard way."

Ryan let the mild insult slide, her mind too full to take on the insignificant.

"Then I have no choice but to accept this task."

It was obvious that Ryan was angry, and that Aeron was inordinately pleased. He spoke, businesslike, as if the outcome had never been in question.

"You have one year, in which to fulfill your duty, and you will report to the Grand Council every three months."

Ryan nodded, her jaw clenched. It appeared that matters were all but settled. The witnesses behind her began to stir in preparation for departure. Ryan's next words stopped them cold.

"I have but one final question."

Aeron outwardly showed no concern. But his sudden stillness indicated he was listening carefully, as were all of the Council members.

"Which is?"

There was a long silence accompanied by a sharp drop in the atmospheric pressure of the room. It was Ryan's turn to examine her fingernails. When she spoke, she enunciated each word clearly and carefully.

"If I am to kill every One of our Kind that I am capable of killing…" She slowly stood, her lithe figure unfolding with a deadly grace. Her words were still spoken softly, but with a dangerous edge.

"Does that include the five before me?"

There was stunned silence in the room, intermixed with a good deal of anger. Aeron's expression was cold and it was evident he was furious. Ala, who was surprised by little, was astonished at the boldness of this One. Marilyn, who knew how powerful Ryan was, kept her thoughts to herself. Abigail, for the briefest moment, actually considered the possibility of the girl's threat.

Only Kusunoki smiled.

Knowing that she would not receive a response, Ryan turned her back on the Council, but Abigail's voice stopped her. "I will speak with you before you leave."

Ryan turned slightly, then nodded deferentially. "I will wait for you."

And the indicted One left the room.

Eleven of the twelve witnesses sat in their chairs, frozen. Edward, the only one who was clear-headed enough to remember protocol, got to his feet. The other witnesses were immobile a moment longer, then scrambled to their feet. They stood stiffly until Aeron waved his hand angrily, ignoring procedure.

"Get out."

The twelve disappeared as if they had never been there.

Ala rose gracefully, and Kusunoki stood, offering his arm to her. Ala took the proffered arm, nodding to the other three Council members. "I am going to retire to my quarters." Kusunoki nodded also, and the two left by the door through which they had entered.

It was quiet, then Marilyn broke the silence. "Well, I thought that went well."

Both Abigail and Aeron turned to Marilyn, her irony unappreciated. Marilyn smiled her wicked smile and stood. "I, too, am retiring to my quarters. I shall have to find a way to release all of the pent-up energy this little gathering has aroused."

Both watched her leave, their thoughts very different on the subject of release, and yet very much the same. It was again silent for a moment, then Abigail turned to Aeron, rising. Her words were both a warning and a parting shot as she, too, took her leave.

"I certainly hope you know what you are doing."

Ryan met Edward in one of the alcoves in the hallway. The subterranean gathering place was filled with corridors, their twists and turns offering opportunities for trysts of all kinds. But as with all political institutions, privacy was at a premium, not because the walls had ears, but because the inhabitants of this structure could hear right through them.

Ryan took that into consideration when choosing the location in which she would speak. She was as far away from the permanent quarters of the Grand Council as possible.

"Well, I thought that went well," she said, unknowingly echoing both Marilyn's words and her sarcasm.

Edward raised an eyebrow. "Ah, yes. I thought your closing statement was particularly effective."

Ryan's mouth twitched. "I believe it was a perfectly valid question."

"I do not think the Grand Council shared your belief."

The dangerous edge returned to Ryan's voice. "They might be in for a very unpleasant surprise."

Edward nodded, returning to the primary matter at hand. "I cannot believe that they would choose you for this task."

"Yes," Ryan mused, "on our return trip you are going to have to educate me further on these 'cleansings.' It seems quite idiotic that I am supposed to run around for a year killing everything I see."

Edward shrugged. "It is an ancient custom. It is normally fraught with political implications, and generally a great honor to be chosen. Although the 'cleansing' is supposed to be without judgment, it rarely is. For the hunter, it is an opportunity to shape the future of our Kind, at least to a degree. Which is why it is so odd that they have chosen you."

Ryan turned to him with a questioning eye, and Edward explained.

"You have no political aspirations and few if any political ties. I cannot see that it would benefit any members of this Council to appoint you, unless they thought they could turn you against another's lineage, thereby leaving their own in a greater position of power."

Ryan pondered his words. "It still doesn't make sense to me. They know I have the ability to decimate our Kind. I almost wonder if this is an excuse to separate me from my father in his time of need."

Edward was quiet. The thought had occurred to him as well. He softly spoke the obvious. "That would imply that someone on the Council knows that he is in fact in need."

Ryan spoke the less obvious. "Or that they had a hand in causing it.

We haven't ruled out non-natural causes."

Edward nodded gravely. That would imply deep machinations on someone's part. For someone to strike at Victor without his or Ryan's knowledge would require great skill and planning. But who would benefit from such a strike? And what was the end result of such an elaborate plan? Ryan would simply be furious and take her revenge on whomever was responsible.

Unless, of course, Ryan was next. All five of the Council members would benefit from the removal of both Victor and Ryan.

Ryan read the concern on Edward's face. She put her hand on his shoulder. "Don't worry about me, my friend. We have no evidence whatsoever to support any of this conjecture, and I did not sense anything from anyone in that room. I do not trust any member of the Council, even those who claim alliance with my father. As powerful as they are, I find it difficult to believe that they could strike at Victor without his knowledge. This situation may be exactly what it seems, and that is exactly how I am going to respond right now."

Edward did not completely understand. "And your response will be?"

"I am going to do exactly what they have commanded me to do. I am going to kill everyone of our Kind that I am capable of killing."

Edward felt a bit uncomfortable. "Should I distance myself from you now or later?"

Ryan rolled her eyes. "I am not going to kill you, Edward. Don't misunderstand me. I am going to do as they have commanded, and I will do it in the way that they expect."

"I am still not certain I understand."

Ryan smiled a humorless smile. "There will be some partiality in my choice of prey."

Edward nodded slowly. "But how will you decide?"

Ryan shrugged. "Now that's where it gets complicated, doesn't it? Deciding who is still standing at the end of the game." Ryan sighed. "You are right, it might be easier just to destroy them all."

Edward glanced over at his young liege; that wasn't what he had said at all.

Ryan eyed her most-faithful servant. "I am not serious, Edward. I swear, sometimes you have no sense of humor at all."

Edward left to ready the jet for departure and Ryan made her way through the underground corridors to the quarters of the Grand Council members. She could feel the power of those present as she approached. She stopped for a moment, letting the sensations flow over her. It was with a certain surprise that she felt Ala and Kusunoki together, although she immediately withdrew her attention out of respect for their privacy. They knew she was here as well.

Ryan continued on until she came to the entryway of Abigail's suite. Each member of the Council had ornate accommodations, a reflection of their power and wealth. The door whispered open, and as Ryan entered she realized each suite was a reflection of the occupant's style and personality as well.

Abigail's suite was a study in timeless elegance and cool beauty. Decorated in brilliant whites and pale blues, it could have been a chateau on the banks of the Garonne river as opposed to a bunker thousands of feet underground. Their Kind had always gone to elaborate lengths to ensure privacy, but were unwilling to sacrifice anything in terms of luxury.

The skin on the back of Ryan's neck tingled as she felt Abigail's presence behind her. The stunning older woman brushed by her, causing the skin on her arm to tingle as well.

"Please, my dear, come sit with me awhile."

With Abigail, even a subtle request held the seeds of command. The fact that Abigail had undergone the Change when physically older than most of her Kind lent her an air of matriarchal authority, even amongst beings whose physical appearance meant nothing. The fact that she was also one of the Oldest of their Kind created an irresistible combination of regal beauty and staggering power.

Ryan was not immune to Abigail's charms. In fact, Ryan's apparent youth created the opposite psychological conundrum. Ryan had been Changed when so physically young, although she was almost seven centuries old, Abigail could still make her feel like a child.

Unfortunately for Ryan, Abigail was very aware of this. "Here, my dear," she said, motioning to the seat across from her.

Ryan obeyed, noting that Abigail had changed from her robes into a striking gown, then noting that she wished she hadn't noted this. She moved further into the chambers and settled across from Abigail into cushions that were a little too comfortable. Their knees nearly touched and as Abigail smoothed her gown, the hem fell across Ryan's feet.

"It is good to see you," Abigail said, noting that the girl had changed into a white shirt open at the throat.

"And you as well," Ryan replied.

"I have not seen you since," Abigail paused and Ryan shifted uncomfortably, "why, since Marilyn had her way with you after the trial."

One of the few human responses that Ryan had retained after her Change was her ability to blush, although Ryan rather considered it her inability to refrain from blushing. She was unable to refrain now, which Abigail observed with pleasure.

The memory of her union with Marilyn brought the full force of another memory. Victor had offered his child to Marilyn in return for her loyalty and assistance in recovering from the near-mortal injuries Ryan had inflicted upon him. He had made the same offer to Abigail. However, to the surprise of everyone Abigail had chosen to delay her gratification and had "saved" her debt, choosing to exercise her option at some unspecified time in the future.

The knowledge of that unfinished business sat heavily in the room at this moment. Ryan knew that Abigail could call the debt at any time. The knowledge sat between them, creating a tension that was not without pleasure. This thought made Ryan angry, or at least made her want to be angry, at her weakness. Abigail watched the girl's struggle, entertained.

Ryan shook her head. "Is there a reason why you have called me here?"

Abigail stared at the girl a moment longer, unwilling to let her little fish loose just yet. When she did release her, it was merely to sink the hook's barb deeper.

"So how is it that you know Aeron?" she asked.

The question slammed into Ryan, and her jaw clenched at the blow. She said nothing, attempting to block Abigail's sudden invasion of her mind. But unlike matters in which she was unequivocal, such as her father, thoughts of Aeron had no such clarity, and were more accessible.

Abigail sensed the confusion and was intrigued. She shifted slightly so that her leg was touching that of Ryan. The contact sent a shockwave through her, almost as if it had opened up a physical conduit between the two beings. Abigail saw that Ryan felt the shock as well and was curious to see if she would withdraw from the connection. As vulnerable as Ryan was, Abigail was impressed that she did not pull away. That did not keep her from pressing her advantage, however.

"Did Aeron force you?" she asked softly.

Ryan was quiet for a moment. "As much as any of our Kind forces one."

Ah, Abigail thought, an interesting admission. The girl had been seduced. She had been privy to Aeron's seduction of others, and it was almost always violent. She would have given almost anything to watch Aeron take this One. She wondered how successful Ryan had been at resistance.

"And did you take his blood?"

Ryan shook her head, her eyes distant. Abigail knew that there was something the girl was withholding.

"Why not?"

Ryan looked down, but her eyes were still focused on a far-away place. She raised her finger to her face, stroking her lip. Abigail was entranced at the unconscious gesture, and struggled to stay on task.

"Victor came, just as Aeron had bled me."

Ah, Abigail thought, the two had been interrupted before the moment of decision had arrived. That would not keep her from finding out what that decision might have been. Her next words were casual, but her question was devastating.

"And would you have taken his blood?"

The question wrenched at Ryan. Her jaw clenched, almost spasmodically. Her eyes, still unfocused, were in a very dark place.

"Would you," Abigail repeated more softly, "have taken his blood?"

Abigail shifted again and her leg was firmly pressed up against Ryan's thigh, opening the conduit wide. Ryan closed her eyes, knowing she could not escape this woman and could not lie to her.

"Yes, I would have taken his blood."

Abigail sighed with satisfaction, settling back into the deep cushions of the chaise lounge. She was not done with her little fish yet.

And would you take my blood?

The words whispered silently through Ryan's head, unspoken but clearly communicated. She stared at the woman across from her. Abigail's knowing smile told her that she did not require an answer because the response was already known.

Ryan's silence was damning, and Abigail's pleasure was palpable. Her next words, ever so casual, were as fraught with peril for Ryan as those that came before.

"And Aeron did not try to kill you?"

Abigail had answered her own question by the way in which it had been asked. And Ryan did not bother to respond, verifying the accuracy of Abigail's answer. Silence, both internal and external enveloped the two.

You were the one who said I could not be killed.

The voice came inside Abigail's head, angry, powerful, and seductive. Ryan's eyes reflected a fire that had no external source and flickered dangerously in Abigail's cool and elegant chambers. It served to remind Abigail that her little fish was in reality a very lethal shark with few if any equals in an endless sea.

"Why are you asking these questions?" Ryan asked quietly, aloud.

Abigail flicked an imaginary piece of lint from her gown. Her words were deliberately casual. "I like to know what motivates the Others on the Council."

Ryan was not fooled by the studied indifference of the answer. "And what motivates you, Abigail?"

Abigail smiled and Ryan swiftly realized she did not want the answer. But it was too late, because the question lay open between them.

"You, my dear," Abigail said simply, but not gently, staring at the girl with the unblinking gaze of their Kind. "You always have."

Ryan stared at the beautiful woman across from her. It was an astonishing admission that should have empowered Ryan, but it did no such thing. In fact, it had the opposite effect as Ryan felt a marked weakness. Ryan sat across from the elegant, enigmatic matriarch and felt a vulnerability that she had felt few times in her life. The seduction Abigail offered was filled with destruction.

Not offering, Ryan thought, that implies a latitude that is not present.

Abigail stood and Ryan felt the anguish of the disengagement, physical and otherwise. Abigail smiled, gazing down at the girl. She reached out and touched Ryan's face, tracing Ryan's cheekbone with her hand. It was all Ryan could do to keep from grasping the hand and pressing it to her chest. She again felt the loss as Abigail pulled away from her.

"As always, I have enjoyed your company my dear," Abigail said over her shoulder.

Ryan realized she had been dismissed. Abigail was gone. She sat for a few moments, dazed by the encounter, the few brain cells left capable of intellectual thought cataloging the event.

As her senses returned to her and the spell lifted, she realized something of far greater importance.

Abigail had quite emphatically served her notice.

"You conveniently neglected to tell any of us that you and Ryan had already met."

Aeron smiled at the voice in his anteroom. He had felt Abigail's approach.

"And how was your visit with our little crown prince?"

Abigail skillfully redirected the conversation without actually changing the subject.

"Enlightening. She told me of your little encounter years ago. Odd that you chose not to share that information with me."

"I thought you would more enjoy hearing it from the whelp."

"Hmmm," Abigail said noncommittally, "yes."

Aeron turned to Abigail, his eyes gleaming. "I am sure she did not do the story justice."

Abigail settled into the chaise across from him. "So perhaps you will?"

Aeron smiled, undeceived by her cool demeanor. "Of course, my dear. I am well aware of your voyeuristic tendencies."

The comment was not an insult, nor was it taken as one. Abigail gazed at him serenely, composed as always.

Aeron reached for his glass of wine. "It was during the time of the Huguenots, and there was much chaos and bloodshed throughout the country, which of course entertained me greatly." Aeron grew thoughtful. "One night I felt a presence passing through my land, and it intrigued me. I began drawing it towards me."

"Like a moth to a flame."

Aeron smiled at Abigail's mocking tone. "Yes, like a moth to a flame, not realizing I was pulling in a full-fledged raptor."

Abigail nodded, and he continued.

"She was dressed like a boy. A beautiful, androgynous little boy. I did not realize at first who she was. I thought 'the boy' might provide a brief dalliance, a bit of a distraction."

"But it ended up being much more than that," Abigail said.

"Oh yes, I realized very quickly she was Victor's offspring, which of course was impossible because we all knew Victor had chosen not to reproduce. He had been past the ability to initiate Change for centuries, long before this child had been transformed."

"And yet there she was," Abigail prompted.

"Ah yes," Aeron said, lost in the memory. "There she was. Impossibly powerful for one so young."

"And so oblivious to her own power," Abigail added, drawn into the memories despite herself. "Ryan has always had an exquisite mixture of power and vulnerability."

Aeron gazed at Abigail shrewdly. "You want her, too."

Abigail gazed back at him. "Everyone wants her."

Aeron nodded, returning to his story. "Which is why I found it so extraordinary that she had never Shared with anyone except Victor. From the moment her blood touched my lips, I was flooded with images that passed so rapidly I could make no sense of it. But there was no one there except Victor."

Abigail was thoughtful. "You know, you may have unwittingly been the one to release Ryan's Memories of her mother."

Aeron turned to Abigail. This was news to him.

"From the pieces I have put together, those few obtained from Ryan and her even-less verbose father, as well as those obtained from the trial, Ryan began to recover the Memories of her birth only after she went through the shock of your taking her blood."

Aeron slowly smiled. This gave him great pleasure. To have unknowingly struck a near-mortal blow at his enemy while committing the symbolic equivalent of rape against his child was brilliant. If only he could take credit for having planned it.

Aeron savored the thought a bit longer, then returned to the conversation. "And you have never Shared with Ryan?"

Abigail smoothed her skirt. "I have a standing invitation."

"Yes, I know, courtesy of her father."

Abigail smiled, remembering the recent events in her chambers. "I do not think the girl would resist, with or without the blood debt."

"But you have not tested the waters, so to speak."

"No," Abigail replied, "so to speak."

She was thoughtful for a moment, then turned her gaze upon Aeron, smiling her cool smile. "There are many paths to domination, some far more enjoyable than force."

Aeron eyed her. "Yes, my dear. I am well-aware of your powers of persuasion. Which is why I avoid the many snares you have laid across the paths of every one of our Kind. Most blindly tumble into your traps and are not even aware they have been taken captive."

Abigail said nothing, merely smiled. If she was at all perturbed by his comments, it did not show. Except, perhaps, in her next words to him, which would be her last for the evening.

"I just hope you know what you are doing. The plan of action you have chosen is going to cause great instability in Ryan." Abigail stood, running her cool fingers through Aeron's hair as she passed. She paused in the doorway, her eyes gleaming in the darkness. "And I know how unstable she can be."

CHAPTER 8

RYAN KNEW SOMETHING WAS WRONG the moment the plane landed. Susan Ryerson's expression would have told her the same thing had she not already sensed it.

"Where is my father?" Ryan asked, coming up the stairs three at a time, knowing the answer.

"He's in his room. He has requested your presence as soon…"

Susan's words trailed off because she was speaking to empty air. Ryan had literally disappeared.

Ryan pushed through the double doors of Victor's room and stopped. Her father lay very still in an immense bed staring out the window. For a moment he simply stared, then slowly turned to face her. Ryan swallowed hard.

Outwardly he had not changed. His handsome face was youthful and unlined, with perhaps just a touch more gray at the temples of his jet black hair. But the exhaustion in his dark eyes brought a fierce ache to Ryan's throat. In an instance she was on her knees at his side, clasping his hand to her cheek.

He gazed down at his golden-haired child, caressing her cheekbone. He placed his fingers beneath her chin, tipping her head up so she would look at him.

"I am going to have to go away for awhile."

Ryan closed her eyes, the words creating an agony within her that no physical pain could match. She clasped his hand so tightly it would have crushed normal bone. Victor held her hand just as tightly.

"We have been apart before."

Ryan shook her head violently. "No, not like this. Even when I thought you were dead by my hand, part of me knew you were still here. But," she shook her head, having difficulty with the words, "I feel you slipping away right now. And I don't know where you are going, or if you will return."

Victor managed a tired smile. "My leaving will give you strength. But I will come back for you, little one. If I can. In fact," he said with emphasis, "I have a feeling you will bring me back."

Ryan shook her head, "I have caused this, I know that I have. You never recovered from my violence."

Victor leaned back on his pillow. "I should not have kept so many secrets from you. I did it to protect you, and now there is no time to tell you what you need to know."

Ryan's jaw clenched and unclenched, the ache in her throat unbearable. Impossibly, a tear began to roll down her cheek.

Victor touched the tiny drop of water in wonder. "You truly are capable of anything."

"I am capable of nothing," Ryan whispered in anguish, "I cannot stop this thing."

Victor again leaned back into his pillow, exhausted. "Perhaps you are not meant to stop it."

Ryan again leaned forward, grasping his hand. "You see the future," she said with insistence, "I know that you do."

Victor turned to his progeny and smiled. "Perhaps."

Ryan clenched his hand even closer. "Then tell me what you see. Tell me that you will come out the other side of this."

Victor closed his eyes. "It is not clear. The future never is."

The answer increased Ryan's anguish, if that was possible. Victor opened his eyes again and reached over, toying with a tendril of her hair. His gesture was playful, but his words were deadly serious.

"You must trust no one, Ryan. No one except yourself. And that you must do absolutely."

Ryan pressed his hand to her forehead, closing her eyes. "I don't understand. What is it that I must do?"

"The Others, those sitting on the Grand Council. You are going to have to," Victor paused, as if the thought pained him, "you are going to have to get very close to them."

Ryan was taken aback, knowing what he was asking her to do. "I cannot," she shook her head at the thought, "I cannot do that."

Victor was firm. "My power has always been my ability to resist desire. Yours," he said, nodding to where her powerful heart sat mute, "might be in giving in to it."

Ryan started to pull away from him but he grasped her hands firmly, and once again his grip was steel. His eyes burned into her. "No one can dance on the edge of death like you can, Ryan. No one. But there is only one way for the Others to learn that lesson."

Ryan swallowed hard. She could not hold his gaze and looked down, but Victor grasped her chin and forced her to look up.

"You will be King, Ryan," Victor said softly, firmly, "it is your fate, and your destiny."

Ryan shook her head violently. "You are my King. You always will be."

Victor smiled and leaned back into his pillow, his strength ebbing. "Hmmm, yes. And look where that's gotten me."

He grew quiet, and Ryan realized those would be his last words.

Marilyn was standing before an open window of her country chateau, gazing out into the well-manicured courtyard. She had returned to France almost immediately after the Council meeting, waiting only for Ryan to depart, which occurred as soon as the girl had left Abigail's quarters.

She had been here only a few hours, and was standing before the open window enjoying the beauty of her country when she felt it coming. Instinctively, she grasped the window sill in front of her tightly, bracing herself for the onslaught.

It rushed toward her, accelerating to an impossible speed, then exploded through the window, ripping through her, burning and shredding everything in its path, leaving only an echo of agony behind.

Marilyn stood frozen, gripping the window sill. Her vision gradually returned to normal. The pastoral scene in front of her was unchanged.

But in fact, everything had just changed.

Ala felt the warmth of her mother sun on her ebony skin, and welcomed the deep, mossy smell of the fecund earth. It was renewal for her; she kneeled and dug her hands into the rich, dark soil of her homeland.

She stood and her consorts stood by respectfully, grateful for their Queen's return. One brought her an elaborately decorated cloth with which to wipe her hands. She took the cloth, honoring the ritual. The hand movement slowed, however, and then stopped. Several of the consorts looked at her with concern as a strange look crossed her features. The cloth dropped to the ground as if in slow motion.

Ala turned to the west, just in time for the wave of agony to overtake her. It sliced through her like shards of ice riding the edge of a bitterly cold wind. It took her breath away, and although she had no need of this air, she felt the loss as keenly as if she did.

She gazed off into the distance, her eyes dark with the knowledge of an approaching storm.

Kusunoki was deep in meditation. His mind was a placid pool, reflecting all and reflecting nothing. Although he had not required oxygen for centuries, he still utilized breathing techniques in his practice. His chest rose and fell rhythmically, the tempo undisturbed by anything in the external world.

Hundreds of years of studied concentration had yielded a mind so perfectly trained that nothing could disturb the utterly still surface of that inner pool. But even so the surface began to tremble, as if agitated by some great force at a distance. Kusunoki attempted to return to stillness, but the surface of the pool began to ripple, then shake violently, as if the force was rapidly getting closer. Kusunoki tried to calm the surface through his iron will, but it was too late, and the pool was caught in a maelstrom, sucked upward into a twisting, violent whirlwind, spraying liquid everywhere.

Kusunoki opened his eyes. He was seated in his meditation chamber, alone. His breathing, which had become harsh and ragged, was stopped. His fists were clenched so tightly that the skin across his knuckles had split wide open. The silence was complete, and the only movement in the utter stillness was the stream of blood that slowly made its way down his arm until it dripped to the floor, forming a perfectly still pool.

Abigail had returned to her private estate, which was decorated in much of the same cool elegance of her Council chambers. As she settled into a pale blue settee, she wondered if the anticipation of an event lessened its impact, or amplified it.

She turned her head ever so slightly to one side. She was about to find out.

The effect was definitely not the former as the anticipation of the force did nothing to lessen its crushing blow. It was impossible to say if the anticipation had amplified the effect because it was of such magnitude, comparisons of size lost meaning.

Abigail let the anguish pass through her like a raging torrent, doing what she could to redirect the flow so that it would damage little and leave her body in the most expeditious manner possible.

When it had passed, she again settled into her settee, gathering her knitting to her lap. Her fingers remained motionless, however, and her eyes unfocused as she stared off into the distance, a look of deep contemplation on her face.

Aeron sat before a chess board whose pieces represented a game four centuries old. He pondered the positions of the pieces, and the knight that had been so boldly moved into a highly unorthodox but brilliant attack. He could not help but smile at the audacity of the move.

However, although fortune might favor the bold, chess could punish them mercilessly. Aeron reached for the rook, ready to counter, but paused when his hand touched the piece. His hand hovered in the air, and he caressed the top of the ivory playing piece with his finger, waiting.

The wave struck him, causing exquisite pain, washing through with a throbbing urgency, leaving only an aching that gave him intense pleasure. He sat for a moment as the feeling ebbed, enjoying every last second of the pain.

Aeron refocused on the board, his hand still on the rook. He smiled to himself as he carefully moved the rook to the square the knight was occupying, and removed the piece from the board.

Edward stood outside Victor's quarters, his head bowed and his eyes closed. There was nothing he could do to assuage his own grief, let alone the agony of his young liege still inside the room. Susan came up beside him and put her hand gently on his arm, and although Edward did not think it possible, the touch brought him comfort.

Minutes passed, perhaps an hour, then both were startled as both doors were thrown open. Ryan strode through the doorway, her face without expression, her mannerisms carefully controlled. She had changed and was now entirely in black, and Edward noted that she wore her father's clothes well.

She turned to him, and her voice was as controlled as her mannerisms. "Prepare my father for transportation, we will be leaving within the hour."

Edward nodded, "And may I inquire as to our destination?"

Ryan glanced at Susan, then back at Edward. "You know where we are going."

"Ah," was all Edward said.

Ryan strode off in the same tightly controlled manner. Susan glanced at Edward uncertainly. Edward touched her sleeve, still watching his departing master.

"I suggest that you and your son prepare yourselves for imminent departure. I think even an hour is a luxury we do not have."

They boarded the plane forty-five minutes later, as Victor's body, draped in black was carefully loaded under Edward's watchful eye. Susan was surprised when Ryan dismissed the pilot and disappeared into the cockpit. Jason, who had been awakened for the departure, had already fallen asleep in his seat, so Susan moved into the seat next to Edward, who was settling in. As far as Susan could see, there was no one else on the plane.

Edward confirmed this. "I am afraid that we are going to a location of such secrecy I am going to have to forbid you to look out the windows." He began pulling down the window shutters. "And you will not be allowed to disturb Ryan in flight."

"Will she be piloting the plane?" Susan asked.

Edward nodded as he settled back into his seat. "She is the only one who knows where we are going."

Susan's head was whirling at what had transpired in the last few hours. Victor's rapid deterioration during Ryan's absence greatly distressed Susan, and although she had made great progress in the brief time in which she had to work, she felt a sense of failure that she had not been able to even slow down the progression of the disease.

If it was in fact a disease, she thought to herself. She wasn't even certain what had happened to him, other than the dramatic rise in histamine in his system she had observed, which made no sense at all.

As Victor worsened, he had been adamant that Ryan was not to be disturbed or called to return. It was only through luck itself or Victor's force of will that he had remained conscious long enough for her to arrive.

Unconscious. Is that what he was now? Or was he truly dead? She had carefully watched his body for any of the initial signs of death, the rigor mortis, the pooling of fluids. There were no markers to indicate he had passed from life to death, only that he was…gone. Whatever had animated his immortal shell wasn't anywhere to be found.

She glanced over at her sleeping son. She had pulled him into such a world of danger. She knew that Ryan would protect him at all costs, but in the last few hours, she was vigorously reminded of how terrifying an individual that Ryan herself could be.

These dark thoughts swirled through her head, and so it was with some surprise, she found herself drifting into a sleep she had not experienced in days.

Ryan sat in the pilot's chair, her hands expertly moving over the controls of the plane. Her passengers were not aware of it, but this was in fact a different aircraft than the one they were used to flying in. Of course, Ryan thought to herself, none of the modifications would have been obvious to anyone other than those deep within the research arm of the United States Department of Defense. And they would be so mortified to learn that the technology had been "borrowed," they would most likely deny all knowledge anyway.

But the very technology she had borrowed guaranteed that the denial would be unnecessary. The design of this plane had only two objectives: speed and concealment.

Ryan glanced at the tactical air navigation system. They were beginning to move northwest, albeit by a very indirect route. Ryan checked the various instruments spitting out electronic countermeasure data. She then checked the readout on the exhaust temperature control system, satisfied. The plane had a tighter thermal signature than a stealth bomber.

Ryan sat back in her seat, relaxing for a moment and pondering their destination. She allowed herself a slight smile, although there was no humor in it.

If the Bermuda Triangle had a Bermuda Triangle, that was where they were heading. But unlike the Devil's Triangle of popular lore, there were no mystical stories about this vortex. There might have been whispers or quiet murmurs, but the few who knew anything about this black hole in the middle of the ocean kept their silence. That was because people disappeared. Not just those unfortunate enough to cross within 500 miles of this particular latitude and longitude, but also everyone who knew those people, and then everyone who knew those people.

Fortunately, outside of all normal shipping lanes, without military significance, and at a deadly confluence of currents, the location was rarely disturbed, and the number of those requiring "silencing" was few.

Susan opened her eyes, confused. She had a moment of complete disorientation before the events of the last few days came flooding back to her. She glanced around for Jason, then saw him playing a board game with Edward. On closer examination, she realized Edward was teaching him to play chess.

As she became more oriented, she realized they were still on the jet. She had no idea how long she had slept, but she had impression that it had been a very long time. She stretched, then stood, just in time for Ryan's voice to come over the intercom.

"Edward, tell Jason to look out the window."

Edward seemed surprised, but opened the window shade. Susan walked over and joined them as they gazed out the side window.

Susan caught her breath, and Jason gazed in wonderment. "It's a castle, mom."

The airplane was winging over an island that looked as if it had just risen out of the sea. It was gorgeous, pristine with an ancient, untouched beauty. The land was bordered on all sides by steep, forbidding cliffs which rose to even more forbidding mountains. There was a narrow ledge high on the cliffs, surrounded by peaks, cut by a million years of wind and rain. And perched, impossibly, on that ledge was a 13th century English castle. A waterfall bordered the west edge of the citadel, falling a thousand feet to the swirling sea below.

No sooner had they passed the castle than the sea just off the island began to churn, as if moved by some great underwater disturbance. The churning became violent, and then a huge mass broke the surface and began moving upward, pushed by some massive, unseen machinery.

It took a moment, but Susan realized there was now a full-sized runway where seconds before they had only been ocean. She and Jason could barely get to their seats before the plane came to a floating, perfect landing. Within seconds, the plane's engines were shutting down.

Ryan stood on the balcony, gazing out at the waterfall. The water was so close she could feel the spray when the wind came up. It was not loud, however, because the water flowed down the smooth cliff for another thousand feet before it collided with the sea. She felt Edward's presence behind her, but did not turn.

"Your father's bod-, I mean your father, is settled in his chambers."

"Very well," Ryan said stiffly.

Edward stood, staring at his liege's back. He finally spoke again. "Dr. Ryerson awaits you in the study."

Ryan stood silently for a moment, then turned. "Then I will see her now."

Susan was seated in front of the fire. Although this island was very green, it was also very cold, making her wonder just how far north they were. She and Jason had already bundled up with the clothes they had been provided by the castle's ephemeral staff.

Susan had been surprised to see that anyone lived in the castle, or actually within a thousand miles of the island itself. It seemed to exist in the middle of nowhere, as remote as inaccessible. The staff did not speak, and she had the feeling she would never hear them do so. She also had the feeling that these people had never left this island, nor would they.

Ryan materialized in the room, startling Susan. She walked to her desk and picked up a newspaper. Susan peered at the header and realized that it was the Wall Street Journal. On closer inspection she realized it was tomorrow's Wall Street Journal. She shook her head. That couldn't be right. She glanced at her watch, wondering what the time difference and date was.

Ryan caught the gesture. "Yes, it is tomorrow's paper, even according to Greenwich Mean Time."

Susan knew she didn't want the answer but could not help herself. "So how is that you get tomorrow's newspaper, or how is that you get a newspaper delivered here at all?"

Ryan skimmed the headlines. "I get the film as soon as it's run. Computers and satellites have made it far easier to obtain information on this island, as isolated as it is."

Susan was processing that, but still didn't understand. "But how is it that it's newsprint, just like a regular newspaper?"

"What?" Ryan said, glancing up from the paper. "Oh, that. There's a printing press in the basement."

"A printing press," Susan repeated, disbelief in her voice.

Ryan was again reading the headlines. "Umm, yes. My father liked to read the newspaper."

Susan shook her head, still not believing. "So this printing press, it prints out one newspaper?"

"Hmmm?" Ryan said. "Oh yes, unless of course I want to read Le Monde or The Guardian, or something. Then it might print out two or three."

Susan sat for a moment, trying to process this piece of information. Ryan folded the paper and tossed it back on the desk. She moved to the seat across from Susan, settling into the dark leather chair.

"I am sorry," Ryan said.

Susan shook her head. "No, I'm sorry. I'm sorry I couldn't do anything to help your father."

Ryan's glanced down for a moment, jaw clenching, then quickly got back on task. "No, you don't understand. I am sorry that I have essentially kidnapped you again."

"What do you mean?" Susan asked.

"Well, several things. I have brought you here because I want you to continue your examination of my father. I don't believe his body will decay. I believe he is," she paused, searching for the words, "in some state of suspension. If there is any way of finding out what is wrong with him, then I believe you are the one who will find it."

Susan was honored at the belief in her abilities, but a little uneasy as well.

"Secondly, politically, there are many very dangerous things occurring among my Kind, and I believe you could be a target both directly and indirectly."

"And a liability," Susan said, saying what Ryan would not.

Ryan slowly nodded. "I would not want to have to choose between protecting you and protecting my father."

Susan didn't want to contemplate the outcome of that choice.

"And finally, I am going to be pulled away to—," Ryan paused, obviously angry. "To attend to some business."

Susan would not ask. Ryan waited to see what Susan's response would be. She did not want an unwilling captive.

Susan shook her head. "I'm never going to get Jason in public school," she mused.

Ryan smiled.

Susan was gratified to learn that, once again, Ryan had amply provided her with research facilities. As she examined the state-of-the-art medical equipment in the laboratory, she wondered how it had been delivered to the island in secrecy. On further thought, she decided she really didn't want to know.

"I hope this meets with your approval."

Susan was again startled by Ryan's presence at her side. "I wish you would make a little more noise when you move around," Susan said.

Ryan merely smiled. "If there's anything else you think you might need, just let Edward know."

Susan turned to her. "Will you be leaving?"

Ryan nodded, obviously displeased at the prospect. "I have some things I have to attend to."

Susan knew better than to probe any further. She turned back to the equipment. "I think what is here is more than sufficient."

Ryan picked up a pair of clamped scissors. "I know that I was gone for only a short time, but did you make any progress in my absence?"

Susan walked over to the charts that had been transferred from the estate. She picked one up with a graph on it.

"In trying to figure out what is wrong with Victor, I am hampered by the fact that I have no idea what might be right." Susan gazed at the chart thoughtfully. "So the only approach that I can use is to compare you and your father and look for something different between you. You two are so genetically similar that you are literally two of a kind, perhaps the only two of your kind."

Ryan replaced the scissors, then picked up a scalpel. "That seems a good approach. Have you found anything, yet?"

Susan showed the graph to Ryan. "Well, I found this, which made no sense at all to me."

Ryan examined the graph, which showed a gradual increase that transitioned into a much sharper increase. "What is this?"

Susan examined the graph herself. "It's the histamine levels in Victor's blood, which rose exponentially the few days you were gone."

Ryan set the scalpel down, puzzled. "And why would that happen?"

Susan was thinking aloud. "Well, I'm not really sure. Histamine occurs in all the soft tissues of the body and is formed by the removal of acid from amino acids, similar to serotonin, dopamine, and adrenaline." Susan traced the line on the chart with her finger.

"Normal blood histamine levels are between 40 and 70 mg. Levels that are too low can cause hallucinations and paranoia. Levels that are too high can cause overstimulation, rapid thoughts, sensory distortion, and a ridiculously high pain threshold."

Susan appeared slightly embarrassed. "And although this is probably not applicable to your father, blood histamine levels in humans directly affect sexual behavior. A low level causes lack of sexual desire and a high level causes over-sexed behavior."

Ryan stared at the chart. Victor's levels had been high from the start, but had increased to pathological levels. "So what do you make of this?"

Susan was suddenly very uncertain. "I have a theory," she said hesitantly, "but it's very speculative."

Ryan glanced up at her. "Please continue."

Susan still hesitated "There is some fairly recent research tying histamine levels in the brain to a physiological state in which central nervous system activity is deeply depressed, maintained at a very low but functionally responsive level." She paused again. "This 'state' allows the body to conserve energy and down-regulate cellular functions such as rate of respiration and blood flow."

Ryan processed the technical information. "And what is this 'state' you refer to?"

Susan cleared her throat. "It's called hibernation."

Ryan stared at the red-headed woman. "You think my father is hibernating?"

Susan's discomfiture was evident. "I don't know. I told you it was very speculative. But I saw something very similar in your system when you were recovering from your wounds the first time I saw you. It is possible that Victor's system knew it was under significant attack and began to shut down in order to minimize the damage."

Ryan was silent for a moment, then spoke quietly. "I think that your approach should also focus on an artificial agent rather than a natural event."

Susan wasn't quite sure she understood. "What do you mean?"

Ryan's words were quiet but there was an edge to her tone. "I don't believe that this is a natural virus or infection. I believe that this was an attack on my father."

Susan considered her words. "Then that would mean that someone has considerable knowledge of Victor's anatomy, that they were able to design a pathogen capable of overcoming his immune system." She shook her head. "I just don't see how that's possible."

Ryan was uncertain herself. "I know. But you have to consider the resources of those who stand against us." She gestured to the roomful of medical equipment. "This is effortless for any of my Kind. They simply have to find the right person to get to."

Aeron sat at his dinner table in a darkness lit only by flickering candles and the licking flames of the fireplace. There were times when he despised the harsh, artificial glow of the modern light bulb. And fluorescent lights were in a loathed category all their own. Halogen, Aeron thought as he gazed balefully at the waiting figure in the doorway, halogen made him want to kill someone.

The frightened servant stepped forward, knowing that the news he had for his master would not be taken well. He stood, nearly shaking, unwilling to speak until spoken to.

Aeron fingered the silverware of his place setting, particularly the knife. It was long, thin, and sharp, appearing to be a utensil more suited for a surgical procedure than an elegant dinner. He tapped his fingers on the crisp, clean, tablecloth.

"Well?" he said finally, his voice smooth and deceptively calm.

The servant swallowed hard. "There is no sign of them, my lord." He swallowed again. "They seem to have disappeared."

"Ah," Aeron said lightly. He rearranged the silverware, as if giving great thought to its relative placement. He was not pleased with the arrangement, and moved it back to its original position. He was considering moving it again when he became aware of the groveling servant once more.

"When?" he asked, his tone still light.

"They were tracked to their primary residence immediately following the meeting of the Grand Council. The residence was placed under observation, but after no signs of movement for several days, the residence was entered. There was no sign of either of the Alexanders. Ryan Alexander's manservant, Edward, was missing, as was the human female doctor and her son."

Aeron nodded, his expression still deceptively calm. "And when do you think they left?"

The servant, uncertain how to reply, made the mistake of stating the obvious. "Sometime between Ryan Alexander's arrival and when we entered the premises."

"Really?" Aeron said. "You think?" His expression grew cold. "Minutes," he said. "She was gone within minutes." He was having difficulty maintaining his air of calmness, although his tone was still tightly controlled. He moved the silverware again. "And, attempts to locate them-?"

The servant shook his head. "All have failed. My lord, it is literally as if they have disappeared off the face of the earth."

Aeron nodded. "Ah," was all he said. He delicately picked up the knife.

CHAPTER 9

Ryan stood at the door of the discotheque. Located in the heart of a monstrous city, it was known to be a hotspot for tourists.

It was also full of Young Ones, Ryan thought to herself, she could feel them in all of their worldly, naïve stupor, intoxicated with new, unimagined pleasures. She entered the club.

At first glance, the scene was so stereotypical of modern vampire movies that she thought it could not possibly be real. No one from her Kind could possibly find this situation interesting or stimulating. She pinched the bridge of her nose in exasperation.

The room was filled with beautiful young people, all in various states of undress, undulating to some horrible electronic noise. The lights were flashing on and off, reflecting from an endless array of mirrors. The air was thick with smoke and fog, pierced only by the red and blue lasers shooting from a rotating ball.

Ryan stared, aghast. Even if she had not been compelled by decree, she would have killed them all simply for subjecting her to such stupidity.

She strolled into the nightclub, a dark-clothed figure who moved almost languorously in contrast to the frenetic movement all around her. She attracted no attention, ignored by Young Ones who still habitually mistook physical appearance for actual age. She walked up to the bar, and the bartender leaned over to her.

"I don't suppose you have any decent wine?" Ryan asked.

The bartender hesitated. There was something odd about the girl's voice. Although the din in the place was deafening, she was speaking in normal tones and he could easily hear her. The voice itself was odd, with a strange inflection and an authority that was far beyond her age. When she turned her gaze upon him, he froze, the glass he had been drying now motionless in his hand.

"I don't think we have anything that would be acceptable to you."

Ryan nodded. "I think you're right."

She turned, and the bartender had the impression that she moved in slow motion, an utter stillness about her in the mass of frenzied, writhing bodies. As he watched her walk toward the door, strangely, the movements seemed to reverse themselves. It was she who now appeared to be moving at normal speed, but the motion of everyone else in the room had slowed to a crawl. The faces and bodies of the dancers were frozen, contorted like those in an unfortunately-timed photograph. All the while the black-garbed figure walked leisurely toward the exit.

The bartender felt ice wash through his body. He dropped the glass and sprang toward the door, but he, too, was frozen in time. As the girl turned and smiled a wicked smile at him, he knew that he would never bridge the gap between them, that she had all the time in the universe, and that she would be a world away before the glass hit the floor.

He was right on all counts but one. The glass never hit the floor because the floor disappeared in an explosion of glass, metal, and fire.

Ryan walked up the steps to the church, glancing at the light streaming through the elaborate stained glass windows. It made beautiful patterns in the night, a stark contrast to the source material of hellfire and damnation depicted in the frames.

She pushed through the doors, brushing by an usher who seemed unaware of her presence, his gaze passing right through her. She pushed through another set of doors and settled into the rearmost pew, one of the few empty in the congregation. Her arrival attracted no attention, caused no interruption in the service.

Ryan glanced around the chapel. The décor was one she associated with modern Christian broadcasts, spectacles she occasionally watched with equal parts horror and fascination. It had that curious mixture of attempted humility and tasteless opulence: an overabundance of gold leaf everywhere, excruciatingly intricate faux woodwork, an immense, oversized cross that Jesus Christ and all twelve disciples could not have carried. Elaborate sconces and candlesticks lit the room, casting flickering shadows on the stained glass that continued its depictions of the most horrific portions of the bible down the walls.

Ryan frowned. The message was clear: self-sacrifice promoted everywhere but here. She leaned back in her seat, her thoughts drifting to her childhood. The Church had been all-powerful then, immoral and corrupt. It had enslaved an ignorant populace, peasants like herself who had been illiterate and incapable of reading the word of God written in the incomprehensible language of Latin. She had killed a priest in the act of raping a child, and in return had nearly been executed. It was only the hidden intervention of Victor that saved her life.

Ryan smiled, and it wasn't pleasant to see. In her seven centuries, she had slain thousands, but the priest had been her first, and one of the most enjoyable.

She turned her attention to the current religious figure, idly examining him. He was handsome enough, with words that had a musical quality, volume that rose and fell, diction that was commanding and cajoling, conspiratorial and patronizing, promising and threatening. His voice drifted over his enraptured congregation, and Ryan felt her irritation stir. If there was anything worse than a religious charlatan, it was a religious charlatan who was one of her Kind.

There was considerable movement in the assembly, and it was apparent some sort of ceremony was beginning. Chalices were brought forward to the altar, and members of the congregation began to pair off. Ryan realized that some sort of communion was being offered, although she doubted this was exactly what Christ had in mind.

A beautiful young woman stood and walked the aisle to the pastor. The rapt congregation waited in a mixture of anticipation, worship, and lust. The woman kneeled, offering her wrists. Attendants to the pastor stepped forward with chalices and jewel-encrusted daggers. Simultaneously, with well-practiced moves, they sliced the woman's wrists and began draining her blood into the goblets. The woman moaned in agony and ecstasy, and the pastor cupped his hand beneath her chin, causing her to rise. The attendants did not spill a drop as they rose with her. The pastor said some incantation, then lowered his head to her neck, slicing into her throat with his teeth.

Ryan watched the spectacle with only mild interest, turning her attention to those surrounding her. They were being driven into bloodlust, stoked by their religious fervor. When the woman at the altar collapsed, they were driven nearly to a frenzy, and began pairing with one another.

Ryan was curiously unmoved by the scene. She had been witness to much depravity during her long life, and this barely on her scale. If these people wished to Share in the context of a religious experience, so be it. But she did have a job to do.

The pastor immediately noticed the tall figure as she stood in the back of the church, incredulous that he had not seen the golden-haired stranger before. She was startlingly beautiful, with a unique presence that seemed to shift the space around her. She was a welcome addition to his flock and he motioned for her to step forward.

As the figure began to walk up the aisle, those she passed broke their bonds, one by one raising their heads uncertainly. Those they fed upon also raised up, drawn to the fair-haired one.

The pastor felt his excitement grow. He could not tell how old this girl was, although he did not think she was as old as his century mark. His congregation was made up entirely of Young Ones, their lust so great they constantly killed one another. It would be pleasant to have someone slightly older, someone more powerful to sate his hunger. His eyes gleamed as the girl approached. He did not know if he could control his own passion, however, nor guarantee the girl's life.

Ryan sensed these thoughts and was amused. Over time she had grown more and more capable of disguising her presence, and at times it was nearly a game to her. The pastor held out his hands to her, but Ryan did not take them. She could disguise her presence, but she could not hide the power in her touch.

The pastor misinterpreted her hesitation. "Do not be afraid, my child.

The Lord will welcome you into his everlasting arms."

Ryan's amusement grew. "I really don't think so. I don't think heaven would welcome me at all."

Evidently, the pastor was also deaf to sarcasm, because he again misinterpreted her meaning. "I am certain you are worthy, my child. Kneel, and it shall be proven so."

Ryan gazed at him. Without revealing the full extent of her power, she began to put pressure on him, subtly at first, but steadily increasing.

"I bow before no one," she said quietly.

Confusion was apparent on the pastor's face. He felt an immense downward force, and the oddest desire to kneel. He withstood the impulse only seconds before he went down on one knee, and then the other. The entire congregation grew silent and still, spellbound and at the sight of their leader on his knees before the golden-haired stranger.

"You do not know me," Ryan said, "but I am going to give you a gift." She raised her finger to her lips and ran the very tip lightly over her front teeth. A drop of blood appeared on the fingertip.

The pastor stared at the finger, as did the rest of the congregation. He was mesmerized by the drop, an infinitesimal amount that created a boundless ache within him he did not understand. He raised his eyes to the girl's, who gazed down at him.

Very slowly, Ryan allowed her presence to be known. And very slowly, those in the room saw her as she truly was. Fear and longing swept through the church, settling most firmly on the pastor kneeling at her feet. His terror was infinite, surpassed only by his craving for her blood.

Ryan stared at the man, then at the drop on her finger. "It will kill you," she said resolutely. "But then again, most vices eventually will."

The drop wavered before him, but there was never any doubt as to his decision. He grabbed the wrist, but could not budge the arm, so powerful was the creature in front of him. Very slowly, Ryan lowered her hand, touching the finger to his lips. She pulled it away instantly, leaving only a touch of red.

The pastor's eyes rolled back in his head, both in pain and ecstasy as the blood shot through his veins like lightning. His last thought was that the agony was more than he anticipated, but worth it all the same.

Ryan turned to the shocked and mesmerized congregation. "You know what I expect of you," she said, her words easily carrying in the silent hall. She stepped down from the altar, and casually walked down the aisle. No one moved until the black-garbed figure had disappeared.

They sat for a long time, staring at one another.

And then they went about the Lord's business.

CHAPTER 10

AERON FELT ABIGAIL'S APPROACH a great distance off. He knew why she had come. Her intelligence sources were as good, if not better, than his own. He had been expecting her.

She swept into his parlor, a cool, elegant, feminine presence in stark contrast to the dark masculinity of his furnishings. He held out his hand and she offered hers. He brushed his lips across her skin, and dismissed her escort with a glance

Abigail settled, smoothing the skirt that never wrinkled. She did not bother with small talk.

"It seems our young prince has resurfaced."

"Oh really," he said noncommittally.

Abigail smiled, not fooled by his demeanor. "Yes. The papers have reported a 'terrorist attack' in which over 400 Americans were killed in a discotheque."

Aeron did not perpetuate his charade of ignorance. "Yes, 380 of which were our Kind. Clever girl," he added, half to himself. "Took out a crowd of Young Ones in a single blow."

Abigail, "And a church."

Aeron raised an eyebrow. This he had not heard.

"Apparently one of our Kind was a pastor who had decided to transform his entire flock, creating one of the many cults among our Kind."

"Ah yes," Aeron said sarcastically, "the inevitable blending of religion, lust, and death from lesser beings who cannot handle the simple fact that we are killers."

Abigail smiled. "In this case, death, as in the 'angel of death,' was the predominant theme. Accounts from the few survivors describe the visitation of 'the bright morning star' who sowed mass confusion, resulting in the destruction of almost the entire congregation."

"She killed them?"

"Oh no," Abigail said, "she didn't have to. They all killed one another."

Aeron contemplated this fact. "And you're certain it was her."

Abigail nodded. "There is no doubt."

Aeron was impressed. An interesting strategy. "It appears our young friend is pursuing quantity over quality, although I must confess the ingenuity of her methods thus far is remarkable as well."

"If you will remember, her father employed the same 'creativity' in his elimination process, although he did not have nearly the mobility or the resources that she has now. And," Abigail said thoughtfully, "I don't believe there has ever been a hunter of this magnitude, not even Victor."

Aeron was silent for a moment. "How many from the congregation?"

Abigail's reply was cool. "Over six hundred."

Before Aeron could fully digest this number, she added. "And that doesn't count those destroyed in the collapse of a skyscraper yesterday, a strategic accident."

Aeron glanced up sharply. "How many total?"

There was a hint of recrimination in her voice. "Nearly two thousand."

Nearly two thousand. Aeron turned the number over in his head. Two thousand in three days. Granted they were the weakest of their Kind, one step from being human, but still…

"We must give an order of dispersal," he said, thinking aloud. "No large gatherings. We can't make it too easy for our little hunter."

Abigail agreed, in principle. "It will be difficult. Our Kind are ever-social, drawn to one another by desire. If Young Ones willingly engage in the act of Sharing knowing they potentially face death, a more 'abstract' threat of death is unlikely to deter them." She paused, deep in thought for a moment before she continued.

"I have the feeling that Ryan is simply sending a message right now, expressing her disdain for this process. She wanted to personalize the initial strikes."

Aeron listened intently. Abigail knew Ryan better than almost anyone else. "And what would you expect her to do next?"

Abigail was thoughtful. "Ryan will not run about killing our Kind, as most hunters have done. It is beneath her. Where others revel in the power and death they perpetrate, Ryan simply doesn't care."

Abigail rose, the movement flowing and graceful. "I believe her strikes will grow more and more impersonal. And because she is in a fragile emotional state, I believe the damage she inflicts will grow exponentially." She turned to face Aeron.

"She will strike against us all, one way or another."

Aeron smiled pleasantly, although it wasn't pleasant to see. "She will not last that long."

There was much activity about the castle, and Susan was curious as to what could cause such commotion. When Ryan strode into the room completely unannounced, she realized the cause. Edward was nonplussed, but she did not know if that was because he had expected Ryan, or simply because he was accustomed to her unpredictability.

Ryan sat down at her desk and began shuffling paperwork. Without looking up, she addressed Edward.

"Are these the census figures I requested?"

Edward moved to her side. "They are not a sampling per se, but they are probably more accurate than a traditional census."

Ryan glanced up at him in question. He leaned down and picked up one particular chart. "Our Kind are notoriously secretive, which makes it difficult to locate them. However, using some very advanced population equations and computer modeling, we have determined what we believe to be an accurate number."

Ryan thumbed through the paperwork. "How many?"

Edward pulled a particular chart from the stack. "Approximately 50,000, worldwide."

"That's impossible."

Both Ryan and Edward looked up at the skepticism from the human occupant of the room. Susan had the grace to appear embarrassed at eavesdropping, but did not relent.

"There is no way that there are that few of your Kind on this planet. As long-lived as you are, with no natural enemies, your Kind should be the dominant species on earth."

"Well," Edward said mildly, "I would make that argument regardless of our number, but I see your point." He picked up another chart and Susan drew close.

"It is not entirely true that we have no natural enemies, because our Kind are both predator and prey internally within the species. And unlike human beings, we enjoy killing our young."

Susan swallowed at the reminder as Edward continued. "Which brings up some interesting dynamics in terms of population control. Our Kind cannot reproduce when young, nor when old, much like humans. The window of opportunity between when One is powerful enough to initiate Change but not so powerful that the human is destroyed is small, ranging from a few decades to perhaps a century in extreme cases."

"Yes," Susan agreed, "but even a few decades is more than enough time to create hundreds, if not thousands of offspring."

Ryan nodded. "If in fact that was a driving force for us. But unlike human beings, our reproduction is not linked to desire, and Sharing with humans is not that pleasant an experience. Nor do we have the evolutionary drive to pass on our genes because we do not face the specter of death." Ryan thought fleetingly of her father, and her expression darkened.

Edward continued. "And you must remember that the population rate is a function of both birth rate and attrition, and although those who survive their infancy are essentially immortal, the attrition rate prior to that is stratospherically high." Edward sighed, as if it were an unfortunate fact of life. "We enjoy killing more than creating."

Susan began to understand. "Your population curve, then must be a steep pyramid."

"Very steep," Edward replied, "although it's not exactly a pyramid, but more like an unbalanced hourglass, with the bulk of the sand at the bottom. The vast majority of our Kind at any given time are Young Ones. There are less than four hundred currently occupying the Middle Ground, those capable of reproducing." Edward nodded toward Ryan, "And as mentioned earlier, there is no guarantee that all four hundred are actively reproducing."

Susan was fascinated. "Then how many Old Ones are there?"

Edward was thoughtful. "If you use the term 'Old One' as anyone who is too powerful to initiate Change and has passed into immortality, there are perhaps fewer than four thousand."

Susan looked at the golden-haired woman. "And how many are there like Ryan?"

Edward smiled. "I would argue only one. But if you are referring to those at her level of power, such as Marilyn and Abigail, there are fewer than a hundred within striking distance, and perhaps two dozen who are even close."

Susan ran the numbers through her head, going back to an earlier thought. "Then that means that almost all of the 45,000 Young Ones who are alive now will die before they reach maturity."

Edward nodded. "Exactly. The attrition rate exceeds 98%. They will not survive complications from their Change, they may be killed by someone older, they may kill one another, or something will befall them before they can pass into immortality. But very few will survive to reproduce."

Ryan had been quiet for awhile, deep in thought. But now she spoke quietly.

"I now understand the significance of the cleansing. It is an unparalleled opportunity to shape the future of our Kind." She paused, her expression dark, "Or to end it entirely."

There was black humor in her words. "For example, if I were to strike at all the Young Ones of Aeron's line, there would be no one to pass into the middle ground to reproduce, and his line would effectively end."

Edward thought through this strategy. "Except there are already those occupying the middle ground who are of Aeron's descent who could create more Young Ones, and who cannot be killed."

Ryan tapped her fingernail on her teeth. "In theory," she said, "only in theory."

Edward shifted uncomfortably.

Ryan abruptly stood, and Edward stood out of protocol. "I am going to rest here awhile, then I will leave for Japan." She nodded to Susan, then turned on her heel. She was halfway to the door when she stopped, turning to Edward. "By the way, you need to adjust your figures downward by two thousand."

Ryan disappeared, and Edward sat down heavily, surprising Susan. She moved to the chair across from him. She was quiet for a moment, respecting his mood. She finally spoke.

"I am not certain that Victor offered me a gift, with a mortality rate of 98%."

Edward glanced up at her shrewdly. "You have only to survive your Change, Dr. Ryerson. None of the other perils will befall you."

This thought did not bring Susan much comfort. The two were quiet for a long moment, then Susan asked Edward a question that caused him a similar level of discomfort.

"So how did you and Ryan meet?"

Ryan and Victor led their horses by the reins, they themselves on foot. They had arrived in the American colonies a few months before, had explored most of what was inhabited, and now were drawn to the wilderness that unfolded endlessly to the west. Towns were growing fewer and farther between on their journey, and they debated leaving the horses entirely, knowing they could travel further on foot. Once they were beyond civilization, no one would question their lack of supplies or choice of transportation.

Victor cocked his head to one side, and Ryan sniffed the air. She could smell smoke from a distant fire, and could hear the faintest sounds of life ahead of them. They were approaching one of the few remaining towns on their chosen route. They remounted their horses, allowing them to pick their way through the forest.

It was apparent as they drew close that some large-scale commotion was occurring. As they exited the forest, they had a clear view across the river. A mob of people were carrying a bound man toward the water.

"I wonder what that unfortunate soul did," Victor mused, idly curious.

Ryan rested her hand on the neck of her horse. "Guessing by the intricate way he is bound, opposite hand to opposite foot, I would say he has been charged with witchcraft."

Victor glanced over at his charge, amused. "Oh, that's right, I forgot you have personal experience in such matters."

Ryan's expression darkened. "Hmm, yes."

Victor allowed his gaze to caress his young companion, quite fetchingly dressed as a boy. He turned his attention back to the drama unfolding across the river.

One man, apparently a preacher, was waving a bible so frenetically he accidentally struck the bound man in the face, causing the man's nose to begin bleeding profusely. Without much more fanfare, the mob carried him into the river and tossed him. He hit the water and immediately sank like a rock.

Ryan shrugged. "Well, you know what that means."

Victor glanced over at his young companion, suspicious at her tone.

"He's innocent," she said, driving her heels into her horse's flanks.

The horse bolted down the bank of the river, leaping into the current. Victor watched as the powerful steed charged through the water. He was always amazed at the battles Ryan chose.

The mob on the opposite bank were stunned at the sight of the striking golden-haired stranger on the jet-black horse barreling through the water as if it were air. A very primitive fear began to develop in all of them, even more primitive than the hysteria of the witch hunt. Their fear grew when the boy stood, balanced effortlessly on the back of his horse, then dove, knifing into the briskly moving current and disappearing beneath the surface.

The horse was still coming at them, full speed, and as it neared the bank, it reared up, kicking its flailing hoofs at them. They fell backward in fear, but the horse turned on its rear hoofs and began galloping back the way it came. As it neared the spot where the boy had entered the water, an arm broke the surface and wrapped itself about the stallion's neck. In a feat of enormous strength, the boy pulled himself back up onto the horse's back, dragging the bound man upward with him. The horse never broke stride, and the boy and the man were free from the water, riding off in the opposite direction.

Victor sighed, then pulled a knife from his belt. He threw it full force at Ryan, and the bound man's eyes widened at the incoming missile. He was astonished when his rescuer plucked the weapon from the sky, slicing his ropes with a downward swipe. The man was then able to straddle the horse properly, and clung to the young stranger's back.

Ryan laughed, entertained by the entire situation as she rode by Victor at breakneck speed. He turned his horse and spurred it, amused at her antics despite himself. They crashed through the forest at a perilous speed until finally Ryan reigned her horse in, wheeling it around. Victor brought his own horse to a halt as Ryan slid to the ground, still laughing.

"Well, that was fun," she said, finally regaining some semblance of control. Victor dismounted with slightly more dignity than his unruly companion. He patted his horse's flanks, calming it.

The man stared down at the two, wide-eyed. It seemed that they had forgotten all about him. He realized he was still wearing a gag, although his hands were no longer tied. He removed the filthy rag from his mouth, and it slipped from his nerveless fingers. The movement caught the dark-haired one's attention, and he glanced up.

"You may dismount," the dark-haired one said mildly, and it was not a request.

The man slid to the ground, stumbling because of the lack of circulation in his legs. The boy caught him, amusement still evident in his eyes.

It was unlike him, but the man was being moved by forces he had never encountered, by emotions with which he was unfamiliar. Without preamble, he fell to his knees in front of the golden-haired one. He grasped the boy's hand tightly in his own, and there was a fierce light in his eyes.

"I will serve you forever, my lord," the man said, his voice surprisingly educated. "And while you live, I will serve no other."

Ryan glanced down at the man, surprised at the refinement of his speech. She extricated herself from him, still mildly amused at the entire situation.

Victor pulled the pack from the back of his horse, speaking over his shoulder with mild reproach.

"Now look what you've done."

Susan tapped the pipette onto the slide and slid it beneath the microscope. She leaned forward to peer into the eyepieces, but stopped when she saw Ryan in the doorway. She was surprised because she knew that Ryan had been with her father.

Ryan pushed away from the door frame. "I understand you coaxed Edward into revealing our first meeting."

Susan smiled. "Yes, very interesting."

Ryan picked up some odd piece of medical equipment, gazed at it with some consternation, then replaced it. "You should feel honored. He doesn't tell that story to just anyone."

"I think he was afraid that if he didn't tell me, you would."

Ryan smiled a wicked smile. "Entirely possible." Her expression sobered once more. "Have you learned anything new regarding my father's condition?"

Susan leaned back. "Well, I don't know how applicable it is, but I keep learning new and interesting things about your anatomy. Do you know anything about mitochondria?"

Ryan settled into an office chair. "I'm sure you're going to educate me."

Susan smiled. "Mitochondria are tiny structures inside of cells that produce energy. They have their own pool of DNA, possibly because they were once an entirely separate creature millions of years ago. One theory holds that these creatures were absorbed by our predecessors and began producing energy."

Once again, Ryan was interested despite herself.

Susan continued. "The DNA inside the mitochondria mutates much faster than nuclear DNA, sometimes 10-20 times faster. One school of thought is that when the mitochondria make energy, there are left-over oxygen molecules that lack an electron and set off a lethal chain reaction that damages other cells. In popular literature, these oxygen molecules are called 'free radicals.' Common wisdom holds that these free radicals damage nearby DNA, causing mutations. The mitochondria are then less able to produce energy and slowly begin dying."

"Okay," Ryan said slowly, "I'm with you so far. And I'm guessing once again that mine are somehow different?"

Susan sighed. "That's the understatement of the year. The energy created in your mitochondria dwarfs that of a normal human being, and the mitochondria create that energy perfectly without throwing off any free radicals or by-products whatsoever."

Ryan was thoughtful. "So, if common wisdom is correct, my mitochondrial DNA mutates very little."

"Yes," Susan said, "and that is in fact the case. Your DNA is identical to what it probably was 700 years ago. Which would be almost impossible to tell were it not for another bizarre feature of your anatomy."

"Which is?" Ryan asked, amused at the description.

"You have Victor's mitochondrial DNA."

Ryan did not understand the significance of this statement, so Susan explained.

"Mitochondrial DNA is passed entirely down the maternal line. Victor should have his mother's, and you should have your mother's. But your mitochondrial DNA is identical to his."

Susan shook her head. "Over ninety-nine percent of mitochondrial DNA is passed through the mother under normal circumstances. But not yours."

Ryan was quiet for a long moment, then spoke. "I wonder if it's possible that some of my DNA was overwritten in my Change."

Susan stared at her. It was a brilliant hypothesis, one she hadn't considered.

"I don't know," Susan said truthfully. "But if I can find out, I will certainly let you know."

"Is there a particular reason why you were looking at the mitochondria?" Ryan asked.

Susan nodded. "Many significant human diseases are caused by some type of malfunction in the mitochondria. Mitochondria are so integral to energy production and general health, I thought it might be a good place to start looking. The problem is that I have no baseline for Victor, other than you, so it is difficult for me to assess mutation."

"Because other than me, you have nothing to compare it to," Ryan finished slowly. "So you are assuming it hasn't changed thus far because Victor's mitochondrial DNA is still the same as mine."

"Exactly," Susan said. "It's not the approach I would choose, but I really have no other choice. And at this point, I'm assuming it's a dead end."

Ryan considered her words. "Because Victor is ill and I am not."

Susan nodded.

Ryan returned to her earlier train of thought. "Hypothetically, if my DNA was overwritten in my Change, is it possible that it's still being overwritten when Victor and I Share blood, and that's why it's still the same?"

Susan had the grace to appear embarrassed. "Um, no. Unless in vivo is significantly different than in vitro."

Ryan interpreted her meaning. "You mixed our blood in a test tube."

Susan nodded. "Some really fascinating chemical reactions occurring when that happens, and I could spend a lifetime looking into those, but DNA mutation is not one of them. That's not to say that it didn't happen at some point in time in the past. But it's not happening now."

Ryan nodded, then abruptly stood. "I will let you return to your work. It sounds as if you have a lot of promising avenues to pursue."

Ryan gave one of her chivalrous bows, and then Susan watched her leave. Susan returned to her paperwork, thinking with irony that for once she wished she had a few less avenues available.

CHAPTER 11

RYAN WALKED RESPECTFULLY TO THE SIDE of the path leading to Kamiji-dori. It was nighttime, and those few souls still out did the same, leaving the path open for the Moon God and his horse. Although she presented a striking figure, they took little notice of her, and she less of them.

Ryan paused, breathing deeply the mountain air and fresh smell of the Isuzu river. This was truly one of the most beautiful places on earth, and although she had little patience for religious institutions, she did find something sacred about this shrine. She took a moment to wander through the structures, amazed at how faithfully they had been reproduced over the centuries. She thought for a moment, trying to remember what year it was, and realized they would be rebuilding it again on the adjacent property in a few years.

She passed through the shrine like a ghost, into the areas where no tourists were allowed, and then beyond those. She passed into the innermost sanctum, but did not stop there, either. Few if any knew that there was anything beyond this chamber.

Ryan paused in front of a door that would not be visible to any but those with preternatural eyesight. She pushed aside the heavy stone that blocked the way, then pushed open the heavy wooden door and started down the stone steps that disappeared deep into the mountainside.

The path was lit by torches, tended by ancient priests who saw that the light in this passageway never went out. She could feel their presence, and they could feel hers. Although she could not see them, she had the mental impression they bowed to her in respect.

Ryan felt the cool air as she approached the end of the tunnel. She exited the side of the mountain into a perfect gorge, lush with surrounding greenery, the true inner shrine. The layout was similar to the two outer shrines, simple gravel walkways, a wooden bridge, a Shinto gate, all leading to a simple wooden structure lit from within. Ryan glanced up at the full moon shining down through the trees. Although she walked on the gravel, there was no crunching noise.

She walked up the wooden steps, and slid the screen to the side.

Kusunoki looked up. "I have been expecting you."

Ryan removed her shoes, then bowed in the doorway before entering. "I expected as much."

Kusunoki watched his former pupil move into the room with the same lithe grace she had always possessed. She moved across from him, and settled into a kneeling position before the small table.

"Would you care for some tea?" he asked calmly.

"Yes, I think I would." She glanced around the room as he poured the tea into a bowl. "I see your accommodations have not changed."

He smiled. "It is all I need."

Ryan agreed. "It is all anyone needs."

She took the steaming tea from him, holding it in both hands, enjoying the sensation of heat.

"I saw your statue in the imperial garden, the one on the horse, it is quite impressive."

Kusunoki said nothing, sensing his pupil's wicked sense of humor coming into play.

"—Although I must say a few of the tapestries made you look a little plump."

Kusunoki smiled despite himself. He inhaled deeply from the green tea, then took a mindful sip.

"So when exactly did you change your name?"

"From what?" Kusunoki asked, feigning ignorance.

Ryan gazed balefully at him over the rising steam from her bowl.

Kusunoki sighed. "Tsukiyomi no Mikoto became a burden."

Ryan nodded in understanding. "But they still revere you above."

The thought gave Kusunoki no pleasure. "I think that all of our Kind have inspired legends at one time or another."

Ryan's thoughts flitted to the discotheque. "I would like to find who is responsible for a few of the more idiotic of those legends."

The two settled into silence and finished their tea. Kusunoki waited patiently for his young pupil to speak, but was surprised by her words when she did.

"Perhaps you could offer me shelter for a brief time," Ryan said. "I feel the need to sleep."

Kusunoki was startled by the request, but quickly corrected his manners. "Of course. You are always welcome here. Forgive me for not offering."

Ryan shook her head. "It is a strange request, I know. But I feel the need to dream much these days."

Kusunoki pondered the words, and their meaning. He would have to spend much time reflecting on this statement.

The two stood simultaneously, and Kusunoki gestured to one of the many sliding doors. "Your previous accommodations are nearly as you left them."

Ryan nodded her thanks and stepped from the main anteroom. The sleeping chamber was exactly as she remembered it. A simple bed, a lamp, a small stone fireplace, and a ceramic washbowl.

She settled on the bed, her long frame taking its entire length. It was limited in terms of comfort, but to her it brought the unparalleled comfort of familiarity.

Ryan rode alongside Victor, enjoying the easy movement of the horse as it clopped along the dirt road. They were attracting a great deal of attention, even more so than usual. It was typical of the handsome pair to draw the eyes of humans, but now their Western features were strikingly different from everything around them. Ryan's fair hair and light eyes were a startling contrast to the predominantly dark-eyed, dark-haired Japanese.

The hooves of the horses made a hollow sound as they clopped across a wooden bridge. Victor pulled the reigns of his horse and dismounted as a priest appeared from the gate. He bowed and took the horses reigns. Ryan nimbly descended from the horse's back, and the priest took her horse as well. She followed Victor through the Shinto gate.

They entered a neat enclosure with several wooden structures spread about. Several priests nodded to them, but did not cease their tasks. Victor and Ryan continued through the shrine until they came to a heavy wooden gate that appeared to lead nowhere. Victor pulled the gate open, revealing a long stairway that disappeared down into the center of the mountain. He began the long trek downward, and Ryan followed, pulling the heavy gate closed behind them.

It seemed they continued for several minutes at a good pace. The passageway was well-lit, although their vision would have been just as clear had it not been. Ryan sensed fresh air ahead, which surprised her.

They exited the tunnel, coming out into a small, beautiful valley. It was a perfect replica of the outer shrine, if perhaps a bit more meticulously maintained. Ryan realized it was probably the other way around, that the outer shrine was a copy of this place.

A handsome, distinguished man stood at the other side of the bridge, waiting for them. Ryan knew instantly that he was one of their Kind, and in fact, had felt his presence for some time. What struck her about him, though, wasn't his power or his beauty, both of which were considerable, but rather the utter stillness about him. It went beyond mere motionlessness, as if the particles in the air itself around him had stopped.

Victor approached him, then stopped about a foot before him, staring at the man. Ryan felt a bit uneasy, uncertain what was about to happen. But the man held Victor's gaze for a moment, then dropped his eyes and bowed deeply from the waist. Victor waited for the man to stand upright once more, then he, too, bowed deeply, returning the respect.

As Victor stood upright, the man's eyes sparkled and he smiled, instantly transforming his forbidding expression to one of mischief. Ryan noted that the man had a dazzling smile. He grasped Victor's forearm with his own.

"It has been too long, my friend."

"Yes," Victor agreed. "Too long. I have been," he paused, glancing at Ryan, "a little busy."

"Ah yes," Kusunoki said, "I can see that."

Ryan felt weight of the man's sudden scrutiny. It was similar to the attention of all Old Ones, both piercing and enveloping at the same time. And yet somehow, this time was different. It was as if the man's perception was tuned to a different place, as if he were searching for, and finding, very different things in her.

"Hmmm," he said, examining the girl, his expression unreadable.

Victor put his hand on Ryan's shoulder. "Rhian, I would like you to meet Kusunoki Masahige."

Ryan wasn't certain whether to bow or offer her hand, but the man solved her dilemma for her. He reached out and grasped her hand. Ryan felt the shock of connection as power flowed through her.

Kusunoki eye's narrowed. He felt it as well.

"Hmmm," was all he said. He released the hand and turned his attention back to Victor.

"I trust you will like your accommodations."

Victor and Ryan settled into adjacent rooms, and it wasn't long before Ryan's inherent restlessness took over and she began to wander the compound. Kusunoki watched her from the front terrace.

"So how did you manage that?" he asked quietly, sensing Victor's silent approach.

"It is," Victor began. He stopped, searching for words. "It is complicated," he finished delicately.

Kusunoki eyed the girl. "Too much motion in that one."

Victor did not respond.

"And not much discipline."

Victor did not mince words. "She is completely wild."

Although Victor tried to sound disapproving, Kusunoki sensed nothing but pride in his old friend. With good reason. He turned his attention back to the girl.

"She reminds me of someone else I used to know."

Victor's tone turned diplomatic again. "Which is why I brought her here. I had hoped you might have the same effect on Rhian as you had on me."

Kusunoki shook his head. "She will be worse."

"Most likely," Victor said agreeably. "But it took ten years of work with me."

"She will take twenty."

Ryan took that opportunity to walk up to the terrace. She stood at the bottom of the steps, lightly kicking the dirt. "You know," she said conversationally, "I can hear every word you two are saying."

Kusunoki glanced over at Victor. "Maybe thirty."

Ryan stood across from Kusunoki in the open courtyard, her heavy English saber held lightly in her hand. He stood across from her, holding what appeared to be farming implements. Ryan eyed the so-called weapons a little dubiously.

"Please," Kusunoki said, as if asking Ryan to humor him. Ryan shrugged and assumed an approach stance. With blinding speed she attacked, thrusting the saber forward with a lightning strike. Just as quickly, the left sai flashed, and then the right, arcing downward in beautiful circles and trapping the sword. When Ryan attempted to withdraw the sword, it was held in place by the triton shaped weapons and Kusunoki's strength. He eased his grip, and the sword was released.

Ryan stepped backward, impressed. Kusunoki resumed his stance, indicating that Ryan should try again. Ryan altered her own stance, and took another tact. Instead of lunging forward, she feinted, turned and brought the sword down in a slashing arc. Again, the left sai was there to catch the sword, while the other one came twirling toward her in a deadly sweep. It was all Ryan could do to duck out of the way, and she had to abandon the trapped sword to do so.

Victor laughed from his seat on the fence. "I see you're having no better luck with him than I did."

Ryan's eyes narrowed. "One more time. But give me that." She nodded toward the sword hanging at Kusunoki's side. Kusunoki glanced down. "You think that you are qualified to wield this sword? Here."

He removed the sword and tossed it to her. She caught it by hilt, and the beautiful blade gleamed in the sunlight. It had a deadly curve to it, and the sharpest edge she had ever seen. She hefted its weight; it was perfectly balanced.

Ryan swung the blade a few times. It was shorter and much lighter than her saber. After a few more experimental swipes, she resumed her stance. "Okay," she said nonchalantly, "let us try this again."

Kusunoki indicated he was ready, but instead of lunging forward, Ryan simply stood there. A stillness descended upon her, as if she were calming the very air around her. Kusunoki could have sworn that the wind itself died down, that the birds and trees silenced themselves at her request.

This time he did not see the attack coming, and it was only centuries of training, and reflexes well into the preternatural realm that allowed him to block the slicing blade. He countered, the sais twirling and flashing in the sun, but the sword was there to meet them both. He went on the attack, turning in a graceful and deadly strike, but the sword flashed here and there, meeting the tritons at every turn. The air was filled with the clanging of metal and flashing light.

Finally, in a stunning acrobatic maneuver, Kusunoki trapped the sword and kicked Ryan's feet from underneath her. She nearly recovered in mid-air, falling only to one knee, but Kusunoki finished the movement, thrusting the sai forward. The sharp tip of the small sword hovered an inch from Ryan's throat.

Ryan did not move, staring at the deadly weapon that held her frozen in place. She slowly raised her eyes to Kusunoki, who stared down at her, curious how she would handle defeat.

It was not what he expected. Her eyes drifted to his chest, and she slowly smiled. To his astonishment, he felt a slight itch and a warm trickle. Without taking his eyes from her, he raised his hand and in disbelief came away with a small amount of blood. His eyes narrowed.

And then the girl did the astonishing. She pushed the sai from her throat as if it were a toy, deeply slicing the palm of her hand as she did so. She stood, and with blood running down her arm, firmly pressed the bloody palm to the narrow wound on his chest.

"There," she said with satisfaction, "now we are blood brothers."

The shock was intense, and it was all Kusunoki could do to maintain his composure. Outwardly, he revealed nothing, his expression as calm and poised as always. But inwardly he was reeling from the connection, and all the deadly desires it stirred up. Centuries of discipline kept him from reacting in any way, but it took every bit of his self-control.

Ryan felt the shock as well, but did not remove her hand. She stood as if analyzing the experience, recording every detail, cataloguing every nuance, every aspect of the bond. Kusunoki's Memories flooded her mind, their presence fleeting but powerful. She finally pulled the hand away, looking at it strangely, as if it had been burned and she wasn't quite certain how it had happened.

There was absolute silence in the courtyard as the two combatants stood a few feet apart, assessing one another. Ryan finally raised the sword, examining the blade in the bright sunlight.

"What is this sword called?"

Kusunoki glanced at the sword, then back at the girl. "It is a Katana. It is unique in its curved design and the sharpness of its edge." His attention grew marked. "It also has the peculiar characteristic that, the more beautiful the sword, the more deadly its blade."

Ryan nodded. "As is true of most of our Kind."

Kusunoki noted that she made the comment as if excluding herself from the reference, when in truth, she was the personification of it.

Ryan handed him the sword with great care, honoring the blade. "Thank you," she said simply. She turned and made her way over to Victor, who was still lounging on the fence. From a distance, Kusunoki saw Victor take her hand and examine the palm. Victor dropped the arm, then ruffled Ryan's blonde hair affectionately. Ryan walked up onto the bridge, leaned over the side and began examining the fish.

Victor leaned back on the fence and turned his gaze on Kusunoki, a knowing look in his eyes. Kusunoki's misgivings were great. His eyes traveled to the girl, then back to her mentor, his indecision pronounced.

Which would be a worse outcome? Having this One remain unrestrained and internally chaotic?

Kusunoki's expression grew dark. Or having her wield that power with perfect discipline and control?

Ryan awoke, uncertain if she had been asleep. She glanced down at her feet, which hung over the edge of the small cot she was lying on. She glanced around the room, and the utter sameness of the furnishings added to her disorientation. She wasn't certain what century it was.

Memories flooded back to her, of her trial, her father's illness, Susan Ryerson, the Grand Council, and she realized it was in fact the 21st century. She sat up in the bed, listening. Although there was nothing to hear, she knew Kusunoki was out in the courtyard.

Ryan stepped down the wooden steps to the gravel path below. She allowed her feet to crunch this time as she approached her old master. He was finishing his meditations, and he rose with suppleness from his kneeling position.

"How long have I been asleep?"

Kusunoki glanced at the sky. "I believe three weeks have passed."

Ryan winced. "I hope you won't pass onto the Council my dereliction of duty."

"I think you were busy enough in your first few days that they are relieved you disappeared for awhile." There was neither approval nor disapproval in his voice.

"Has there been any word?"

Kusunoki finished the sentence for her. "About your father? No."

She glanced over at him. She would not answer, and he would not ask. The matter slipped away from them.

"So what do you think of this 'cleansing'?"

Kusunoki shrugged. "It is an ancient custom. Quite frankly, I think it is long overdue."

Ryan glanced at him, surprised, and he explained.

"There are many of our Kind creating inferior offspring. And many of the controls of the past are no longer in place. The world has become so large and so small at the same time."

Ryan waited in silence for him to continue.

"Those of us who are far beyond the ability to reproduce must face the consequences of the choices we made hundreds of years ago."

Ryan nodded her understanding while Kusunoki continued. "Those whom we felt might carry our line with honor failed to do so. Or," he said, "perhaps their offspring failed. Or their offspring's offspring failed."

"So why don't you take matters into your own hands?" Ryan asked.

"I could," he replied. "I could certainly take care of the weaknesses in my own lineage. But I don't imagine the Others, especially my 'peers' would appreciate my exercising that sort of discretion over their own. And it does little good to pull the weeds in your own garden when your neighbor refuses to tend his."

Ryan realized how complex this situation truly was. "I still don't understand why I was the chosen one."

Kusunoki glanced over at her. "I would have chosen you, my only concern being that you had the ability to annihilate generations. I think Marilyn and Ala would have chosen you as well, even though Ala had never met you."

Ryan looked sideways at him. "And why is that?"

"She likes your father," Kusunoki said, his emphasis on the verb a bit too pronounced.

"Oh really," Ryan said dryly. She brought her attention back to his previous words. "So who did make the choice?"

Kusunoki was thoughtful. "It was Aeron, the one who in hindsight appears to have the most to lose by you being named the hunter."

"Aeron is in love with death," Ryan said contemptuously. "He may have chosen me just to satisfy his own perverse sense of humor."

Kusunoki looked sidelong at his pupil, but said nothing.

The two settled into a comfortable silence, which Ryan finally broke.

"You know, the human doctor who examined me discovered that my sleep is more akin to a meditative state than to actual sleep."

Kusunoki snorted. "Lazy as always. Taking the easy way out and relying on raw talent instead of practice and training."

Ryan smiled, knowing there was no bite to her master's words. "So, lazy am I? Perhaps you would like to spar a bit, to see if I have been practicing after all."

Kusunoki smiled. "I live for the possibility."

They walked to the wall of the nearest structure where weapons were displayed on wooden pegs. Kusunoki was surprised that Ryan bypassed her preferred Katana for a pair of sais. Kusunoki, too, removed a pair of the forked weapons.

Ryan swung the weapons, as if loosening up and accustoming herself to their feel. Kusunoki was not fooled. She required neither a warm-up nor adjustment to the lethal swords. He assumed a ready stance.

In a flash, Ryan was upon him, the two short swords spinning and arcing so rapidly that they were only a blur. Kusunoki parried, his swords moved as quickly as hers. Had anyone been watching, they would have had only a vague impression of whirling swords, supported by the constant "ting-ting-ting," of the metal strikes.

Kusunoki went on the attack, bringing the swordplay up a level. The footwork became elaborate, the swords moving so quickly that attack/counter-attack became meaningless. The battle had transformed into a ballet of deadly grace, the skill transcendent.

The dance shifted, and it was now Ryan who led. The swords moved so quickly they could not be seen, only arcs of light and a constant "tinging" that sounded like a single, prolonged musical note. Kusunoki's face was expressionless, but he began to give ground, no longer attacking but merely countering defensively. Ryan's speed and timing went beyond preternatural, as if she were now violating the laws of physics themselves. Apparently quantum mechanics had decided to work on a larger scale and favored only her.

Finally, in a move beautiful in both tactic and execution, Ryan trapped both of Kusunoki's swords. He had only one option left, and powerfully bent both his wrists. This had the instant effect of shattering all four swords, effectively disarming them both.

Ryan gazed down at the hilt of the sai, all that remained in her hand. "Strike too hard and the sword will break," she said, repeating ancient words.

Kusunoki nodded. "I see you remember much of what I taught you."

Ryan dropped the hilt to the ground. "I remember everything you taught me." She stood upright and bowed deeply.

Kusunoki stood upright as well. "It is I who should bow to you."

Ryan shook her head. "I may have mastered the physical act of fighting, but I do not have your mental control."

Kusunoki was silent, knowing what was coming.

"I must ask something of you."

"What can I give you?" Kusunoki asked quietly.

Ryan appeared to be in some great internal struggle. She finally spoke. "I need your Memories, but I cannot return the gift."

Kusunoki pondered her words. When he spoke, Ryan was surprised by both his words and by the manner in which he spoke them, for he was no longer speaking to his former pupil but rather to the heir apparent of their Kind.

"Rhian, as powerful as you are, you probably could have taken my Memories. And as compelling as you are, you probably could have seduced them from me."

Ryan did not speak, so Kusunoki continued. "I know you cannot Share your mind because you hide your father there. And no one, not even me, needs to find him."

Ryan did not confirm or deny his words.

"I will give you my Memories."

Ryan still said nothing, simply nodded.

Kusunoki sat in the mediation chamber, his mind prepared. He was utterly still, his eyes closed. A small sword lay across his lap. Ryan sat across from him, also deep in meditation. Their eyes opened simultaneously, knowing the time had arrived.

Ryan stood and moved behind Kusunoki, kneeling. With the solemnity of a religious ceremony, Kusunoki raised the blade of the short sword, then slowly ran it across the skin of his neck, slicing through the jugular vein. Blood began to flow down his side.

Ryan leaned forward and the last coherent thought that Kusunoki had was surprise at how gently her lips covered the wound.

The shock that went through his system, however, was anything but gentle. It was as if lightning had struck the side of his head and went ricocheting through his body, seeking but not finding ground. The agony was intense, but it was also intensely pleasurable. Kusunoki fought to maintain mental control, but for the first time in centuries, also found himself wanting to let go.

Ryan also felt the powerful shock and struggled to reorient herself. Kusunoki's blood flowed into her, and the lightning began burning a path through her veins as well. Her heart strained under the exertion, momentarily faltering, but that powerful organ responded to one even more powerful as her mind took over for her autonomic nervous system.

Kusunoki felt his own heart falter, but then regain a different rhythm, as if Ryan's heart were now driving his own, demanding absolute synchronization. It beat harder, faster, an utterly merciless yet wholly benevolent master.

And then her mind touched his.

And the lightning in his head increased in temperature to that of the core of the sun.

Kusunoki felt a pleasure that he had only dreamed about. It was as if the act of Sharing had moved from the physical into the entirely cerebral, as if Ryan were not content to merely take his blood, or even simply his Memories, but wanted his mind itself.

And Kusunoki wanted to give it to her. He briefly considered resistance, but the thought flitted away, given no weight at all. He opened his entire consciousness to her, offering her an unlimited expanse of awareness.

All was suddenly still for Ryan. She stood on an endless plain bordered by an infinite lake. All was motionless, utterly silent. She turned to Kusunoki, who was at her side.

"I need to see."

Kusunoki smiled and pointed to the infinite expanse of sky. Ryan turned, and the sky was filled with images, Kusunoki as a child, as a young man, as he was transformed into an immortal, as he lived and Shared and fought for centuries, as he became the revered moon god, then the most honored shogun in all of history. She saw Victor, long before Ryan's birth, and the time they spent together taming Victor's restless spirit. She saw the Others, some that she knew, countless that she did not know. She saw Kusunoki's lineage stretch outward, multiplying toward the future they now occupied.

She saw it all in an instant, yet felt it as if she were living every moment of his very long life. For a moment she saw through his eyes, not only seeing as him, but feeling as him, knowing as him, believing as him, being him.

And now she remembered as him.

He put his hand on her arm, and she turned to him. He smiled at her gently, but there was a fatigue about him that caused her concern. Ryan turned to the sky, which was darkening to a deep red. In the distance ominous drums beat out a steady but ever-increasing rhythm. She turned back to Kusunoki.

"And will you kill me?" he asked softly.

"No!"

The blood-red world disappeared as Ryan jerked away from Kusunoki's limp body. The exclamation echoed loudly in the otherwise empty meditation chamber.

Ryan looked down at the pale figure of her master, who appeared to be halfway between exhausted sleep and death. She put her hand on his chest and was relieved to feel a faint, thready pulse, although in truth that meant nothing. She stood, then gently lifted Kusunoki over her shoulder. She carried him to his sleeping chambers and laid him on his cot, carefully arranging his limbs so that he was comfortable. She knew that he would sleep a very long time.

She started to leave, then stopped. She leaned down very closely to Kusunoki, gazing at his peaceful, beautiful features. She leaned even closer, her lips nearly brushing his ear.

"I will repay in kind when this is over."

Ryan left the shrine. She now knew without a doubt that Kusunoki had no part in her father's betrayal, although she had never really suspected him. But Victor had told her to trust no one, and Ryan had chosen Kusunoki first simply because she did want to trust him. And now she could travel through his lands, using the exact discretion he would have used in culling his line.

Kusunoki awoke when one of the priests tending him brushed his cot. The priest nodded to him, silent as always, and bowed while backing from the room. Kusunoki looked out his window. The sun sat lower in the sky and the shadows were longer. Many weeks had passed since he had Shared with Ryan.

The memory shot through him, causing him equal parts pain and pleasure in his head. He turned the memory over and over in his mind, reliving every aspect of the matchless experience. His pupil truly had become a master.

His expression darkened. And she was indeed powerful. He wondered what the Others would think if they knew she had nearly killed him by accident.

Kusunoki sat up, thoughtful. He did not know if Ryan could have actually killed him. There was no record of any such thing among their Kind. Old Ones were assumed immortal simply because none of them had ever died. And even with all of their internecine squabbling, none were capable of killing each other, even in the act of Sharing.

But that did not mean it was not possible.

Kusunoki thought back to Ryan's thinly-veiled threat at the Council meeting. He wondered if she had any idea that she might actually be capable of carrying it out. He did not think so, gleaning what little he could from her mind. He did not have her gift—he could not see her Memories without Sharing her blood. But he did not sense she had any grasp of her true abilities.

Kusunoki grew more thoughtful. It would come down to a mental battle. And what gift did Victor have, that he could foresee how important the psychological battlefield would become? All of the Old Ones were equally matched, creating a tenuous détente. Ryan had, in a sense, "caught up" with many of the Old Ones in terms of physical prowess and sheer magnetism, the hallmarks of their Kind. She had done so through her unique birth and through Sharing with the most powerful of their Kind, her father. She now sat in a position as powerful as it was dangerous, both to herself and others.

For Kusunoki realized one very important fact: in order for Ryan to take Kusunoki to the brink of death, she had been required to go there herself. And someone else with less pure motives might take advantage of that door that only Ryan could open.

These thoughts occupied Kusunoki for a very long time. And although he would spend the next weeks in meditation, it would be awhile before his mind would return to the reflection pool it once was.

CHAPTER 12

THE GREAT TABLE DOMINATED THE SPACE in the internal meeting place of the Grand Council. It was a less formal setting than the Great Hall, designed only for the secret meetings of the members of the Grand Council themselves. Bordered on all sides by walls ten feet thick, its function was to allow the Council members to speak frankly to one another without the possibility of preternatural ears overhearing. It was also regularly swept for electronic devices that might overhear as well. On this date, it would serve as pre-assembly prior to Ryan's arrival, who was due to report on her progress. Only Ala and Kusunoki had arrived as yet, and as Kusunoki settled into his chair, he was very aware of Ala's scrutiny.

"You seem different somehow, my old friend." Ala said, her rich, melodic voice both suspicious and knowing.

Kusunoki did not react, his expression inscrutable as always. "I cannot imagine how."

"Mm-hmm," Ala said, "perhaps you could Share the experience with me later."

The double entendre was not lost on Kusunoki, nor the invitation. He did not react, however, saying only "Perhaps."

Their discourse was interrupted by Aeron and Marilyn, who quite surprisingly came in on Aeron's arm. He led her to her seat, solicitously holding her chair for her as they finished their conversation.

"Yes, she was quite talented at obtaining information, even as young as she was. I quite enjoyed the exchange." Aeron glanced at Kusunoki as he took his seat. His tone was mild and mildly threatening at the same time. "I can't imagine what she is like now."

Kusunoki gazed at Aeron, expressionless. Aeron stared at him for a long moment, then turned back to Marilyn, his demeanor still wickedly charming. "We could all just hold her down and take turns."

Marilyn's eyes gleamed as she entertained the thought, then shook her head with some regret. "Knowing her as I know her, that might be more difficult than you think."

"Ah," Aeron said, "the joy might be in just trying."

"And you would pay for that attempt," Abigail said as she entered the room, "probably in ways you could not possibly imagine."

Aeron smiled. "But you would finally get the opportunity to collect your debt."

Abigail settled into her chair, unperturbed. "That opportunity is ever-present." She glanced pointedly at Aeron. "And I do not require assistance to collect it."

Ala cleared her throat, "Perhaps we could move to the business at hand."

Aeron smiled to himself, still enjoying the vision of Ryan being held down. He was gracious to Ala, however, the perfect gentleman.

"Of course." He grew more businesslike. "Does anyone have an educated guess as to how many Ryan has managed to destroy?"

All were silent for a moment, unwilling to show their cards or reveal the extent of their intelligence networks. It was Kusunoki who finally broke the impasse.

"She has been particularly industrious in Asia. I do not have an exact number, but I would estimate she has destroyed in excess of six thousand on that continent alone."

There was a marked silence at the table as Kusunoki's words sunk in. Even Ala turned to Kusunoki, surprised at the number.

Aeron did not believe him, and his tone was scathing. "I find it difficult to believe her capable of such destruction in the span of three months. It is not so easy to kill our Kind, even the Young Ones."

"Two months," Kusunoki said evenly, his gaze unwavering. "She slept for nearly a month."

Abigail's gaze flicked to Kusunoki, aware of the significance of his words. She would have to reflect upon this development, and the danger of any type of alliance between Ryan and the shogun master.

Kusunoki was not finished. "And she did not stop with the Young Ones, nor did she waste any time with them." His voice was entirely conversational, as if relating temperate weather conditions. "She destroyed a dam in the southern part of China, which created tidal waves for hundreds of miles downstream. It wiped out two full clans of my line, not to mention a hundred thousand human beings, burying them under mountains of rock and debris."

Abigail paid no notice to the collateral damage and keyed on what Kusunoki had said earlier. "What do you mean she did not stop with the Young Ones?"

Kusunoki took a deep breath. "Apparently she is capable of destroying those who occupy the middle ground as easily as the Young Ones."

"That is impossible," Aeron said.

Kusunoki's gaze did not waver. "I spoke with a survivor personally, with whom Ryan had left a message. She said, 'Many things are impossible. Now I have done them all'."

Abigail and Marilyn exchanged glances. Ryan had used that exact phrase the night she had "murdered" her father, and Victor had spoken the same phrase at Ryan's trial in reference to her birth.

Kusunoki continued and his tone grew darker. "Lest you forget, I spent several decades with Ryan when she was little more than a Young One. Even then she was one of the most efficient predators I have ever seen. There is no moral ambiguity within her. She is following her father's edict right now, which is absolute. And to complicate matters, she is being driven by an immense pain," he gazed at Aeron, his words suddenly biting, "the cause of which I cannot determine."

Aeron gazed at the shogun warrior coldly, but said nothing. Ala, who had been assessing the implications of Kusunoki's words, turned to him. "How many of those in the middle ground has she taken?"

"Twenty-five, perhaps thirty."

Aeron's fist smashed downward, creating a split down the middle of the heavy table. "That is not possible," he said through clenched teeth.

Kusunoki's gaze was as cold as Aeron's and his words were steady. "Do not make me repeat her words again."

Abigail interrupted the rapidly escalating situation. "I suggest we wait to hear those words from Ryan herself, who will be here shortly." In a display of extreme matriarchal authority, both Abigail and Ala stood, effectively ending the meeting.

The twelve witnesses stood stiffly, their attention wholly focused on the figure seated in the center of the room. "Seated" was once more a generous term, as the position was more akin to an elegant sprawl. It was hard to determine if the sprawl was an act of deliberate disrespect, or one of complete inattention, as the figure was so obviously lost in thought.

"Disrespect" became the more likely suspect as the Grand Council entered and the figure, although aware of their presence, did not move. When she did move, it was not to stand, but rather to shift position slightly, crossing one long leg over the other.

"Please be seated," Aeron said with mild sarcasm, and the witnesses took their seats.

Edward glanced over at Ryan. He had not seen her in weeks. She had stopped in several times, but her visits were brief, primarily to check on Victor and to speak with Dr. Ryerson. She rarely stayed for longer than a few hours, and most of those she spent kneeling at Victor's side, her head on his silent chest.

He looked more closely at her. He knew Ryan extremely well, and there was something not quite right about her right now. As if reading his mind, she turned to him, and as clearly as if she had spoken in his ear, he heard her words.

Do not worry about me.

Abigail noticed the exchange, but so powerful had the girl become, Abigail was unable to grasp the content of the message. Then, as if sensing the attempted interception, Ryan turned to the matriarch, staring at her intently.

And do you stand against me as well?

Abigail felt the girl's presence in her mind, and was angered at the intrusion while stimulated by the exercise of power. She was intrigued by the dangerous edge that Ryan possessed right now. The girl seemed positively reckless, seething in a tightly controlled manner.

Marilyn also noted the girl's unusual demeanor. She had seen the girl like this before, when she had been furious at Victor many centuries before. She knew that were she to touch Ryan's skin right now it would be on fire. That thought brought its own heat to Marilyn, and she smiled at the memory.

Again, as if reading her thoughts, Ryan turned to Marilyn, and there was a wicked glint in her eye.

And are you the One to put out this fire?

Marilyn, who had never been caught off guard in the game of seduction, was nearly so by the surprise attack. But not quite.

I have put out that fire before, little one, came the whispered voice inside Ryan's head.

Ryan looked down at her hands, smiling to herself at the memory. This fascinated Marilyn, who had never seen Ryan quite so injudicious.

It fascinated Aeron as well. The girl was positively taunting the members of the Council, fanning flames that would not be easily extinguished. He again had his vision of her being held down, but the outcome was less certain this time. He could now see the Old Ones tearing each other apart for the opportunity to take what she was so impudently dangling before them.

If her actions up to this moment were startling, her next act was fairly astonishing. She turned her full attention to Aeron, and, shifting slightly in her seat, addressed him directly.

"And perhaps you and I should just end this charade and I should kill you now."

There were audible gasps and several of the witnesses drew backward at this affront. Abigail's expression immediately reverted to an unfathomable state while Marilyn raised an eyebrow. Kusunoki and Ala both looked over to gauge Aeron's response. It was not what they expected.

Aeron stared down at the girl, and very slowly, he smiled. His pleasure was evident. "You could try, my dear, which would probably be extremely enjoyable for both of us," he said in his clipped, aristocratic tone. "In fact, we could go back to my chambers and settle this right now."

Ryan also slowly smiled, not giving ground for a moment. "Could you at least wait until we are through with this meeting?"

"Why not?" Aeron said expansively, "I have waited this long."

"Very well," Ryan said mockingly, "then let me give my report as required." She glanced over to Edward, nodding.

Edward stood, withdrawing a folded paper from his breast pocket inside his robe. Apparently Ryan was going to dispense with the pretense that he was an objective observer to the proceedings, which was fine with him. His sense of refinement was failing him; he wanted to kill half the people in this room as well.

He cleared his throat. "The numbers to this date are as follows: 8,132 dead, 196 missing and presumed dead, and 221 missing, status unknown."

There was utter silence in the hall. No one moved. And although no one required oxygen, the fact that no one breathed was evident as well.

Ryan stood, unfolding her long form with cat-like grace. "Well," she said casually, "if that's all, I will be in my father's chambers if anyone needs me."

And before anyone could say anything, she was gone.

Edward stood, still holding the paper, all eyes now turned to him for lack of a better target. He carefully folded the paper, placing it back into his breast pocket with great deliberation. He cleared his throat, uncomfortably aware of the intense scrutiny. "I," he cleared his throat again. "I will be retiring as well."

He bowed to the Grand Council, and made it three steps toward the door before he was abruptly stopped by Aeron's voice behind him. Aeron's tone was quiet, but there was an underlying steel in it that allowed it to easily carry in the vast hall.

"Edward-"

Edward turned to face the head of the Grand Council, bracing himself. Aeron gazed down at the man with unblinking ice-blue eyes. His words were measured, completely controlled, deceptively light. "You tell Rhian I expect her in my chambers within the hour."

Edward gave a short bow. "I will deliver the message, my lord." He quickly disappeared.

Ala nodded to the nearest witness, indicating that they should leave as quickly as possible. No sooner had she given the silent order than the eleven remaining witnesses disappeared nearly as quickly as Edward, simply grateful to be out of the presence of such terrible power.

There was a prolonged silence among the five remaining Old Ones. It was finally broken by Ala, who stood. When she spoke, her voice was smooth, like fine mahogany. "I am afraid I must depart for my homeland immediately." Her white teeth flashed brilliant against her ebony skin, although her words were filled with meaning. "I believe I will soon have a visitor."

Abigail stood as well. She moved to leave, but stopped at Aeron's side, speaking to him quietly, but loud enough for the Others to hear. Her tone was as deceptively light as his had been earlier.

"You may have unleashed something that will destroy us all."

Ryan was preparing to enter Victor's chambers when she felt Kusunoki's presence behind her. She turned to her old master, bowing. She felt Ala's presence in the shadows, and she nodded deferentially to her as well.

Kusunoki mentally reached out to his pupil. Ryan allowed him to touch her, and he was shocked at the chaos within her. He had a sudden, troubling premonition of how much danger they all were in due to the power she wielded and the condition she was in. He wondered what could have caused such a disturbance in the girl, and he was now greatly concerned for Victor.

"Do not worry about me, my master," Ryan said quietly, "or my father."

Kusunoki gazed at the striking, androgynous creature before him. "I fear for us all right now."

Ryan nodded, but did not reply. She was silent for a moment, then changed the subject. "And have you fully recovered?"

"Yes…"

Ryan glanced over at him

"…and no."

Ryan again nodded her tacit understanding. She raised her hand in offering, her palm flat and facing him. He raised his hand and joined it with hers, pressing palm-to-palm. He spoke quietly.

"I am recovered, but I am no longer complete."

Ryan knew that such an admission of longing from the great man could only come from his great strength. She cleared her throat, looking away for a moment. She then looked into his eyes and spoke as solemnly and with the same simple emotion.

"When this is finished, I will make you complete again."

He gazed into her eyes, his own dark eyes the color of a starless night. "I know," he said simply.

Kusunoki dropped his hand, breaking the connection. He turned to leave, and then was gone. Ala was gone as well.

Ryan stared off into the dark and empty hallway. She sighed heavily, then turned to enter her father's stateroom. She paused, however, and turned back to the hallway as Edward approached.

He stopped in the alcove and started to speak. He stopped and shifted uncomfortably. Ryan raised her hand, saving him from having to deliver his message.

"I know," she said. She gestured to the double doors that she still had not entered. "When I return, I will stay the night in my father's chambers. There is a second suite that I understand is quite comfortable. You are welcome to stay there."

Edward bowed. It was a great privilege to stay in the chambers of the Grand Council, and although Ryan cared nothing for ceremony, he was honored nonetheless.

"I will prepare the quarters for your return."

"Very well." She turned, and Edward watched her stalk away with deadly grace, again struck by how similar she and her father moved.

Ryan approached Aeron's chambers. She hesitated briefly before the ornately carved doors, then pushed through them into the anteroom. Aeron was seated at a table reading the newspaper.

"Please come in," he said with mild sarcasm, still reading the paper.

Ryan smiled, completely amused. She took the opportunity to examine him. The years had done little to change him. He was still wickedly handsome, with chiseled, aristocratic features, ice-blue eyes, and hair so fair it was a stark contrast to his light tan. He sat, casually elegant with one long leg crossed over the other, a dangerous litheness about him. He had broad shoulders and a strong chest tapering to a slender waist, and Ryan noted that he had changed into a white, collared shirt that he wore open at the throat.

"Would you like me to disrobe?"

Aeron had stopped reading the paper and was watching her pointed examination of him. Rather than being embarrassed, however, she was further amused and allowed her eyes to flick up and down him once more.

"Yes, could you?"

Aeron folded the paper without taking his eyes from Ryan. He was amused despite himself. "Perhaps another time," he said. He allowed his own gaze to flick up and down the girl, taking his own assessment. Time had not changed her, either. She was still strikingly beautiful, with high cheekbones and a perfect mouth, and the peculiar ability to pass as either a boy or girl and still remain a perfect specimen of both. She was tall with a deceptively slender build that he knew disguised incredible strength.

"So," he said casually, "perhaps you could tell me why you have chosen to go about your duties in this way."

Ryan was deliberately obtuse. "Whatever do you mean?"

"I mean," Aeron said, standing, "that you have killed more of our Kind in three months than have been killed in the cleansings of the last two hundred years."

Ryan was thoughtful. "Hmmm, I see your point. I shall have to pick up the pace."

Aeron moved around the table toward her, and Ryan nonchalantly moved around the table away from him. Aeron was not fooled by the tactical maneuver, nor by the indifferent manner in which it was executed.

Ryan continued moving with deliberate casualness and deliberate intent. She maintained a strategic distance between her and Aeron, but stopped abruptly when something caught her eye.

It was a chessboard, set up in a corner of the room. It was beautifully constructed, with hand-carved figurines that were horrifying, intricate renditions of the standard chess pieces. But it was not the horrific interpretation of the classic pieces, nor the obvious skill that went into the hideous artwork that attracted Ryan's attention. The positions of the pieces, even from across the room, were instantly recognizable to her, representing a game that was over four centuries old.

Ryan slowly moved to the game board, disbelief and curiosity on her face. She noted that the knight that she had moved had been taken by the opposing rook. With only a brief examination of the new positions, she picked up an ebony rook and moved it across the board.

"An interesting move."

Ryan was startled by the whisper in her ear. Aeron stood behind her, so close she could feel his shirt collar brush the back of her neck. He encircled her wrists in his hands and pulled her forcefully toward him, and she could now feel a good deal more than his shirt.

"You should give up now," she said, still facing forward, her voice steady.

He was not fooled by her calm demeanor. He marveled at the sensations flooding through his body from the simple physical contact with her. Although he had not engaged in any sexual act in centuries, he found himself idly wondering what it would feel like to have her naked form fully pressed against his own. He made a note that he would have to explore that at some time in the future.

He leaned over her shoulder and brushed his lips on the side of her neck. It was all Ryan could do to keep from blacking out, so electrifying was the sensation. She struggled to maintain her composure, knowing that if he chose to slice open her neck now, she was not in a position to resist him.

His teeth did not go through the skin, however, but his lips continued down the now-throbbing vein in her neck.

"And why is that?" he asked, his words partially muffled by his continued torturous actions.

Ryan was amazed that she managed to keep her tone even. "Because I have already won."

Aeron smiled, but did not stop what he was doing. He instead moved his head from one side of her neck to the other, now feathering the artery on that side. Ryan felt her knees buckling, as did Aeron, who caught her about the waist, pulling her even closer. With one hand now free, he grasped her hair gently and guided her head backward, exposing her throat even further. Now having pulled her off-balance and completely supporting her, he spoke.

"Oh really?" he asked, his amusement evident. He lowered his head further, toying with a small vein that branched out near her collarbone.

Ryan closed her eyes, then forced them open to focus on the chess board. Her words were suddenly very clear, with a distant other-worldly quality. "It is twenty moves out, and you cannot see it, but you have already lost."

Her words stopped him, and he raised his head to look at her. In his current position, he was leaned over her shoulder. Before Ryan could completely think about what she was doing, she leaned sideways toward him and brushed her lips across the veins in his neck, biting him gently without breaking the skin.

The shock was instantaneous, causing Aeron a sharp intake of breath as his back arched. The dark desire uncoiled and began twisting inside of him, and any illusion that he had that he could maintain control in this situation was immediately banished. His involuntary response allowed Ryan to free her wrists and regain her leverage, but instead of pulling away, she turned to face him. She grasped his shirt collar in her hand, uncertain if she was going to push him away or pull him close.

She wasn't given the liberty of deciding. As soon as she turned to face him, Aeron wrapped his arms around her sinuous frame and pulled her to him. Without hesitation, her teeth were again at his throat, torturously biting without breaking the skin. Aeron wanted to moan with pleasure and scream in agony at the anguish this child was inflicting upon him.

Ryan was in her own agony, wanting so desperately to pierce his skin and take his life into her body that she felt her insides writhe in torment. She wanted to take this man's blood more than she had wanted anything in her entire life.

But instead, she turned her head and with immense effort, pushed him away.

The two mortal enemies stood feet apart, staring at one another across a chasm that had just grown deeper but more narrow, seeing in an instance an outcome that was both impossible and inevitable.

Ryan did not know what to expect from Aeron, did not know if he would be furious with her, or if he would take her by force, which he was surely capable of. And, she admitted to herself, it would only be by force for so long because her embattled will would quickly fade.

He surprised her, because he did none of these things. He stood without moving, then slowly smiled. His eyes gleamed in the candlelight.

"You are even more than I had hoped for."

Ryan's eyes narrowed, but she said nothing. Aeron continued.

"When I take you," he paused for emphasis, "and let there be no doubt that I will take you. I expect that it shall be the most extraordinary experience of my life."

Ryan's eyes flashed in anger. "And your life might end shortly thereafter."

"Perhaps," Aeron said, amused. "But I think not."

He reached over to the chessboard and moved his queen across the board, removing the rook that Ryan had just placed there. He set the castle to the side with the other captured pieces.

Ryan gazed at the board for a moment, then turned to leave without a word. But halfway to the door, she paused, then turned around. There was a dark intensity in her gaze.

"Nineteen," she said, nodding to the board. "Now it's nineteen."

And then she was gone, leaving Aeron staring at the empty space where she had been, marveling at the audacity of the girl.

Edward stood in the anteroom as Ryan pushed through the double doors of Victor's chambers. He did not speak, and nor did she until she was at the door leading to the inner stateroom. There she paused and turned to him.

"I require nothing further this evening, other than not to be disturbed."

Edward nodded and disappeared into the adjoining suite.

Ryan pushed through the door into Victor's chambers, and was so suddenly overwhelmed by his presence that she stopped short, closing her eyes. As the door whispered closed behind her, she breathed in deeply, inhaling his scent, his very essence. The longing welled up in her, so different and so similar to the ache she had just experienced.

She glanced around the room at the furnishings, as masculine and elegant as her father. She walked over to a highly polished mahogany table and picked up an ancient book. It was an original copy of "Le Morte D'Arthur," the same one that he had given her as a gift centuries before. It was probably priceless now, one of the few still in existence. She smiled at the thought that he had kept it.

She wandered through a few of the rooms, wondering if this is where he had spent time recovering from her attack on him. She had to move quickly from this thought, because it reminded her that she might well be responsible for his current condition.

She moved into the bathing room, which for her father was always one of the most elaborate living areas. He had gained his appreciation from the ancient baths in Damascus. Prior to her birth, he had been a great admirer of Turkish medicine, far more advanced than its barbaric European counterpart. And although he had no personal need of medical care, he had an intellectual appreciation of their sophisticated knowledge.

Ryan smiled in remembrance. Prior to her Change, Victor had been a shadowy figure in her life, protecting her from afar as she was raised as a boy by a peasant family. He felt that she would be safer that way, hidden from the Others and protected from his own dark desire. He did, however, lay out certain seemingly arbitrary requirements of her human parents, one of which was that she had to bathe everyday, fully clothed. In a modern context, it did not seem unusual, with the possible exception of bathing fully clothed, but in a medieval context, it was unheard of. The filth they unknowingly lived in was obscene by modern standards. It was likely that Victor's understanding of the connection between hygiene and disease, gained from the Turks centuries before, kept Ryan from contracting any number of the hideous maladies that plagued medieval peasants. Ryan smiled at her father's foresight. Bathing fully clothed had not only disguised her sex, but had made her wash her clothes as well.

She moved into his sleeping chambers, gazing at the huge, ornately carved bed. It was neatly made, as if awaiting his imminent return. She ran her fingers over the smooth lines of the dresser, then moved to the closet. She found a comfortably loose pair of nightclothes and changed into them, and was again overwhelmed with Victor's ghostly presence. It brought her solace, however, and when she settled into the luxurious bedding, the comfort it brought was immense.

She stared through the darkness at the ceiling. As thick as the walls were, she could still here the murmurings of the Others as they went about their various trysts and assignations. She shut them out, returning to her examination of nothingness on the ceiling.

She wished desperately for Victor's counsel now. She wondered if he would change his mind about telling her to Share with the Old Ones if he knew what she had gotten herself into. Having Shared with no one other than him for centuries, and now having done the deed with both Marilyn and Kusunoki in such short order, it seemed as if her dark thirst was growing. Victor's power had so satisfied her that she rarely wanted. But now, paradoxically, it seemed her appetite was growing by satiating it.

And it did not seem an entirely physiological thing, although the pleasure was almost unbearable. The psychological aspect of it was as addictive, if not more so, than the physical. The interplay of power and relationship, of role and role-reversal, was both arousing and disturbing.

Ryan stared up into the darkness. She wondered if this was the conundrum of the Old Ones, that the more powerful they became, the less likely they were to be satisfied by anyone or anything. She wondered if they would eventually move to a place where they would never be satisfied at all. She marveled at how neatly Victor had side-stepped the entire issue by creating her, and was oblivious to how dangerous a position this placed her in.

She closed her eyes, inhaling deeply. She could smell the wonderful spice scent of her father and ached from missing him. It seemed she could open her eyes and see him, and she avoided doing just that so she could maintain the illusion.

But as she lay with her eyes closed, a different scent wafted toward her, one of cinnamon with a touch of ginger. She spoke into the darkness without opening her eyes.

"Remind me to fire Edward."

Marilyn kneeled on the bed and ran her hand through Ryan's hair.

"Ah, ma Cherie, maybe he thought you needed company."

"Hmmph, not likely," Ryan said, rolling on her side to face the woman. "It is more likely he was bewitched by your rather lethal charm."

Marilyn gazed down at the girl, eyes gleaming in the darkness. "And why is it that I do not have that affect on you?" She shifted so that she was closer. "Or perhaps I do." Her hand settled lightly on Ryan's waist.

Ryan suppressed the urge to pull away, as well as the urge to do its complete opposite. Marilyn glanced down as something caught her eye, and she lifted Ryan's wrist for closer inspection. There was a light bruise circling it, one that was rapidly fading, but still visible. She looked to the other wrist, which had similar bruising. She gazed at the girl with amusement.

"Ah, little one, I see you have been playing with Aeron."

Ryan raised an eyebrow. "And is this the voice of experience talking?"

"Perhaps," Marilyn said. She examined the injured wrist. "He is an indulgence best partaken of infrequently."

Ryan rolled onto her back, looking up at Marilyn. "And why is that?"

Marilyn caressed the bruise on the wrist she still held in her hand. "Because he is a very dangerous man, ma Cherie. Particularly to you."

Ryan was having a difficult time concentrating on the conversation, as serious as it was. She brought her attention back to the matter at hand. "And why not to you?"

Marilyn held Ryan's gaze as she raised the wrist to her lips. "Because I am not a threat to him," she said, kissing the bruise. She feathered her lips across the veins on the inner wrist. "I am not the crown prince of our Kind."

Ryan was really having a hard time concentrating now. The importance of the conversation was being overshadowed by the sensations shooting up her arm and spreading out to the rest of her body. "I have a hard time believing you're not a threat to everyone," she said, half under her breath.

Marilyn smiled. "You don't have to be afraid of me," she whispered, "I won't hurt you."

She then did just that as she sank her teeth into the bruised skin. She did not bite deeply however, just breaking the skin enough so that a small amount of blood began to seep.

The pleasure at the first bite was so intense that the darkness in the room was filled with stars for a few seconds until Ryan's vision cleared. Marilyn still held her wrist, now toying with the small wound she had inflicted, her eyes locked with Ryan's. To make it worse, it now seemed that Marilyn was going to continue to have a conversation with her, as casually as if they were speaking over dinner.

"But Aeron," she said, suckling the wound, "Aeron wants to kill you." Her lips traveled up Ryan's arm toward the veins on the inner forearm. She pulled back slightly, examining her target. "Or worse," she said as she again sunk her teeth into the arm.

Ryan arched her back at this puncture, but not in pain. The bite was again minor, and Marilyn covered the wound with her mouth before it could spurt, drawing the blood into her. Ryan stared down at her, mesmerized by the sight of her lips on her arm.

Marilyn's movements were still entirely casual, as was her tone. "You will find that Aeron is very different from your father."

The reminder that Marilyn had Shared with Victor angered Ryan, momentarily clearing her senses. She started to pull away, but Marilyn skillfully twisted her wrist, exposing the inside of her bicep and the brachial artery. In a second, the dark-haired woman severed the artery and pressed the wound to her lips.

Ryan wasn't certain if she had blacked out for a moment, or merely tightly closed her eyes to fight against the sensations that were tearing through her. It was possible for Marilyn to completely bleed her from the large artery, and Ryan steeled herself to put a stop to the seduction. Instead, Marilyn caught her off guard and chose again to defer her pleasure, sating herself for a moment with a lengthy drink. Ryan inwardly cursed herself for the urge to beg her to continue. Marilyn leaned back, putting pressure on the wound as it quickly healed, staring down at Ryan.

Ryan held her gaze, fighting the daze. Marilyn had already taken so much of her blood she felt light-headed and lethargic, which was not an unpleasant feeling. Marilyn had also always had the ability to entrance her, sapping her will. No matter how powerful Ryan had become, it was an irrelevant ability if she would not use it.

Marilyn returned to the wrist, brushing her lips across the bruised flesh once more. She still seemed completely in control, as if the outcome of their little tête-à-tête was not in question.

"So are you at all curious how they are different?"

Ryan gazed at her suspiciously, then realized what she was saying. "You could show me," she said.

"I could," Marilyn said, as if the thought had just occurred to her. Her gaze returned pointedly to Ryan, and her tone confirmed that the thought had pre-existed. "But what do you have to offer me in exchange?"

Ryan's eyes narrowed. "I could simply take what I want."

"Hmmm, yes," Marilyn said, glancing at the girl's somewhat vulnerable, supine position. "I almost believe that you could."

Ryan wasn't certain if she were being mocked. In a flash she was upright, pinning both Marilyn's wrists in her grip and twisting. In an instant she had thrown the other woman on the bed, pinning her beneath her.

Ryan stared down into Marilyn's eyes, which were now filled with wicked amusement. Ryan cursed herself. Marilyn's other gift was the ability to manipulate her into exactly what she wanted Ryan to do.

"You are right, ma Cherie," the dark-haired woman said, glancing down at the lithe body that now lay on top of her "This is much better."

Ryan stared down at her, now in the awkward position of not having any idea of what to do, or how to disentangle herself. Marilyn saved her from any more difficult decisions and pulled her firmly downward, slicing into her neck with perfect, razor-sharp teeth. It briefly occurred to Ryan that it was dangerous allowing Marilyn access to her mind, but she thought she could resist the mental aspect of Marilyn's Sharing more successfully than she could Kusunoki's.

All physical aspects, however, were open to contest. Ryan arched her back and resisted perhaps a second before the events of the day took her headlong into Marilyn's embrace. The pressure that had built in her veins during her exchange with Aeron was screaming to escape, and Marilyn was only too willing to provide that release.

Aeron stood in his chambers, staring at the wall. Abigail stood a few feet away, watching his struggle, entertained as always at the anguish of their Kind. In a startling move that did not startle her, Aeron punched his fist into the wall, sinking the fist into the solid rock up to his shoulder. He pulled the appendage from the rock, glanced at the damage to his hand, and thought about doing it again.

Instead, he regained control, and turned to Abigail who gazed at him coolly from across the room.

"Marilyn can be quite opportunistic."

Aeron glared at her. "If she does not cease tempting me, she will have the opportunity to regret it for the rest of her life."

Abigail smiled. "I don't believe it is you she's tempting right now."

Aeron's jaw clenched spasmodically, and Abigail relented.

"The girl has always had a weakness for Marilyn. It is an interesting phenomenon, because Ryan is the more powerful of the two."

Aeron glanced at her sharply. "You know this to be true?"

Abigail was always reluctant to reveal her sources, but in this instance it did not matter. "Marilyn as much told me so herself, and she was quite pleased at her findings."

Aeron absorbed this information, filing it for future reference. If the girl had caught and even passed one of Marilyn's stature…

"And have you any verification on the numbers?" he asked, changing the subject.

Abigail nodded. "My reports are preliminary, but it seems the girl was telling the truth. There are thousands missing."

Aeron silently fumed as Abigail continued.

"There are reports that some are killing themselves at her request, while others have taken it upon themselves to self-sacrifice."

Aeron was furious. It was just like the girl to seduce them into doing her job for her.

"And is there any word of Victor?" he asked, his gaze burning into the rock wall.

"None."

"Well," he said sarcastically, "she must be far more hardy than her father. Who thought that she would still be standing at this point?"

Abigail kept her own counsel. She had previously been quite forthright with her opinion.

Aeron was running the facts through his head. "First Kusunoki, now Marilyn. What do you think she is doing?"

Abigail was thoughtful. "I believe she is looking for information. She is quite gifted, I understand, at obtaining the Memories of Others when in the heat of the passion." She cleared her throat delicately. "I believe you have some personal knowledge of that yourself."

Aeron's eyes narrowed at the memory, even though it also gave him pleasure. The whelp had touched his mind before they even touched, and had seen his Memories without a drop of blood passing her lips.

"So you think she is seeking the One who betrayed Victor?"

Abigail stood, smoothing her skirt. "Perhaps." She touched his cheek as she passed him, stopping only when she reached the door. She turned back to him.

"Or perhaps she's just enjoying herself."

The door closed behind her, but she could still hear the sound of the fist shattering through the rock.

Ryan was held in the steel of Marilyn's embrace, who had nearly bled her dry. She enjoyed the feverish, light-headed sensation of emptiness, the deep lethargy that came from being so close to death. She could hardly keep her eyes open, so languorous was the feeling.

Marilyn had a similar sensation for the opposite reason, she was completely sated. She languidly toyed with the girl's hair, who lay on her light as a feather. Marilyn did not believe it possible, but this Sharing was as powerful and satisfying as the one before. Marilyn could tell that Ryan was withholding her Memories from Marilyn during the act. Although capable of forcing disclosure, Marilyn did not pry. She was too busy enjoying the sheer physicality of the powerful union. It seemed that Victor's progeny had his gift for consistent and continual gratification.

She knew that Ryan had seen her Memories of Aeron, seen his sadistic passion and brutal domination. He was dangerously seductive, violent in the act, and rarely fulfilled. The union of he and Marilyn had been physically satisfying for both of them but emotionally bereft. Both enjoyed the game of seduction itself almost as much as the outcome, and they were perhaps too alike in that sense to create any of the enjoyable, uncertain tension of the hunt.

Marilyn glanced down at Ryan. Unlike this one, she thought. She never knew what to expect from this girl. One moment stumbling about endearingly like a bashful adolescent, bringing out the predator in all of them. The next moment turning into a devilishly charming, near invulnerable individual who made them all want to throw themselves at her feet. And neither personality was the least bit affected or artificial, nor, oddly enough, in conflict with the other.

Marilyn grew more thoughtful. Perhaps it was because they were both true. Was it possible that Ryan had not yet reached anywhere near her potential? Was it possible that she still was nothing more than an adolescent, as old and powerful as she was? Had Victor indeed rewritten all the rules in creating Ryan?

Although the thought might have brought others resentment and fear, it brought Marilyn nothing but pleasure. The girl was clever, charismatic, and impossibly alluring, but lacking in the guile of the Old Ones. Marilyn would greatly enjoy watching her mature.

Marilyn thought for a moment that the girl was asleep. She gently rolled Ryan onto her back, then sat up to leave. She was halfway standing when her movement was abruptly stopped by a hand encircling her wrist in a grip of iron.

"And where are you going?"

Marilyn sat back down on the bed, amused. She leaned over Ryan, who had not released her wrist. "You have what you want, ma Cherie. And

I have what I wanted."

Ryan gazed up at her, idly toying with the wrist she still held imprisoned. "I don't think you've completely fulfilled your part of the bargain."

Marilyn raised an eyebrow. "Oh really, ma Cherie." She thought Ryan might have been implying that she had withheld information, but noting the mischievous glint in Ryan's eye, she realized that wasn't the case at all. She did not suppress the tingle of excitement that ran along her spine. "I would hate for you to go away unfulfilled," she said, with emphasis on the final word.

Ryan brought the wrist to her lips, her eyes locked with Marilyn's as she feathered a kiss on the now-burning veins.

"I do not have my father's sight. But I do not foresee that happening."

Marilyn laid with the girl for hours, feeling the heat emanating from the sleeping form pressed against her. Marilyn finally pulled away, only because she had pressing business to attend to. Otherwise, she admitted to herself as she departed, she might well have never left again.

Ryan lay on her stomach in a feverish, exhausted sleep. Normally, even soundly unconscious, she would have been aware of anyone's presence in the room. But this particular presence was used to moving about clandestinely, ethereal and undetectable.

Abigail stood at the foot of the bed, gazing down coolly at the prone figure. She moved alongside the bed, trailing her hand up the girl's calf, along the length of her thigh, then across the tight muscles of the her back. She brushed her hand lightly along the girl's cheekbone, tracing its outline. She ran her fingers through the blond hair, causing the girl to stir and murmur in her sleep.

Abigail allowed her presence to settle on the girl like a mantle, calming her and keeping her from awakening. Although there were no outward cues that the girl had fallen into a deeper sleep, Abigail knew it was so.

Abigail stood in the darkness gazing down at the sleeping figure thoughtfully far into the night.

CHAPTER 13

THE FIGURE MOVED THROUGH the dense tangle of the jungle. Completely covered in an elaborate pattern of black and green paint, it was difficult to tell if the person was wearing clothing, or indeed, even if it was male or female, as it shifted ephemerally in and out of the forest. It would seem that the paint was for camouflage, so perfectly did it blend into the dark vegetation. But that theory was shattered by the shock of pale hair that was uncaringly exposed. As the figure loped through the forest like some great jungle cat, the grace and power on display made it apparent the figure had no need for disguise, and that the paint was merely for effect.

And a terrifying effect it was, yielding something fierce and primordial. Even the huge, coiled pythons and the occasional mountain gorilla gave this one wide berth.

Ryan smiled, and her teeth were blinding white against the dark green paint. This place stirred something deep within her, something primitive and primeval. Perhaps it was because she had Memories of this place, but they were not her own. She inhaled deeply the fecund, verdant earth, the wondrous deluge of smells that competed for her senses. She wondered why she had not spent more time in this birthplace of humanity. She glanced at a parrot on a nearby branch, who gazed at her curiously but unafraid. A nearby bonobo monkey screeched an alarm and raced off to tell his family of the strange animal he had seen in the jungle. She again smiled and continued on her way.

It began to rain again, and Ryan lifted her face to the dripping water. The water gave life to the rubber trees, the oil palms, the banana, coconut and plantains. It nourished the teak and the ebony trees, the cedar and the mahogany, and created the monstrous redwoods that dwarfed her, both in size and in longevity. She touched one great trunk, marveling that it was a sapling at the time she was born, when the black prince ruled England and the French and the English were gearing up for a war that would span lifetimes. The water ran down her arms, down into the earth, snaking into tributaries that ran back to the massive river that ran for thousands of miles through the heart of this country.

Ryan began climbing the gradually rising series of plateaus that bordered the east. The physical effort required of her was minimal, but she paced herself out of habits acquired centuries before. The Great Rift Valley was still miles away.

Time passed, and the sun rose and set. The vegetation began to change, becoming near impenetrable. Ryan again smiled. An excellent location, the approach nearly impassable and deeply hidden. There would be a few recreationally scaling the mountain peaks from the other side, and there were many who lived in the shadow of Nyiragongo, close enough to be subject to the volcano's whims. But there was no one here. At least no one human.

Ryan began to feel the presence of those in the jungle around her, circling warily, uncertain of the One who was walking through their midst. Ryan stepped into a beam of light filtering through the trees. She concentrated, blurring her mental impression. There was only One who could now see her as she truly was, and that One already knew she was coming.

Ryan continued through the trees, feeling the Others as they got closer. She was surprised at their great number. It seemed she was to receive quite a welcoming committee. But then, she imagined they received few visitors here. When she knew she was completely surrounded, she stopped.

The jungle around her barely moved, so quietly did they step. But Ryan heard them as clearly as if had they been thundering through the undergrowth. She stood, blurring her presence further until it was as camouflaged as her skin.

The first One stepped from the jungle in front of her, and from an ancient world.

Ryan had seen many soldiers in her journey across Africa, but they had been modern solders with assault rifles swung over their shoulders and bandoliers across their chests. They rode about in dusty jeeps with surly expressions, scattering hungry children, and emaciated livestock. Had she been less focused on her mission she would have slaughtered them all, save for perhaps the child soldiers, and even they might have been too indoctrinated to allow to live.

But this One stepping from the forest night was an ancient warrior. Magnificently tall, his ebony skin gleamed in the darkness. Naked to the waist, he wore an intricately woven necklace and full headdress. He carried a spear, which seemed more for show than from actual need. He was Old, perhaps older than Ryan herself, and very powerful. Ryan had to concentrate greatly to deflect his probing.

Another stepped from the jungle, this One dressed in more elaborate garb, perhaps that of a holy man. He, too, probed Ryan with ancient senses. There passed some silent communication between the two men, and then the jungle came alive as dozens, perhaps hundreds appeared. They were all glorious, with beautiful features and flashing white teeth, sinewy muscles flexing beneath gleaming skin barely covered with intricately woven skirts. Some wore detailed masks, and others wore beards, but most were clean-shaven.

They all stood staring at the strange creature before them, who seemed to shift before their gaze. The girl was a foreigner and garbed strangely, not simply from another tribe, but from another planet.

Ryan stared back at them, fascinated. They were her Kind, but different from the Others, possessing an amazing physicality and a primal energy. Drums began off in the distance. There seemed to be some silent debate among the leaders as to the next step, but that was quickly decided. They as one moved toward Ryan, and as one seized her arms and legs, thrusting her toward the sky. They began moving as a great blanket of humanity, picking their way effortlessly through the thick tangle of vines and branches. Ryan felt herself tossed above the great wave, handed from person to person as they ran en masse in one direction.

Ryan relaxed, staring upward as the canopy overhead flashed by. It seemed that regardless of time, place, or culture, she could always manage to anger the locals sufficiently for them to execute her. Burned at the stake, drowned as a witch, pulled apart by horses, they were all attempted assassinations she could claim on her résumé.

As they stepped into a clearing in the shadow of the mountain, Ryan inwardly cursed the not-so-subtle influences of Christianity on the African culture. She was dumped unceremoniously to the ground in front of a twelve foot high cross. Apparently she was going to be able to add crucifixion to her list of accomplishments.

The night was falling and torches were lit, casting flickering shadows across the clearing. A Young One grabbed her arm and before she could suppress her preternatural reflexes, she had flung him halfway across the court, knocking two of the flaming torches to the ground. She was quickly set upon by a group of the muscular warriors, and she ceased resistance.

The cross was removed from the deep hole that held it upright and laid on the ground behind Ryan. Her arms were pulled to an outstretched position and she was pulled backward onto the cross. Ropes were tied tightly about her ankles, and around both arms, pinning her to the wooden frame. The Old One who had first stepped from the jungle approached, a great mallet in his hands.

Kokumuo stared down at the girl lying on the cross. Oddly enough, she showed no fear of what was about to happen, nor did she appear to be offering any resistance, other than flinging Kijana across the clearing like a toy. He again tried to get a fix on this one, tried to get a feel for her power. But she gazed at him impassively, and if he could get a singular emotion from her, it was that she was mildly entertained.

That would change soon enough. He motioned for the iron spikes, and two men rushed forward, placing the spikes in the center of the girl's palms. She did not even curl her fingers.

Kokumuo straddled her and slammed the mallet downward, hammering the spike through the flesh and into the wood. There was no scream of pain, no writhing in agony. The girl did wince, but it was a reaction more commensurate with the stubbing of a toe than the damage he was inflicting. He slammed the mallet down on the other spike, and it again went through the flesh and into the wood with a loud "thwack."

The girl winced and twisted slightly, this reaction more appropriate to an attack of mild indigestion. Kokumuo frowned and stepped back, motioning for the holy man to approach. The holy man stepped forward and gestured impatiently to the group hovering a safe distance off. They rushed forward, uprighting the cross and returning it to its hole in the ground. Ryan again winced as it jarred, settling into place. The drums increased their tempo.

The holy man drew his Nsakara blade, and it was Ryan's turn to frown. Now this was probably going to hurt. He approached her, and, mumbling some ancient incantation, drew a line of blood from Ryan's left shoulder to her wrist. The wound began to seep immediately. He carved another line down her right arm, then two across her torso, intersecting at her sternum. All of the wounds began to seep blood, running down her body and dripping into the dirt below.

There was a sudden shifting in the throng at the sight of the blood. None of their Kind was immune to the bloodlust, no matter the ceremony. Ryan stared down insolently at Kokumuo. She sensed his hunger increase exponentially. She held his gaze and, for just the briefest of moments, revealed herself to him.

Kokumuo staggered backward. His thoughts coalesced at frightening speed, and he lunged forward to stop the holy man, but he was not quick enough.

The holy man plunged the blade into Ryan's left side, just beneath the ribs and upward toward the heart. This caused Ryan significant pain, and she muffled a centuries-old expletive under her breath. She closed her eyes and shifted uncomfortably at the pain of the impaled weapon.

The drums stopped abruptly and there was complete silence in the torch-lit courtyard. A murmur went through the crowd, and Ryan opened her eyes. The throng was parting like a great sea before a gorgeous, ebony goddess. The woman was dressed in elaborate robes, intricately decorated with symbols of the night sky. She gazed at the girl on the cross, her eyes following the rivulets of blood that streamed down the lean, muscular frame. The goddess stopped before the girl, her eyes caressing each crimson path. She finally turned her attention upward, and her tone was unaccountably amused.

"I find you most curious, Rhiannon Alexander," Ala said.

The name sent a ripple through the throng, and those who had dared raise their hand in the crucifixion took a step backward. Ryan stared down at her wordlessly as Ala continued.

"And why is it that you have allowed them to do this to you?"

Ryan smiled a wicked smile. "Because you wished it."

Ala felt the subtle sensation pass through her, the invitation, the enticement. She stepped forward, pretending to examine the impaled weapon thoughtfully. She then grasped the hilt of the knife and pulled it sharply downward. Ryan muffled a groan, shifting again. Actually, she thought, that felt a lot better.

Ala raised the crimson blade, touching it to her lips. Ryan felt the tremor pass through her as Ala tasted her blood. Ala held her gaze, invitation in her own eyes. She lowered the blade.

"You have allowed yourself to be sacrificed to honor me." She glanced at the unique markings on Ryan's body. "And I see that you have honored me further by dressing in so ancient a way that even the oldest here would not remember it. And how is that you discovered this array?"

Ryan, although completely caught up in the moment, could not control her wayward sense of humor. "Internet," she replied.

Ala smiled, amused despite herself. That information was not available anywhere on that living web of knowledge. It could only be obtained at great effort and great expense.

"Hmmm-mm," was all she said on that matter. She turned slightly. "Well, my sacrificial lamb, come down off of your cross."

Ryan sighed with mock relief. "I thought you would never ask."

With little more of a flexing of her shoulders, Ryan snapped the cross lengthwise, splintering the wood in all directions. She shrugged, and the ropes snapped, whipping wildly about as she landed lightly on her feet. Now, attached only to the crossbeam by the spikes, she braced herself, and pulled sharply forward. The nails came free of the wood, still impaled in her palms by her clenched fists. The heavy beam fell to the ground with a thud. Ryan gazed at the nails, puzzling how to remove them since both hands were affected. She was about to use her teeth when that mellow, melodic voice stopped her.

"Allow me to help you with those," Ala said, holding one injured hand. She pulled the spike from the center of Ryan's hand, then raised the hand, palm upward. She gently kissed the injury, then repeated the process with the other hand. Ryan's eyes were locked with hers over the already healing flesh. Ala felt the shiver of excitement the girl tried, and failed, to suppress.

Ala did not release the girl's hand, but rather placed it on her own and began leading her from the courtyard. The two ancient Ones walked from the clearing arm in arm, disappearing into the side of the mountain.

Kokumuo glanced over at the holy man, who was staring after the two. He would not want to be him at this moment. He looked back at the side of the mountain. He was not real happy about being himself.

Ryan was shown into a sumptuous room decorated with African and Egyptian artwork from across the centuries. Steps wide enough to comfortably sit on were carved from solid rock and led down into the center of the room. To the left on a raised platform was a sleeping area draped with translucent veils. There was the sound of running water from a waterfall that flowed from a hole in the ceiling and disappeared into the floor. A depression around the waterfall was worn into the wall, creating a natural shower. Ryan walked over to the waterfall and put her hand into the stream of water. It was frigid, obviously warming little with its trip down the mountain. She glanced over next to it, where steam rose from a raised bath.

A beautiful young woman came in carrying another jug of hot water. She added it to the steaming water. She lowered her eyes demurely.

"Would you like assistance bathing?"

"Ummm," Ryan said uncertainly, "I don't think so. Thank you."

The woman nodded, her disappointment obvious. She disappeared from the room.

Ryan quickly removed what little clothing she was wearing and stepped into the waterfall. The shock of ice cold water felt good, as did the spice scented soap which lathered her skin. She scrubbed the paint from her body with the pumice stone, careful to avoid her injuries. She took a moment to examine them. The shallow cuts down her arms and across her chest had already begun healing. They were now thin red lines. She glanced at the back of her hands, then turned them over to look at the palms. The wounds had closed on both sides. She flexed the hands experimentally.

She turned her attention to the knife wound in her side. That was a different story. That cut had been much deeper, and although it was healing quickly, it still seeped a small amount of blood. Ryan put pressure on it, as if willing it to close.

"I trust your injuries are not causing you too great of discomfort."

Ryan glanced over her shoulder as Ala entered the room, then back down at her wound. "It's but a scratch."

Ala settled onto a cushion on an upper step and took the opportunity to examine the girl's physical form. She had a great appreciation for the aesthetics of their Kind, and this One was exceptional, especially for a European. Standing over six feet tall with well-built shoulders and a muscular back tapering to a slender waist, the girl had the sinews of a lioness. Her lower body was built for power and speed, with long, slender legs and well-developed muscles that rippled beneath the skin when she moved.

Ryan was aware but unabashed at the keen inspection. It was not a question of immodesty, but rather that she felt no more vulnerable naked than she did fully clothed. She stepped from the frigid waterfall into the nearby bath. The huge temperature differential brought its own pleasure as she settled into the steaming water up to her neck. She was about to comment on how well these accommodations integrated with the natural surroundings when something in the corner caught her eye.

"Is that a satellite receiver?"

Ala was amused. "We are not savages, my dear. We honor an ancient way of life, but that does not mean we have not evolved. I do enjoy occasionally watching CNN."

"Hmmm," Ryan said, "and the crucifixion, was that part of the old world or the new one?"

Ala smiled. "Kokumuo is greatly embarrassed. You hid yourself well, and he is ashamed both by the way you were treated and the fact that he did not detect your identity."

"And why would Kokumuo care who I am?"

Ala hid her smile. The girl was once again oblivious to her sovereignty, which carried authority even in this place. Ala chose not to explain the former, but rather the latter.

"Your father is revered here, and not in some foolish 'superior white man' way."

Ryan sat up in the bath, curious. She had seen Memories from this place, but they were ancient and unclear. "And why is that?"

"Long before it became a more common name, they called him Shombay, or 'he who walks like a lion'." Ala's melodic voice deepened, taking on a mesmerizing quality. "The original chieftain here, over a thousand years ago, was an evil man." Ala paused, lost in her own thoughts for a moment. She continued. "Given immortality, he chose to crush any of those not of his tribe. He created internecine warfare that lives to this day in the children of Africa."

Ryan listened thoughtfully as Ala continued, wondering what this had to do with Victor. Ala answered her unspoken question in her next sentence.

"Your father destroyed him in the first millennial purge."

Ryan's thoughts deepened, and she had a sudden prescience. "This chieftain was your mentor."

Ala nodded, her dark eyes gleaming. "You have much of your father's insight."

Ryan shook her head, abruptly standing up in the bath. She grasped a towel from the rack and stepped onto the smooth floor. "I have none of my father's sight," she said, wrapping the towel about her waist. She pulled another towel from the rack and quickly dried. She examined some cloth that was also draped over the rack, then pulled a simple patterned one. She expertly tied the sarong about her waist, then another one about her upper body. She turned to Ala, and the distance between them seemed to disappear. The silence in the room was complete, and outside as well, as if everyone and everything within a thousand miles had frozen in place.

So what is it that you want from me, Rhiannon Alexander? Ala said without speaking.

The words whispered through Ryan's head as she gazed across the room at the primordial goddess.

"You know what I want," Ryan said, speaking aloud.

Ala smiled, her white teeth startling against the darkness of her skin. "I will not offer you the same bargain that Kusunoki did."

Before Ryan could object, she continued. "And you have nothing to hide because I already know of your father's illness."

Ryan stared at her. She had suspected as much. "You have the sight as well."

Ala shook her head. "I have the second sight, Victor the third. I see things as they are now, Victor sees things as they will be."

Ryan could not keep the bitterness from her voice. "And is your sight clearer than his? For it seems he could not prevent his fate."

Ala's voice was suddenly gentle. "Perhaps he did not want to, child."

Ryan looked down, clenching her jaw and her fists. "He said the future was unclear. That he didn't know if he would come out the other side."

Ala nodded. "That is the way it is. Like a reflection in muddied water." She watched the girl for a moment, watched the emotions flicker across her face, saw the faraway look in her eye and wanted to go there with her. Her voice grew more gentle, but full of meaning.

"So, my sacrificial lamb. You are going to have to satisfy more than just my curiosity."

Ryan glanced up, immediately drawn to the power of that mellow voice. She felt the great tendrils of Ala's power branch out and wrap around her, holding her tight. She stood for a moment, eyes closed, feeling the magnetic pull of the earth itself emanating from the woman across from her.

"Come here, child," Ala whispered.

And Ryan moved to her, stopping but two steps beneath her and kneeling but one. Ryan leaned forward into the great expanse of her breasts and Ala welcomed her into that motherly warmth. The tendrils wrapped tighter. She cradled the girl's head in her hands, and brushed her perfect teeth across the girl's neck. The vein opened and began to spill its dark power into her body.

Ala shuddered from the monstrous yet delicious sensations that tore through her body. The visions came to her immediately, briefly indistinct then springing into painful and beautiful clarity. She saw the girl's life stretch out before her, saw her as a child, as a soldier, as a Young One who was never truly Young. She saw Ryan's passionate couplings with Victor, and Kusunoki, and Marilyn. She saw Abigail's long and convoluted seduction that had not yet come to fruition. She saw the dangerous game Ryan played with Aeron, and saw perhaps clearer than the girl did how intensely he desired her.

Ryan saw Ala's life as well, and it rushed toward her in all its sensual spirituality. She saw Ala's birth, and her Change. She saw Ala conspire with Victor to destroy her mentor, and she smiled at a recklessness she had never know him to have. She saw Kusunoki, and the deep relationship he had with Ala over the centuries. She saw Ala create Kokumuo, and saw her withdraw into the mountains of the Congo, tired of the senseless strife of humanity. She saw her deeply divided over that withdrawal as the Europeans came and stole the princes and princesses of Africa, enslaving them. She saw Ala pondering the approaching storm, when the Europeans and their children would exhaust the resources of the kingdom of Babylon and again turn their attention to the riches of her dark continent.

The world turned blood-red, and Ryan was again in the netherworld. She stood at the edge of this world, the red sky at her back, staring into the blackness. It was as always, a vast nothingness, a yawning abyss that called to her.

But this time it was different. Ryan strained, peering into the darkness. She could see nothing.

"I must see more."

Ala leaned back from the girl, who although far from death had weakened considerably. The girl was barely conscious, whispering something. Ala shifted her position slightly, cradling her on her lap. "Here," she said, "take this."

She brushed her teeth across her own wrist, bringing the blood to the surface. She pressed the wrist to the girl's lips, returning the power she had only so recently taken.

Ryan gasped at the shock, grateful for the dark gift. Although the physiological satisfaction was immense, Ryan was more focused on returning to the edge of the darkness. "I need you to continue feeding," she murmured, "I need your sight."

Ala raised an eyebrow. "You don't have to ask me twice, child." And she sliced open the other side of Ryan's neck, drawing her blood into her.

The bond created by their simultaneous feeding was powerful, and Ryan was instantly back in the netherworld. She sensed Ala behind her, farther from the edge than Ryan and closer than she wanted to be. Ryan turned to her and Ala saw how truly powerful this child really was. She stood at the edge of death, unafraid, glancing back with mischief in her eye.

Don't you want to come with me?

Ala shook her head, scolding. Do what you came for.

Ryan turned back to the darkness and took a step closer. There was something there, the barest hint of a presence. Ryan extended her senses warily, then withdrew in shock.

The presence was powerful, more powerful than anything Ryan had ever felt before. More powerful than she could even comprehend. It had a prehistoric, monstrous quality to it, an alien, reptilian impression that made Ryan feel as if she were suddenly covered with hideous crawling insects. Ryan stepped backward. Being irreligious became irrelevant; the presence was demonic.

The words came whispering towards her in a strange tongue that somehow she could understand.

"I'm...Coming—."

The words hissed out of the darkness at her, sibilant and terrifying. They cut through her like shards of ice and she stumbled backward in horror. She felt a hand grab hers, and suddenly she was not in the netherworld but in Ala's chambers in the middle of the Congo. The woman held her, staring down at her in concern.

"What is it, child?"

Ryan realized that, although she had taken Ala to the edge, Ala had not seen what she had seen. She closed her eyes, immediately shuttering the image and placing it far away.

"Nothing," she mumbled. "Nothing at all." She held herself stiffly for a moment, then buried her head against Ala.

Ala stroked the girl's hair, concerned. She had enjoyed the union immensely, but toward the end something had changed.

For the most infinitesimal of moments, she thought the fearless One had been afraid.

CHAPTER 14

THE JET WAITED NEAR THE PRIVATE HANGAR off the runway of the Ndjili International Airport. Although privately owned, the plane was outfitted with the latest military hardware. Large enough to act as a cargo carrier, its primary mission was to transport personnel.

Numerous black-garbed figures milled about outside the plane, wearing dark sunglasses and cradling automatic weapons. As if the weapons weren't threatening enough, there was a sinister, other-worldly quality to the men themselves. They seemed to move with an unnatural grace and strength.

As one, the men became aware of something, although what it was did not become apparent until several moments later when a string of black limousines with heavily armed escorts passed through the gate. Impossibly, this seemed to make the men slightly nervous, although it was difficult to imagine that anything could frighten them.

The limousines came to a stop in front of the jet, and numerous men began exiting, again all dressed in black with dark sunglasses. Finally, the occupant of the lead car exited and it became apparent what the men were frightened of

Well over six feet tall and cruelly handsome, Muenda surveyed the surrounding men with a piercing stare. His name, "one who cares for others," was a great irony for Muenda cared for no one but himself. He ruled his followers through fear and punishment, and terrorized any who stood against him. Many followed willingly, but it was only because Muenda allowed them to sate their bloodlust in every base way imaginable.

Satisfied with his inspection, Muenda boarded the plane, as did nearly all of the men. They settled into the luxurious accommodations inside.

The plane taxied on the runway and took off to the west. Muenda was impressed with the pilot's touch on the controls; he was getting better. Muenda settled into his seat, his ugly thoughts his own.

Although his Change centuries before had given him immortality and untold power, it was one of his few regrets that he had lost the ability for sexual congress. He was looking forward to Rwanda. As was his custom, he would arrange for women to be raped for his enjoyment while he satisfied his bloodlust with one of his Kind. The only difficulty was finding suitable virgins, which was getting more and more challenging. Somehow the superstitious fools had gotten it in their heads that they could cure AIDs by having sex with a virgin. Now the only virgins they could find were girls of seven or eight years old.

Muenda smiled. That was all right with him. He settled deeper into his chair, the images his thoughts brought him unpleasantly entertaining. This occupied him for some time until he felt a subtle shift in the flight path of the airplane. He frowned. Perhaps this pilot wasn't as good as he thought. Muenda was just preparing to send someone forward to berate the man when the airplane dramatically increased airspeed, violently lurched, then went into a 40 degree angle dive nose down.

Anyone who was standing was thrown rearward in the plane, and the g-forces were so great it pinned everyone in place. Although every creature in the plane possessed preternatural strength, without leverage to fight against the terrific strain of gravity, the strength was useless. A few tried to claw their way forward to the cockpit, but merely ended up tearing off whatever piece of metal or fabric they were clinging to.

The pilot in the cockpit, however, was well-prepared and had arranged straps to give her the needed leverage. Ryan held tightly to the metal mesh, locking the plane into its intended path. Exerting tremendous effort, she pulled a 9 mm handgun from her coat and shot out the side window, creating an immediate, powerful suction with the dramatic pressure change. With one last glance at the looming mountain and one quick adjustment of the controls, she let go of the mesh strap, allowing herself to be sucked out of the plane.

She regained control of her body in the air, enjoying the sensation of floating. She did a quick somersault with a twist, so she could get a better view of the plummeting aircraft. It was a perfect missile, heading directly into the gaping maw of Nyiragongo. And Nyiragongo had opened that maw wide, spewing lava in a fiery welcome.

Ryan congratulated herself on a perfect plan, then looked down at the rapidly approaching ground. No, she thought, a perfect plan would have entailed a parachute. Invulnerability often made one overlook the simplest of details. This was probably going to hurt.

She hit the canopy of a huge redwood, which hardly slowed her descent. The eighty-six branches that she hit on the way to the ground did slow her slightly more, but she still hit the ground with an impact severe enough to imprint her five feet deep into the damp earth.

Ryan lay on her back in the hole, covered in dirt and vegetation, gazing up at the light filtering through the trees. After the constant roar of the air rushing past her during descent, the forest was eerily silent.

Of course, she thought, it could have been the impact of the bomb that just plummeted to earth that silenced the jungle creatures. She was fairly certain she had broken every bone in her body. She shifted slightly in her hole and confirmed it. This would take at least a week to heal.

Ala sat within her chambers, Kokumuo nearby. The tendrils of her senses were stretched out through the darkness of the jungle, collecting sensations from the flora and fauna throughout. She enjoyed the various impressions of sights and smells that drifted back to her through this extended web.

She cocked her head to one side. There was a great disturbance rippling across her web, but it almost seemed to come from the air above. She stood and moved from her chambers into the outer clearing, turning her gaze to the sky. Kokumuo followed her curiously. He looked up into the sky, but he could see and feel nothing.

But then he felt what Ala felt. In fact, even the youngest among them turned, and all as one turned to distant Nyiragongo. Multiple cries of fear and pain swept through the collective conscious of their Kind, and then were abruptly and emphatically silenced.

Ala listened intently to what could not be heard, testing for the survival of any of those she had sensed. It did not seem possible, but there was no sign of the presence of any of them, even the most powerful among them.

She turned to Kokumuo, who did not understand what he had sensed and looked to her for response.

Ala smiled, and it was blinding in the darkness.

Kokumuo made his way through the jungle, easily sensing ahead of him what he was searching for. As he neared, he glanced up at the path of destruction that came downward through the branches of the giant redwood. He looked to the base of the tree, where the path ended in a hole shaped in the outline of a spread-eagled figure. He walked to the edge of the hole, peering down into it.

"Habari," Ryan said, greeting him in Swahili. "I hope you're not going to crucify me because I'm really not up to it right now."

Kokumuo gazed down at the prone figure, assessing her injuries. "If you were more forthcoming with your identity, you would probably be greeted more appropriately."

Ryan shifted in her hole, causing her to wince in pain. Even so, she could not contain her sense of humor. "I don't know," she said, "many might consider crucifixion an appropriate greeting for me."

The handsome black man tried to maintain his stern demeanor, but failed, his teeth white against his skin. He motioned to several of the warriors who accompanied him, and they rushed forward, bearing a litter. Under Kokumuo's watchful gaze, they carefully extricated Ryan from the pit and gently placed her on the stretcher.

The movement was painful to Ryan, but not unbearably so. She relaxed in the sling as they began their trek back through the jungle.

Kokumuo gave one last look at the broken branches of the redwood, then walked next to the stretcher.

"So," he said conversationally, "did you think you could fly?"

Ryan winced at a slight jar, then relaxed again.

"Oh, I don't know," she replied, staring up at the passing canopy. "I try to stay open to new things."

Ryan awoke in the chambers she had vacated only a week before. She corrected herself. Only a week before she had flown Muenda into an active volcano. She had no idea how long she had been asleep.

Ala entered, sensing that the girl had awakened. She read Ryan's expression, answering her unasked question.

"Only two weeks, my dear."

Ryan appeared relieved. "I don't want the Grand Council to think I am sleeping through my duties," she said with mild sarcasm.

Ala smiled. "I will be sure to report of your diligence on my continent. You were quite busy in the short time you were here."

Ryan said nothing, so Ala filled the space.

"The collapse of the South African diamond mine. The opened floodgates of the Kariba dam. The renewed internecine warfare across the entire continent. All reported in world news, but missing the common thread woven throughout.

"Which is?" Ryan asked, knowing the answer.

"That all were intentionally caused, and resulted in an abnormal number of our Kind destroyed, either directly, or by their slaughter of one another.

"And do you mourn the innocents lost?"

"None of our Kind are innocent," Ala said, a dark look in her eye. Her manner grew casual once more. "And as for the loss of human life? I have much blood on my hands already, simply from my past inaction."

Ryan was curious. "And why is it that you have chosen inaction when you could be the supreme ruler of all of Africa, if not more?"

Ala looked at her shrewdly. "And why is it that you are not Emperor of the United States, or of England?"

Ryan was thoughtful for a moment. "Because I really don't care much about the affairs of humans."

Ryan paused, then continued. "A human once noted that 'life in an unregulated state of nature is solitary, poor, nasty, brutish, and short.' He concluded that humans accepted the moral constraints of civilization as an alternative."

Ryan looked up. "I see no superiority in their choice."

The two settled into silence, which Ryan finally broke. "I don't know if Muenda is truly dead. He was very ancient and very powerful, and it is possible he survived."

Ala nodded. "Even if he survived the impact, and if he survived the lava, and if he survived being buried in the center of that mountain, it will be many centuries before he fully recovers." She shrugged. "And I do not sense his presence at all."

Ryan agreed. "I do not sense him, either."

It was Ala's turn to be thoughtful. "If you had any concern for the 'innocents' yourself, you can be secure in the knowledge that your removal of Muenda will save many more than you would ever kill. You have interrupted a blood line that needed to die."

Ryan took odd comfort in that fact, and again drifted off to sleep.

CHAPTER 15

RYAN AGAIN SAT, OR RATHER AGAIN SPRAWLED, in the Great Hall of the Grand Council. The twelve witnesses stood stiffly at attention in their semicircle behind her.

She shifted in her chair, wincing slightly. Although her bones had knit cleanly, she was still a bit sore from her fall from the sky. This tended to make her a bit irritable. The hovering of those behind her made her more so.

"Oh, for Christ's sake, would you all sit down!" she finally blurted out.

The twelve sat down with alacrity, and Edward hid a smile.

Ryan rubbed her head, wincing. The crack in her skull had been particularly slow to heal. And there was little she could take for the pain, as her body treated most drugs with total disregard. She shook off the mild irritation. She had been in far worse pain.

Ryan thought back to her Change. When Victor had first transformed her, the alteration to her physical form had been so dramatic it had been agonizing. The Change was always painful, and the vast majority of times lethal. But Ryan's had been particularly intense because never in the history of their Kind had anyone been Changed by One so powerful. The pain and exhaustion she had endured resulted in a sleep lasting nearly 14 years immediately following her transformation, during which Victor never left her side.

Ryan became aware that she was under significant scrutiny. She looked up. The five members of the Grand Council had filed in and were already seated, staring at her with expressions ranging from curiosity to amusement to total irritation.

"Are we disturbing you?" Aeron asked sarcastically. He was already angered at the fact that the witnesses were seated. He was more so by the fact that the girl seemed oblivious to them.

"No more than usual," Ryan said, her focus and humor returning with deadly precision.

"I understand you have been very busy, ma Cherie," Marilyn said, dispensing with all formality, irritating Aeron even further.

"I am merely following the edict of this Council."

Marilyn smiled. "I do not think your actions have anything to do with the desires of this Council."

Ryan smiled as well. "Or perhaps they have everything to do with the desires of this Council."

Abigail watched the girl carefully. Her recklessness seemed even more pronounced. She noted that the girl shifted with visible, physical discomfort, but if Ryan had sustained the injuries attributed to her, she probably shouldn't even be conscious yet.

"Is it true that you fell 20,000 feet?" Kusunoki asked, giving voice to Abigail's thoughts

"Hmmm," Ryan said thoughtfully, "I think it was probably closer to 15,000, but it was difficult to tell at that velocity."

"Then you did kill Muenda," Abigail said slowly.

The room grew silent as the words and their implications sunk in. Ryan looked at Abigail, then shifted her gaze squarely to Aeron.

"It is likely that he is dead," Ryan said.

Aeron stared at the girl in cold fury. Never in the chronicles of their Kind had anyone managed to destroy an Old One. None had existed when Victor had performed his duties as hunter, and few had even been as old as he at that time. Although there had been many pitched battles over the years that had resulted in temporary disabling injuries, none of those occupying the upper echelon had ever managed to kill one another, creating a frustrating but secure détente.

That détente had ended. And it wasn't even the method that she had used, ingenious as it was, that was the most troubling. It was the fact that she could effortlessly penetrate Muenda's inner circle, disguise herself and her intentions from his entire entourage, and remain completely hidden to Muenda himself, arguably the most paranoid and security-conscious of all of them. That bespoke a mental power and discipline that was inconceivable and incredibly dangerous.

Aeron stared down at the girl. Under normal circumstances, the greater the power of their Kind, the more difficult it was to hide, especially to those of equal or greater power. Their auras shone like fire on a moonless night, easily veiled to the eyes of Young Ones, but blindingly obvious to any beyond the Middle years.

And this girl had an aura like the sun. It was impossible that she could have passed unnoticed.

Ryan was aware of but ignored his scrutiny. "Edward has the current numbers, which once again are easily verified."

Edward stood, clearing his throat. "The numbers now stand at 16,498 dead, 542 missing and presumed dead, and 456 missing and unaccounted for."

Ryan sat, examining her fingernails as silence again descended on the Great Hall.

"And which category did you put Muenda in?" Ala asked, her lack of concern for the stratospheric figures evident.

Ryan glanced up, then returned to her perusal of her fingernails. "Until he crawls out of that volcano, I'm going to assume he's dead," she said casually.

Abigail glanced over at Ala, her outward expression impassive and her inner guarded as well. She noted that Ala in no way seemed disturbed by the massacre of her kin, and actually seemed pleased. Abigail turned her attention back to the girl. How Ryan had managed to destroy over 16,000 of their Kind without creating enemies of the sovereigns of the continents most affected was astonishing.

Just like Victor, Abigail thought. She had both his finesse and his judgment, and the devastating charm that made her the perfect predator.

Aeron gazed down at the girl, stroking his chin thoughtfully. Once again he was caught between cold fury and pure lust. He wasn't certain if he wanted to leap across the table and snap her spine or leap across the table and take her to bed. The thought of doing both, perhaps not in that order, gave him great pleasure.

Ryan held Aeron's gaze, her amusement evident. Try either, her expression said, and you may not survive the attempt.

Aeron smiled, drumming his fingers lightly on the table. When he spoke, his words surprised just about everyone in the room.

"Would you care to join me for a drink in my chambers?"

Ryan was not surprised by the invitation but by the very public way it was offered. It was as if suddenly she and Aeron were the only ones in the room. She raised an eyebrow.

"And what are we drinking?" she asked.

Aeron allowed his gaze to flicker to her lips, then back to her eyes. "Whatever you would like."

The tension in the room was palpable. Ever attuned to the subtle, sensual interplay amongst their Kind, all were fully aware of the dark dance the two were engaged in. They were also very aware of the underlying power struggle taking place. Whoever yielded to temptation first might not survive the outing.

"Very well," Ryan said. "I will join you shortly."

Without waiting for permission, Ryan stood. She glanced at Marilyn, who seemed amused by their exchange. Marilyn was unconcerned, jealousy a known but infrequently experienced emotion with her. As Ryan unwound from her seated position, Marilyn took the opportunity to admire the girl's physical form. She knew whom she was betting on between the two combatants.

Ryan nodded to Kusunoki and Ala, who both returned the gesture. Ryan then looked to Abigail, holding her gaze for a long moment. Abigail's expression was impassive.

Ryan then turned, as did Edward, and both disappeared.

Ryan stood before the ornate double doors, but before she could knock, the door whispered open. Aeron stood in the doorway.

"Welcome back, my love."

Ryan brushed by him, raising an eyebrow at the somewhat sarcastic endearment. Out of the many words she could use to describe their relationship, love wasn't on the list.

Aeron followed her into the room, offering her a place on the settee. She ignored the offer and instead settled into a chair across from him. He sat down as well.

Ryan's eyes drifted downward to the small table between them. The chess board sat there, the twisted pieces in the positions of their last parting. Ryan assessed the positions for a moment, then leaned forward, moving a bishop across the board.

Aeron eyed the piece. It was a curious move, almost completely at random. He evaluated the overall positions a second time to make certain he was not missing something, then moved his queen into a position of attack. There was no defense for the bishop; he would take it on the next move, or the one after that.

Ryan leaned back, unconcerned for the vulnerability of the chess piece. She locked gazes with Aeron, who was openly examining her, his eyes lingering on her lips, then caressing her throat. He allowed his gaze to flick down her body, noting once again how perfectly she was formed.

"Would you like me to disrobe?" Ryan asked, her amusement evident.

"Yes, would you?" Aeron said.

"Perhaps another time," Ryan said.

"Another time," Aeron agreed, his voice drifting off. He was thoughtful for a moment, then spoke.

"So you are the product of Victor's union with a human woman."

Ryan was wary of the sudden change in direction of the conversation. Despite her attempt at an outwardly cool demeanor, she felt her jaw clench. "The circumstances of my birth are public record from the trial."

Aeron smiled his shark's smile. "Unfortunately I was not at your trial, although I'm quite certain I would have enjoyed the proceedings." Aeron savored the thought for a moment. "And I certainly would have come up with a different punishment for you than returning you to Victor."

Ryan looked away, as if dismissing the conversation, but Aeron would have none of it.

"So is it true?" he asked softly.

"Is what true?" Ryan asked, unable to quell her irritation.

Aeron did not alter his conspiratorial whisper. "Am I the one who set those Memories free?"

Ryan's jaw again clenched, and Aeron thought she was going to refuse to answer. Without moving, he reached out to her, allowing the full power of his influence to settle on her.

Ryan felt the embrace, felt the pull, both welcome and unwelcome. She tried to shrug it off but was unable, and the encirclement tightened. She felt herself flashing back to the first time she had met Aeron, when he had taken her so easily. Although she was much more powerful, so was he, and it seemed their battle had only changed by degree.

Ryan shook her head, uncertain where such defeatist thoughts were coming from. She looked Aeron in the eye.

"Yes," she said simply, "when you fed upon me, you released Memories that I myself had not seen."

Aeron took pleasure in the admission, but was relentless. "And so how did it feel, to see your dear father rape and kill your mother?"

Ryan's jaw clenched tighter, and she avoided those piercing blue eyes. But they found the answers that they were looking for.

"Ah," Aeron said with satisfaction. "that's right. You have such an extraordinary ability to look into the minds of others. So you didn't merely see your father do it, you experienced it firsthand. So I guess my question should be, how did it feel to rape and kill your own mother?"

Faster than any eye could see, Ryan was across the table and upon him, one hand clenching his shirtfront, the other his throat. "I have my mother's blood too, you bastard. Maybe you should ask me how it felt to be her."

Aeron was fascinated as he turned this improbability over in his mind. He ignored the tightening hand at his throat, continuing his train of thought aloud. "So you experienced it from both perspectives. You were both the rapist and the raped, and ultimately the progeny from that forced union."

Ryan shoved him away in disgust, standing abruptly. "Whatever perverse pleasure you are getting from this conversation is over. Your hospitality is sorely lacking."

She made as if to leave, but it was Aeron's turn to use his preternatural speed. He stood and grabbed her arm, turning her forcefully to face him. He twisted the arm behind her, causing her to press up against him. They were now face to face, centimeters apart. His eyes lingered on her lips, then traced the line of her cheekbone, then moved to the throbbing vein in her neck. He leaned forward, brushing his lips across the blood vessel straining under the skin.

Ryan's fury had stoked her bloodlust, perhaps Aeron's intention all along. Rage and desire were at times so physiologically alike for their Kind, it was hard to differentiate between the two. She forcibly clamped her jaw shut, grinding the teeth to keep them from rending his flesh.

Aeron twisted the arm tighter, creating the other paradox of their physiology; the very fine line between pleasure and pain. They were now so close their lips were nearly touching.

"So, my dear," he whispered, "do you think you are capable of reproducing as your father did?"

Ryan leaned tantalizingly close, nearly brushing his lips, then pulled away. "Even if I am capable of reproducing," she said, quietly sarcastic, "what makes you think you are?"

Aeron merely smiled at the insult. He again allowed his eyes to linger on her lips. "I'm not certain," he said, "but I shall enjoy trying."

Ryan's eyes narrowed at the prospect, but she would not give him the satisfaction of a reply.

Aeron continued. "And lest there be any confusion, my dear, we *will* try."

He released her and Ryan stepped back, flexing the arm he had twisted. Her shoulder settled back into place with an audible pop. She gave him a look indicating his proposal was the least likely thing to occur in her lifetime, then moved to the chessboard. Without hesitation, she moved a knight over a space and then up, ignoring the sacrifice of the castle.

Then, without a backward glance at him, she left the room.

She quickly met up with Edward in Victor's chambers.

"Will you be staying the evening, my lord?" Edward asked politely.

"No, I don't think so, Edward. I'm going to be spending some time in Europe. It will be some of my more enjoyable hunting," she said, her expression dark as she thought about Aeron. Her head hurt, and she winced as pain shot across her temple.

Edward noted the gesture. "Still recovering from your fall?"

Ryan frowned. "I imagine so, although I have been hurt worse and healed faster. This seems very strange." She turned as if to leave. "It makes me feel a good more empathy for my father after I tried to kill him."

She had taken two steps when her own words stopped her cold. She stood there for a moment, her thoughts racing. Empathy. Her father's pain. Her pain.

"Is something wrong, my lord?" Edward asked.

She slowly turned to him. "I need to get above ground and get a secure signal to Dr. Ryerson."

They had barely lifted off the runway when Ryan opened the video line. The screen showed static for a few seconds, then sprang to life. Susan Ryerson was on the screen.

"Ryan, what is it?"

Although the technology was state-of-the-art, there was still a slight delay due to the distance the signal had to travel, and due to the encryption process it went through. Ryan was impatient with the delay.

"Have you found anything regarding my father?"

Susan was concerned. Ryan seemed slightly agitated, which was very unusual for her.

"No, I'm following up on several promising leads, but I still haven't identified anything I think might be causing his illness."

Ryan shook her head. "You need to change your strategy."

Susan ran her fingers through her red hair, a gesture betraying her apprehension. "What do you mean?"

"You need to stop looking for something that's different between my father and I and start looking for something that's the same."

It took a few seconds for Ryan's words to sink in, and when they did, Susan's concern grew exponentially. "Ryan, are you all right?"

Ryan nodded, visibly angry. "Yes, I'm fine for right now. And I'm on my way there, now. But start looking for something that I may have transmitted to my father, or that he might have transmitted to me, and that I myself might be infected with."

It seemed the hidden runway had barely settled beneath the sea before Ryan was striding into the laboratory. Susan looked up from her microscope and Ryan noted how exhausted she looked.

"It seems you were right," Susan said.

"About-?" Ryan asked.

"Whatever is affecting your father is probably beginning to affect you as well."

Ryan settled heavily into a chair. "How can you tell?"

"I took your advice, and no longer eliminated the possibility that you could both be infected, which caused me to revisit the data from the mitochondria. Instead of comparing Victor's DNA to yours, I compared his current DNA to an older sample of his DNA. What I found is amazing, even for your anatomies."

Susan again placed a few slides on the overhead projector, and Ryan gazed at the smug little organelles as Susan continued. "The mitochondrial DNA is mutating, and at an astonishing rate. Normal mitochondria can mutate over years, centuries, and sometimes over millions of years. But yours is mutating so fast that I can't measure it with even the most advanced techniques—the typing is just too slow."

"If Victor's DNA is mutating," Ryan asked uncertainly, "then how can his and mine still be the same?"

Susan could not keep the incredulity from her voice. "Because yours is mutating as well. And it's mutating in an identical fashion to Victor's, which is why I missed it." Susan put up another chart. "I compared blood samples taken from you on the same dates that Victor's had been taken. Your and

Victor's mitochondrial DNA profiles on the first date were identical, and the profiles on the second date, although dramatically different from the first date, were still identical."

"How can that be?" Ryan asked.

Susan shook her head. "It can't be. It's impossible." She gestured to the charts. "And yet it is. I was afraid that I had mixed the samples, so I recreated the experiment three times. I am certain if I took your blood today, your mitochondrial DNA profile would still be identical to Victor's, although you are both apparently undergoing random mutations."

"Is it possible that they are not random, but rather by design?" Ryan asked.

"I thought about that. I think the overall strategy, i.e. the implementation itself is by design, but the mutations are completely random. Although I haven't isolated the exact mechanism, the exact trigger for the mutation, I do know what is occurring."

Susan again stood, returning to her charts. "It is a three-pronged attack, and Victor's system is capable of withstanding one, perhaps two of the attacks, but is folding under all three." She pointed to a profile. "The DNA is mutating, and the mutations are not beneficial, which is attack number one. Under normal circumstances his system would simply repair the damage. But the rapid mutation is creating a domino affect, damaging other nearby cells and lessening their ability to create the energy to recover, which is attack number two. And the damaged cells are creating additional free radicals, which are in turn creating their own mutations, which is attack number three."

Ryan was perplexed. "I still don't understand how apparently random mutations are occurring identically within our bodies when there is no physical connection."

Susan shook her head. "I don't understand, either. I don't have anything to compare it to."

The two were silent for a long moment, then Ryan spoke.

"Maybe it has less to do with microbiology and more to do with physics," Ryan quietly mused.

Susan raised an eyebrow as Ryan continued.

"I read about a very odd phenomenon that has been observed

numerous times. Paired electrons spin in opposite directions, and when one reverses its spin, the other reverses as well. It doesn't matter how far apart the electrons are, they always seem to know what the other is doing, whether they are inches from one another, miles from one another, or clear across the universe from one another." Ryan was thoughtful. "I find it a very elegant phenomenon." She shook her head. "That still doesn't explain why I am not being affected as my father, or why it is taking longer."

Susan was apologetic. "I am so sorry, Ryan. I just don't know. And I'm still not sure what has been the trigger for the rapid mutation, whether there has been some sort of radiation damage, some external agent…". Her voice drifted off, her frustration evident.

Ryan placed her hand on Susan's shoulder, and Susan was surprised by the comforting gesture. It was also an incredible shock to her system.

"You have already done so much for my father and I. And you have given me some sort of hope."

Susan looked up at her uncertainly.

Ryan examined the charts. "This theory gives credence to your other theory about my father hibernating. If his system is as intelligent as it seems, then perhaps it did go into stasis to limit his need for energy."

Susan hadn't considered that, and nodded slowly. "Yes, limiting the body's need for energy would slow down the entire destructive process."

Ryan nodded. "Then that would mean that the condition that he is in is not a result of the damage being done…"

"But rather a response to it," Susan said, finishing the sentence. She looked to Ryan with concern. "But then that would mean that your body will begin to take that route as well, to protect itself."

Ryan's expression was resigned. "Then that means I am running out of time."

CHAPTER 16

THE HANDSOME YOUNG MAN WAITED in the shadows. The beautiful girl said she would meet him here, and he waited anxiously for her. Although he attracted many of his Kind, there seemed to be something special about her, something different from the self-absorbed crowd he was used to. He was taking a great chance, inviting her to such a secret gathering, but he desperately wanted to impress her. Introducing her to the Old Ones, or at least, what he considered to be Old Ones, would hopefully make her wish to keep his acquaintance.

He shifted from foot to foot, thinking of her. God she was beautiful, with golden hair and eyes that changed from blue to green to gray depending on her mood. He thought she might be American, although she spoke French fluently. He had no idea how old she was, but thought she might be close to his century mark. That would make them some of the youngest ones at this gathering. He frowned slightly. That would be dangerous. Still, he thought, she really wanted to come to the gathering.

His heart jumped as he saw her approach, and he rushed to take her hand.

"Bonsoir, comment ca va?"

"Ca va," she responded, "thank you for inviting me, Jean-Luc."

He smiled, clutching her gloved hand and pulling her with excitement. She laughed as they rushed off to their destination. It was a short distance away, then down a dark alley, then down a deep stairwell. They stood at the door as a small window slid open and they were inspected. Apparently they passed muster, and the door opened inward. The young man gripped her hand tightly as they were ushered in.

Ryan held the young man's hand, feeling oddly protective of the youngster she had just duped. She was carefully controlling her aura, which had been simple enough to do with this infant, but it was just about to get significantly more difficult.

She inwardly smiled. Not as hard as Muenda, though.

They were welcomed into a large foyer, and Ryan had to struggle to keep from bursting into laughter.

The room was decorated in the most melodramatic, gothic way imaginable, filled with thin, pale creatures lounging about on overstuffed couches draped with dark silk fabrics. The creatures were dressed in clothing that might have been fashionable in Victorian France, with lace cuffs and cravats in glorious abundance. Dark eye make-up seemed to be popular with both sexes, although it was difficult to tell them apart even without it. All held large, jewel-encrusted goblets that they sipped from.

Ryan carefully controlled her demeanor, although it was extremely difficult considering she could barely control her mirth. She was decidedly underdressed in her blue jeans and simple black turtleneck and jacket. She and her companion were the center of attention as they entered, with numerous predatory glances sizing up the newcomers.

Julien eyed the two Young Ones. The boy was handsome enough, but otherwise unremarkable. The girl, on the other hand, had a certain "je ne sais quoi," about her. Strikingly beautiful with a perfect, athletic form, she wore her simple clothing with more elegance than the fully-dressed fops in the room. He watched them carefully.

Jean-Luc was searching for a place for them to alight, someplace out of the center of the room and out of the center of so much attention. It was with some relief he recognized Didier, who rushed up to them.

"Jean, you know you're not supposed to bring strangers here," he whispered furiously, although everyone in the room could hear him. Didier eyed the girl. "Julien will not like this."

Julien materialized at Didier's elbow, startling him. "And since when do you speak for me, Didier?" he asked smoothly. He offered his hand to

Ryan, who tried to appear flattered as he brushed a kiss across the back of hers. There were several titters from the shadows. It appeared poor Jean-Luc would not be leaving with whom he came, and the poor girl might not be leaving at all.

Ryan quickly assessed Julien. He was likely the oldest One present, perhaps even four or five centuries. She would not really consider him an Old One, because he lacked the stunning magnetism of the truly aged, but he was definitely in the upper ranks of the middle ground. He was assessing her as well, but with decidedly more lust and less accuracy than her appraisal of him.

"Won't you and your companion join me?" he asked Jean-Luc, motioning to a small seating area off to the side.

Jean-Luc nodded, but wasn't certain he was happy with the invitation. Although it was a great honor to be noticed by someone of Julien's stature, it was also very dangerous. He held the girl's arm and they settled on a couch, sitting very close to one another.

"Would you care for a drink?"

A woman of reasonable attractiveness in a low-cut gown leaned over, a goblet in her hand. Her breasts nearly spilled out of the blouse, and Ryan and her companion had a hard time not staring at the twin globes of flesh on the verge of exposure.

The woman felt a flush of warmth from the girl's steady gaze, which was odd coming from one so young. She was oddly flattered by the attention, again, a feeling completely incongruous with the youth of this girl.

Ryan finally managed to make eye-contact. "I'm sorry," she said, feeling the heat rise in her cheeks, "what did you say?"

The woman was completely enamored with the reaction, as was Julien, who watched it closely.

"I asked if you would like a drink. It is blood from an Old One."

Ryan cautiously leaned forward, sniffing the glass. Unlikely, she thought. It wasn't anyone she knew.

She delicately took the goblet, and after a good deal of hesitation, tentatively took a sip. She immediately choked and spit the blood out on the ground, evoking laughter from those around her. They were all greatly amused, mistaking her disgust for weakness.

"It is powerful, eh?" the woman asked.

Ryan wiped her mouth, wishing the foul taste were gone. "Um, yeah, powerful," she said weakly. She handed the goblet back. "Do you have any wine?"

This evoked additional laughter, but she was brought a goblet of a mediocre French merlot, which at least rid her of the aftertaste. She leaned back, sipping the wine.

Jean-Luc, flush from the blood he had been given, tried to make conversation.

"So, Julien," he said, overly friendly, "any word of the hunter?"

Ryan was suddenly very alert, although outwardly she appeared completely relaxed on the couch.

"Rhiannon Alexander," Julien said with a degree of disgust, "she will not come here."

"Why not?" Jean-Luc asked, feeling slightly reckless.

Julien eyed the boy, finding him annoying. But his companion was growing more and more relaxed, which was a good thing.

"Because our lineage protects us. We are the offspring of Aeron, the true leader of our Kind. Why do you think she has not set foot on this continent?"

The woman took a sip from her goblet. "And what about Victor Alexander? I think he might have something to say about who is in charge." She leaned back dreamily, "I saw him once. He's very handsome."

Julien's arm shot out, slapping the woman's face so hard he drew blood. She raised her hand to her face, stunned, then stood and ran from the room. The sudden violence and appearance of blood raised the tension in the room dramatically, and several followed the woman, most likely with less than honorable intentions.

Jean-Luc stirred the liquid in his goblet with his finger, then licked it. He took another deep drink from the goblet. "It's so odd that no one has pictures of her. In this day and age that seems like it would be such a simple thing."

Didier had strategically moved to take the chastised woman's place as soon as she left, hovering about Julien. "I heard that anyone who has a picture of her has been killed, and the pictures immediately destroyed."

Julien snorted in disgust. "I weary of this talk of the 'hunter' and these 'Alexanders.' The stories we have heard of the Cleansing have been greatly exaggerated. I have heard from good sources that Rhiannon Alexander has been able to kill fewer than a hundred, and all of those were Young Ones, one step from being human."

Jean-Luc and Didier both nodded sagely at the wisdom of his words. It was likely true.

Ryan took a long drink of wine, finishing the glass. Julien watched her carefully. She seemed almost drugged. His influence was working.

Ryan stared at the wine glass in her hand, and was surprised to see two of them. It was not possible for her to get drunk, so there was definitely something else wrong. She glanced up, and the room appeared to be swimming, the figures elongating and twisting. She felt suddenly very dizzy and nauseous, and she could feel the fire rise in her veins. She struggled to bring the room back into focus, knowing that if she lost mental control her identity would quickly and emphatically become known.

Ryan cursed the virus, or whatever it was, that was in her system. Its timing was inopportune to say the least. She focused on Julien, and was relieved to see that he suspected nothing. Even in her current pained state, it amused her to realize he thought he was the cause.

Julien watched the girl carefully. He motioned for Jean-Luc to move, who did so reluctantly. Ryan felt Julien settle in beside her, and any goodwill she felt toward her companion immediately dissipated with his next comment.

"Can we at least watch?" Jean-Luc asked.

Julien nodded, his irritation obvious. He returned to his prey, and again there were titters from the shadows as all watched him seduce the Young One. He kissed her throat sloppily, and Ryan had to will herself not to move as another wave of dizziness overtook her. She could not, however, control her thoughts.

He certainly doesn't have any of his "father's" finesse, she reflected, then was angry at herself for the reflection.

The anger somewhat cleared her vision for a moment, and she saw Julien in a state of massive self-absorption, preparing to bite her neck after his miniscule attempt at foreplay. He leaned downward, lost in his passion, preparing to take what was his.

But it was not to be, for he was stopped by something that felt like a vise grip. He opened his eyes to find the girl calmly looking up at him, holding his throat between a thumb and forefinger. She gazed at him curiously, turning her head slightly as if she examining some strange insect she had found. She began to sit up, and astonishingly, Julien felt himself lifted upward. She stood to her full six-foot-plus height and he felt his feet dangling off the ground.

She brought him very close to her face, tightening her grip on his throat, causing him to claw helplessly as his eyes bugged outward. She leaned forward even more, now centimeters from his face. Her eyes were aflame but her words were calm.

"My father, Victor Alexander, will always be the leader of Our Kind," Ryan said between clenched teeth, "and in his absence," her grip tightened further, "I am King."

She flung him across the room as if he were a rag doll. Her comment brought immediate pandemonium to the room, which was amplified by the fact that she released the perceptual veil she had been hiding behind. Those in the room were horrified to realize that the hunter was in the room with them.

And more horrified to realize that Rhiannon Alexander was far more terrifying than they had imagined.

Ryan felt the heat rise in her veins, both from her fury and from the virus. Normally she could control the violence that spilled out of her, the ferocity that Kusunoki had spent decades teaching her to restrain.

But the virus seemed to add fuel to a fire that was already burning out of control, and Ryan's vision went blood red as she stared at the frozen sheep in the room.

And then, quite surprising her, it went black.

Ryan's head was pounding, and her mouth was painfully dry. A dim light shown through her closed eyelids, and she opened them slowly to see a beam of light shining through a pair of ripped curtains. She closed them again, wincing at the brightness. She sat up, leaning back on her hand as she did so.

She opened her eyes again, raising the hand to her face. It was covered in blood. She slowly focused on what was beyond the hand, and she swallowed hard.

The room was in shambles, and there was blood everywhere. There appeared to be body parts lying in some of the larger pools of blood, but they were so mangled it was difficult to tell what they used to be. There wasn't a single piece of furniture that wasn't in splinters.

Ryan slowly stood, and looked down at herself. She was covered in blood, from the top of her head to the bottom of her feet. And none of it appeared to be her own. She looked back at the room.

I did this, she thought. I killed them all, and I don't even remember it.

She slowly moved through the wreckage, wondering if anyone was left alive. There had to have been almost a hundred people in the room. She moved down a hallway where the carnage continued. She didn't even remember being here.

She staggered out into the alleyway, which was now lit brightly in daylight. The blood on her clothes was garish in the sunlight. She glanced down at a huddled form near a trash dumpster. It was the woman who had offered her the goblet. Ryan wasn't certain if the woman was still alive, but didn't think she had been the one to attack her. The figure shivered, although it wasn't cold, and turned to look up at Ryan.

Ryan gazed down at her, unblinking. Although expressionless, the woman realized Ryan was not going to kill her.

Ryan gazed at her a long moment, then spoke. "You were right," she said, still slightly unsteady. "My father is very handsome."

In a flash, Ryan was gone, moving too quickly for anyone to see the blood, or in fact, see anything at all.

Abigail picked her way delicately through the ruins, dabbing her nose with a scented handkerchief. The blood had dried, but the body parts remained, and they were beginning to smell. Preternatural senses were not always advantageous.

Aeron walked through the debris as well, glancing around him. He was followed by Kusunoki, who had come because he had to see this for himself.

"Well," Aeron said, unperturbed, "I'm impressed. I didn't think she had it in her."

Abigail glanced around at the slaughter, less disturbed by it than one would think. "She did try to eat her father," Abigail reminded him.

"Oh, that's right," Aeron said with obvious pleasure. "I forgot."

Abigail assessed the bloodbath without emotion. The actual killing did not concern her. Ryan was a predator, and had killed thousands long before she had been tasked with the cleansing. But she usually did so with cold efficiency, without passion or sentiment.

This was an act of pure, unadulterated rage.

Kusunoki agreed in his own, lyrical way. "I spent decades caging the dragon." He turned with obvious disapproval to Aeron. "And now you have released it."

Aeron did not take kindly to being scolded by some would-be samurai. He turned sharply to Kusunoki, staring down at him. "Maybe I like the dragon," he said bitingly.

Kusunoki was not the least bit intimidated. "You will not like it so much when it comes for you."

Abigail put her hand on Aeron's chest, pushing him gently but firmly away. He stepped back, but only because he had nothing more to say.

"These were your offspring," Abigail said.

Aeron shrugged, "The nearest was fourth or fifth generation, and none that I was particularly fond of." He was thoughtful. "The girl does have a knack for taking out the least desirable amongst our Kind."

Kusunoki bit down hard to keep from adding to that comment. The dragon would be visiting him for sure.

"I understand there was a survivor?" Abigail asked calmly.

"Hmm, yes," Aeron said. He motioned to someone standing in the doorway, and the woman whom Ryan had allowed to live was brought in.

Abigail stared at the woman curiously. There was nothing particularly noteworthy about her, and she wondered why Ryan had spared her. The woman was obviously terrified, and Abigail calmed her, not out of any altruistic motive but because she needed information from her.

The woman felt the calmness descend upon her, and relaxed in spite of circumstances. First she had come face-to-face with the hunter, and now she was in the presence of power she had not known existed. These Old Ones made Julien look like an immature fool.

"Perhaps you could give an account of what transpired here?" Abigail said, more than a hint of suggestion in her voice.

The woman nodded, and began relating how the young, beautiful stranger came with Jean-Luc.

"And no one recognized her?" Aeron asked in scorn and disbelief.

The woman shook her head. "She appeared to be nothing more than a Young One. Julien insulted her father right in front of her, then disparaged her."

Ah, Abigail thought, there was the spark that lit the inferno. And most likely the former rather than the latter.

"Did she say anything while she was here?" Aeron asked.

The woman again nodded. "I saw and heard from the doorway," she said, motioning to what was now a gaping hole in the wall. "Julien thought to feed from her."

Aeron's blue eyes grew icy. Good thing for Julien that he was already dead.

"She had Julien by the throat, dangling him above the ground. And she said, 'my father, Victor Alexander, will always be the leader of our Kind'." The woman's voice trailed off, and Aeron knew there was more.

"And what else did she say?" he prompted, vaguely threatening.

The woman swallowed hard. "She said, 'And in his absence, I am King.'"

Abigail glanced at Aeron out of the corner of her eye. She now knew why Ryan had spared this insignificant. She had left a message for Aeron.

And Aeron had certainly received it, although he did not react as expected. "That cheeky little whelp," he said with more amusement than anger. The girl was continually full of surprises.

Abigail motioned to the woman, who bowed low and backed quickly from their presence, disappearing. Abigail took one last look around at the carnage, then turned to both Kusunoki and Aeron.

"So how does one slay a dragon," she asked, "when the dragon cannot be slain?"

CHAPTER 17

RYAN KNELT BESIDE VICTOR'S BED. He lay in peaceful repose, unmoved from the last time she had seen him. She held his hand for a moment, then settled into a lounge next to his bed, extending the footrest outward so she had a makeshift bed. She leaned her head back into the soft cushion, gazing at his beautiful features with unblinking eyes.

She was trying to will the pain from her head to go away. She knew it would eventually subside, but it seemed to be staying longer. This forced her to visit the island more often, and to stay for longer periods of time. Fortunately she had already done ample damage in her hunt, and was no longer concerned about the Council's edict. She had obeyed Victor's wishes, and that was sufficient.

Ryan returned her gaze to her father, feeling a great heaviness descend upon her. Susan was working feverishly, but had found nothing substantial since her discoveries with the mitochondria. Ryan still did not understand why the internal damage was not affecting her the way it had affected her father.

Ryan became aware of Edward's presence in the door. He was mindful of her mood and stood respectfully at a distance. But the pain in her head was passing, and her thoughts were returning to coherency.

"Edward, I need you to do me a favor."

Edward bowed low. "Anything, my lord."

Ryan was thoughtful. "I need you to pull all the records from the hospital we purchased, the one that Dr. Ryerson used to work at."

David Goldstein sat in the dimly lit cafeteria of The Sister Guadalupe Hospital, wondering how his life could have come to this. At the height of his career, he had been a well-paid, highly-respected doctor at a major medical research facility. Now he was working graveyard shift in this dive, treating uninsured patients for whatever exotic diseases they had smuggled across the border. Although he couldn't say exactly how, he was certain that Susan Ryerson was somehow responsible for this.

He smiled bitterly. His only consolation was that, after her brief stint in the limelight, Susan Ryerson had dropped off the face of the earth. After he had been "let go" by the hospital's new management for a series of trumped up sexual harassment charges, he had tried to track her down, certain she had been the one behind the allegations. But she had been impossible to find.

He leaned back in his chair. He had been briefly flush with funds after his windfall, thanks to the blood sample he had stolen from Ryerson's laboratory. But he had gone through that money quickly. And now he was forced to make ends meet by treating the dregs of humanity in this hellhole.

"Dr. Goldstein, we have a patient coming in by ambulance."

Goldstein gave the nurse in the doorway a look of irritation. "I'll be there in a minute," he said. Probably another drunk Mexican, he thought to himself, fresh from driving his family into a tree.

Goldstein stood, tripping over the leg of his chair then kicking it in frustration. He didn't see how this night could get any worse. He was given an immediate answer when the lights flickered and then went out.

"Well, that's just fucking great," he muttered under his breath. The electrical system in the place was about as reliable as a condom made of cheesecloth. He smiled to himself. That was pretty funny. He'd have to remember to use that later in front of the ladies.

What little light in the room slowly disappeared as the door whispered closed. Goldstein's irritation grew. "That's real fucking funny," he said loudly, his words echoing in the sudden silence. The refrigeration unit to the vending machine kicked on, startling him. He turned around and gave it a kick as well, cracking the plastic logo.

"You seem to be having some difficulty with inanimate objects."

Goldstein whirled at the voice from the shadows. It was smooth with an indefinable quality to it, something both ancient and young. He heard the sharp strike of a match and an outlined form was briefly illuminated in the flame. The figure cupped the match, expertly lighting a small thin cigar.

"Who the fuck are you?" Goldstein demanded with far more bravado than he was feeling.

A striking golden-haired woman stepped into the dim glow of the vending machine. Under normal circumstances, Goldstein would have let his appreciation for such a fine specimen be immediately, and probably tastelessly, known.

But these were not normal circumstances.

"I'm surprised you don't recognize me," the woman said, blowing out a fine stream of smoke. She gazed at the glowing end of the cigar with unblinking eyes. "Of course the last time you saw me, I was dead in the emergency room."

Goldstein's eyes narrowed. He tried to get angry at the preposterous statement, but a very primitive fear in him was beginning to grow. The girl did look familiar.

"Uh, yeah, whatever. I have an ER to get to," he said. He started to push by her, but her next words stopped him cold.

"So what did you do with the research you stole from Dr. Ryerson's laboratory?"

The name inspired fury in Goldstein that overwhelmed his common sense. "That bitch, if she said—."

Goldstein could not finish the sentence because his ability to speak was compromised by the grip at his throat as he was lifted off the ground and slammed backward into the wall. Peeling plaster crumpled on his head as he flailed about like a garroted fish.

At that moment, the door whispered open, and a tiny, rotund Hispanic nurse leaned in. "Dr. Gold—"

Her voice trailed off as she took in the scene. A very tall woman dressed in black held Dr. Goldstein off the ground by the neck with one hand. The woman casually held a cigar in the other.

"Dr. Goldstein will be with you in a moment," the woman said politely.

The tiny nurse nodded, and with wide eyes backed from the room, letting the door whisper closed once more. She thought about calling security, but then thought again. Dr. Goldstein could be a punta. She crossed herself, asking forgiveness for the foul language, and headed back to the ER.

"Or maybe not," Ryan said casually, turning back to Goldstein. "That depends on what you tell me."

Goldstein's eyes bugged out of his head as he clawed for air.

"Oh that's right," Ryan said, "you probably can't tell me much of anything right now, can you?"

Goldstein tried to shake his head.

"Very well, then, blink once for yes, twice for no. Do you understand?"

Goldstein accidentally blinked twice, then blinked once trying to make up for it.

"Okay, that was three times. Are you a complete idiot?"

Goldstein blinked frantically.

Ryan took a long draw from her cigar. "Hmmm. That's debatable." She flicked some ashes from the glowing end. "Just so you know, Dr. Ryerson did not say anything to me. That was quite a lucky guess on my part. A review of the files recorded after I purchased the hospital revealed you were one of the few employees to be let go. You also happen to be the only one to deposit a large sum of money shortly thereafter."

Goldstein's eyes bugged further. This couldn't be the person who had bought the hospital.

"So what did you take?" Ryan asked, releasing her grip just enough to let him speak.

"Bl-," he tried hoarsely. "Blood. Just a vial of blood."

Ryan's eyes narrowed. This was much worse than she thought. She leaned very close to the terrified man, her grip tightening once more.

"You stole my blood."

Goldstein shook his head frantically. "No, it couldn't have been," he croaked. "That was a synthetic. It couldn't have been human."

Ryan leaned even closer, and blinked without closing her eyes.

Goldstein had a terrifying flashback to a shark documentary. He could hear the guide's conversational discussion of the shark's second eyelid, used only in the midst of a bloody feeding frenzy.

"Do I look human to you?" Ryan whispered through clenched teeth.

Goldstein blinked four times.

"I didn't think so."

Ryan abruptly released him and he fell into a crumpled heap on the floor. He tried to huddle in the corner. Ryan took a deep draw on the cigar, blowing the smoke on the cringing man.

"Who did you sell it to?" Ryan asked.

Goldstein was far beyond his fear of consequence from any human adversary. He gave up the name instantly

"Grant," he said hoarsely, "Alan Grant from Grantech International."

Ryan sat perched on the edge of the skyscraper like some great gargoyle, some forty stories above ground. The penthouse lights cast eerie shadows, throwing her into odd relief. She could see her reflection and was amused by it. The dramatic uplighting reminded her of modern monster movies.

Of course all movies were modern to her, she thought, so that didn't narrow it down much.

She sat patiently, entertaining herself with her last image of David Goldstein, stuffed into the vending machine, the neon logo flashing off and on as it sparked above his head. She knew that Susan would have enjoyed the overall composition and theme of her performance art.

Ryan's expression darkened. When Ryan told Susan of the theft of the vial of blood, Susan was greatly concerned, as well as mortified at the compromise of her research. Ryan dismissed her concerns over the theft, but shared her concern at the item seized. At least the knowledge that it was Ryan's blood allowed Susan to begin to narrow the scope of her current search.

Ryan's attention was brought back to the matter at hand when the glass door slid open and her prey stepped out onto the balcony. She eyed Alan Grant, trying to control the rage that was burning its way through her veins. She was concerned for a moment that the virus was making another appearance. She could not afford to lose control, black out, and dismember him.

At least not until she had the information she came for, she thought, her eyes narrowing. Then she could dismember him.

She leaped down lightly behind him, landing like a jungle cat. He was oblivious to her presence as he leaned over the balcony. It was apparent by his body language that he was not completely comfortable at that height, although that did not stop him from making a rude noise and spitting his effluence over the edge.

"Classic."

Alan Grant turned toward her and Ryan hit him solidly in the chest with the flat of her palm, toppling him backward over the edge. She caught him easily by one ankle, stepping up onto the edge as she did so.

"Do not scream Mr. Grant, or I will drop you."

Grant had started to scream, but it was cut off when he smacked his head on the side of the building. Ryan gave him a little shake to make certain he was paying attention as she balanced precariously on the edge.

"I am going to ask you some questions, Mr. Grant, and I want you to answer them quickly and without prevarication, because I have little time and less patience."

Grant looked down at the ground, his eyes wide with fear. It was a little-known fact that he was terrified of heights. He tried to look up at whatever was holding him so effortlessly by the ankle. When he caught sight of the stunning but demonic creature holding him, he looked back at the ground as the lesser of two evils.

Ryan shook him again, smacking his head against the building once more. "Do you understand me?"

"Yes! Yes!" the petrified man said.

"Good. Your accomplice, David Goldstein was a little slow on the uptake. But he eventually got on board with the program."

Grant frantically searched his memory banks for the name. It sounded familiar, but he couldn't place it. The demon helped him.

"David Goldstein sold you a vial of blood that he stole from the research laboratory of Dr. Susan Ryerson."

The memories locked into place. Grant knew immediately what she was talking about.

"You're with that other man, aren't you? The creepy British guy?" Grant asked, horrified. That old bastard had scared him to death with his obscure threats.

"Creepy British guy?" She was thoughtful. "I'm not certain Edward would approve of being called the 'creepy British guy.'" The demon found this terribly amusing. "No, I'm fairly certain he would not approve at all."

Ryan raised him higher so that he could somewhat see her face. She leaned closer. "And just so you know, Edward is like," she paused, searching for the appropriate phrase, "he is like a little brother to me," she finished.

Grant could not control his bowels. If that madman was like a "little brother" to this one…

Ryan wrinkled her nose. "You know, I have an excellent sense of smell. You are not giving me much incentive to hold on to you."

"Jesus, lady. Whatever you want from me, I have money," Grant said, tears streaming down, or rather up, his face, which was turning red from hanging upside down.

Ryan's mocking tone turned serious and deadly quiet. "I could buy you a thousand times over," she said. She had to close her eyes a moment to control the rage that was rising in her. She felt the virus stir, felt the blood red haze fall upon her. She opened her eyes, forcing herself to focus.

"All I want is information. I want to know who you sold the vial to."

Grant shook his head violently. "I don't know."

Ryan started to lower him, and he choked on a scream.

"I mean I really don't know!" Grant began babbling almost incoherently. "I was going to use the blood to develop drugs for Grantech. But then I was approached with an offer that I couldn't refuse."

Ryan leaned forward again. "What kind of offer?"

"A hundred million dollars," Grant said, sobbing. "A hundred million dollars for a simple vial of blood."

Ryan felt the rage rise again. She smacked his head hard.

"You sold my father for a pittance," she said through gritted teeth.

Now Grant had no idea what she was talking about, although he was quite certain she was insane. He hoped the hell her father wasn't going to show up, too.

"And who gave you the hundred million dollars?"

"I don't know," he again sobbed. "It was a brokered deal through four, maybe five intermediaries. Whoever bought it didn't want to leave a trail."

Ryan was thoughtful. "But I'm sure that you kept some kind of records, yes?"

Grant grasped at this straw desperately. "Yes, yes, of course. They are all in my computer in there. The laptop on my desk. It's encrypted, but I can give you the key codes."

Ryan glanced in the window. She could see the computer from where she stood. She looked back out over the city. She was about to reel Grant back in when she felt a wave of nausea wash over her. She swayed, causing Grant to scream, then scream again when his head smacked the building once more.

But Ryan could no longer hear him, because she was no longer standing on the edge of the skyscraper, but on the edge of the blood red netherworld she had only ever seen while Sharing. She was curious. How is it that she could be in this place now?

She stared into the blackness, warm and enticing as always. Part of her wanted to simply lean forward and fall into that welcoming abyss, letting it envelope her and fill her with nothingness.

But there was something cold in the darkness. Ryan reached out tentatively. She could sense the same presence that she had felt before. Something ancient and reptilian, something scaly and terrifying, something so enormously powerful it dwarfed anything she had ever felt before. It seemed closer now, its razor-sharp claws snaking out of the darkness as the alien words came whispering toward her.

"I'm...Coming—"

The sibilant words again sliced through her, shredding through flesh and bone like a thousand needles with a single trajectory.

"I'm...Coming...for...You!"

Ryan staggered from the mental assault, and could not maintain her balance, falling backward into the endless pool of blood.

But she did not go far, merely falling onto the balcony of Alan Grant's penthouse. She held her head, deeply confused for a moment, trying to focus and make sense of the suddenly very normal world around her.

She stood, blinking in the darkness, still unsteady. She realized the virus must have taken hold of her system once more. Odd, she thought, looking around. She didn't see Alan Grant anywhere.

Ryan peered over the side, somewhat relieved that she did not see his mangled body forty stories below. She shrugged. It wasn't that she would have minded killing him. She would just like to be there for the experience.

She couldn't bother herself with such minor details at this stage of the game. She opened the sliding glass door and lifted the laptop, tucking it under her arm. She took the elevator down to the street below, and disappeared into the night.

The homicide detectives trying to piece together the murder of Alan Grant spent weeks trying to reconstruct the events preceding his death. It just didn't make sense. First off, they couldn't even identify the exact scene of the crime, although his body had been shoved through a plate glass window and remained there until found by a cleaning lady. The problem was, the plate glass window was thirty stories above ground, and Grant had been shoved from the outside in.

As if that weren't odd enough, the glass window was eight city blocks from his penthouse, and no one could see any connection between his domicile and his eventual resting place. Various scenarios were put forth, including the most likely, in which he was thrown from a hovering helicopter. Even that seemed far-fetched, however, as no one had reported seeing or hearing any helicopter in the area, and the force and trajectory weren't quite right for a hovering aircraft.

Having run out of ideas and prepared to close the case, the lead detective joked that the only true scenario that fit all the facts was that he had been fired out of a cannon from his penthouse balcony, or that someone had picked him up by his ankles and thrown him clear across the city.

CHAPTER 18

RYAN PUSHED THROUGH THE DOORS of the city library, sensing the presence of Young Ones. Because of her preoccupation with tracking down David Goldstein and Alan Grant, she had not been as vigilant in her 'cleansing' this past month. It would be a simple enough matter to add quickly to her numbers.

Ryan frowned at the thought of Grant. She had read the accounts in the newspaper and realized that she had killed him in another one of her black-outs. Fortunately Edward was already fast at work following the money trail from the data on the pilfered computer. In his last communiqué with her, Edward relayed he was getting close.

Ryan's expression grew more grim. It wasn't as if she couldn't guess who was behind it. She just needed to know the degree of participation from the Others, and needed the proof prior to the next Council Meeting.

Ryan entered the elevator, extending her senses upward. She looked at the available buttons and smiled. She pressed one that was unmarked, and the elevator lurched upward.

The doors opened and she stepped out onto the floor of what looked like a normal library. The only difference was that those milling about were all her Kind. They looked up, surprised when they did not recognize her.

Ryan quickly masked her presence, curious about the Young Ones. They sat about, engaged in serious conversation or studying. Others sat before computer terminals, turning slightly at her arrival.

An attractive girl in glasses approached her. She reminded Ryan somewhat of Susan Ryerson.

"Hi," the girl said uncertainly, "Um, welcome to our library."

"Thank you," Ryan said politely. She took in the room with a single glance. "Do you mind if I look around?"

"No, of course not," the girl said quickly. "I will introduce you. My name is Courtney."

"Courtney," Ryan said, trying the name out as if it were something new. "My name is Ryan."

The girl smiled. "Ryan, excellent." She grabbed Ryan's sleeve and began leading her reluctant guest around the room. "This is Troy."

Ryan nodded to a young black man seated in front of a computer screen. He waved awkwardly.

"This is Michelle." Courtney pointed to a dark-haired girl peering shyly over a textbook.

Ryan continued nodding as Courtney whirled her around the room, introducing her with great enthusiasm. She was greeted with degrees of curiosity and timidity. Ryan was greatly amused by this gathering, never quite having seen anything like it.

"So," Courtney asked, "what do you think?"

Ryan had no idea what she was talking about. "Um, very nice," she said.

"Yeah, it seemed that there was just such a need among our Kind."

Ryan glanced over at her, hoping she would continue so she would have some idea of how to respond.

"If we're going to be immortal, it seems that there should be some attempt to stay abreast of knowledge. To be a kind of repository of science for our people."

"Ah," Ryan said with dawning understanding. "There is a word for you." She glanced around the room. "It is a modern word, and I am not completely familiar with it."

"Geeks?" Troy offered helpfully.

Ryan shook her head. "No, no, it is something similar to that. But that is not exactly it."

"Nerds?" Michelle proffered.

"Yes," Ryan said, pointing to her. "That is it. You are," she paused, carefully trying out the unfamiliar word, "nerds." She raised an eyebrow, commenting under her breath, "Marilyn would be so surprised."

"Who is Marilyn?" Courtney asked, puzzled.

Ryan shook her head. "Never mind. If you are to be the repository of knowledge for our Kind, don't you think you should have someone older in your group?"

"Well," Courtney said, wrinkling her brow, "how old are you?"

Ryan cleared her throat, but before she could respond, the elevator doors opened. Courtney squealed in delight.

"Oh great, Raphael is here."

A devilishly handsome black man stepped from the elevator. His close-cropped hair accentuated his fine features, and his teeth shown brilliantly when he flashed a smile to the group.

"Hi all," he said. He slowed when he saw Ryan.

Ryan quickly took his measure. Two hundred years, no more, but he was obviously the oldest member of the group. He maintained his friendly demeanor, but was cautious. That did not stop him from extending his hand to her in greeting.

"Hi. My name is Raphael."

Ryan took his hand, and time stopped for Raphael.

"You are the hunter," he said quietly, both fear and resignation in his voice.

Ryan sensed the fear was for his companions, the resignation for himself.

"Yes," she said simply. "I am." She released his hand and turned from him, suddenly tired. "But I am not hunting today."

Raphael was not certain he understood. "Why not?"

Ryan turned back to him, amused. "Are you asking me why I won't kill you?"

Raphael's words tumbled out. "No, of course not. I mean, forgive me, my lord." He started to bow on one knee, as did the others in the room.

Ryan waved her hand in exasperation. "Please stop that. It gets very old after awhile."

Raphael stood uncertainly. "So why is it that you are here?"

Ryan sprawled into one of the overstuffed library chairs. "I was just making my rounds."

The others in the room were stunned into immobility, because as Ryan sat down, she no longer hid her presence from them. They could feel and see the full force of her magnetism. It inspired both fear and longing in them, creating desires that were previously unknown.

Ryan, of course, was oblivious to this. She pinched the bridge of her nose, then rubbed her temple.

"Is there-" Raphael approached hesitantly. "Is there something I can get for you?"

"Mmm, no," Ryan said, "thank you. I should probably be on my way before too long." She gave him a sidelong glance, "I do have a job to do right now."

The others who had been surreptitiously listening all found something with which to occupy themselves. They were all suddenly very industrious.

Raphael glanced around, then back at Ryan, grinning. Ryan assessed him once more. He was very charming and charismatic, courageous without being too bold.

"How old are you Raphael?"

Raphael seemed a little embarrassed. "I was born almost 200 years ago. I was Changed when I was twenty-eight."

Ryan quite openly examined him, continuing her mild interrogation. "Are you capable of initiating the Change?"

Raphael gave the appearance of blushing, quite a feat considering the darkness of his skin. "I, I think so," he said nervously. "I'm not sure."

Ryan raised an eyebrow. "You've never tried?"

"I mean I Share and all that," he said uncomfortably, "I just never—."

He stopped, then looked Ryan square in the eye, getting to the point. "It's a lot of responsibility," he said. "Or at least it should be. I don't want to do it with just anyone."

"Hmmm," Ryan said, "as I said before, Marilyn would be so shocked."

Raphael at least knew who Marilyn was. "You have met the mother of our line?"

Ryan nodded. "Oh yes, I have known her for many centuries."

Raphael's eyes gleamed at the thought. "I would like to meet her some day."

"Be careful what you wish for," Ryan said, more to herself than Raphael.

Ryan abruptly stood, and the room again went silent. Ryan extended her hand to Raphael, who took it, bowing deeply.

"I live to serve you, my lord."

Ryan nodded. "I will see you again, Raphael. Probably sooner than you know.

Raphael again bowed, but Ryan was gone, using neither the elevator nor the stairs, but simply disappearing.

CHAPTER 19

RYAN HAD BUT A FEW DAYS before the next Council meeting. The virus was stirring more frequently in her system, and she had a desire to see her father before she met with the Others again. Edward was not present at the island when she arrived, but Susan relayed that he had left to handle a few business affairs in Europe prior to their rendezvous at the meeting. Ryan's return was fortuitous in timing because within hours of her arrival, Susan had substantial news.

"I think I know what is causing the uncontrolled mutation."

Ryan was cautious but hopeful. "That is excellent news. What word?"

Susan dumped a load of charts onto the table in front of Ryan, but for once did not use them.

"I think someone examining the 'I' compound in your genetic make-up discovered it could be used as a mutagen because of its unique pairing capabilities. The discovery was probably completely accidental, because that is how I stumbled across it."

Ryan was trying to sort through what she was saying. "The 'I' compound was the unknown base in our genetic profile, the one that does not exist in human beings."

Susan nodded excitedly. "Or in any of the Others, at least those I have examined. But it did have the ability to pair with any of the other bases in the nucleic acid. Someone genetically altered strands containing this particular base and somehow re-introduced it to you and Victor. The mutated structure continued to divide within cells unchecked, much like cancer."

"So someone basically turned our own anatomy against us."

Susan nodded. "And did so in a way that would affect only you and Victor, based upon your unique genetic profile."

"So," Ryan said thoughtfully, "I am back to the original question of why it is not affecting me as it is my father."

Susan shook her head. "I'm not certain. It might be because Victor was infected first, or it might be because the pathogen was created from your blood, giving you more natural immunity."

Ryan thought through the implications. "The most obvious method of transmission would be through the act of Sharing. Prior to my father falling ill, I had Shared with only him and Marilyn. My father also Shared with Marilyn, and perhaps Abigail as well."

"Do you think Marilyn was the carrier?"

"If she was, then she was unaware of it, of that I'm certain." Ryan's expression darkened. "Although I know for a fact that she Shared with Aeron. It is possible that he infected her, either directly or by passing it through himself."

"I'm not certain I would try this on myself, even if I knew genetically it would not affect me."

Ryan's expression was still dark. "But he would have no qualms experimenting on Marilyn."

As Ryan was speaking, she was reliving Marilyn's Memories, sorting through them rapidly, looking for any clue. The images flew at her with great speed until abruptly, they stopped. Ryan was looking down at herself, seated on the chair before the Grand Council. Her hands were crossed in her lap, and her head was down. Slowly, through Marilyn's eyes, she turned to the left, catching a significant glance pass between Abigail and Aeron. She had missed it in the Council room because her head was down and her thoughts were of her father. But Marilyn had not.

Ryan snapped back to the present, her face white. Susan looked to her with concern.

"Are you alright?"

The color returned to her face with full force, so great was her anger. But her words were tightly controlled as she changed the subject.

"So what do you think will happen to me?"

Susan's expression was bleak. "I'm afraid that you will eventually shut down like your father. And although I do not think he will pass, I think he will stay in a period of equilibrium, as he is now. Although…".

Ryan turned to look at Susan, and Susan hesitantly continued.

"There is one notable difference between you and Victor genetically, which is the additional X chromosome. Obviously, males normally have one X chromosome and one Y chromosome, and females have two X chromosomes."

Susan could not disguise the marvel in her voice. "Victor has two Y's and two X's, and you have four X's."

"And why would that be significant?"

"I'm not certain. Normally in a human female, one of the X chromosomes is inactivated, but I have no idea which of yours might be expressing itself. Only one might be working, or it might be all four. If a human female's spare X chromosome is incompletely inactivated, it causes significant defects. However, an extra gene here or there for you seems to have no negative effect." She returned to her generalized discussion. "Human males are sometime at a disadvantage when a defect is carried on one gene in the X chromosome. Women have a spare that can be activated. That's why many diseases are considered 'sex-linked' and occur only within males."

"I'm still not certain why that might be significant."

"Well, a lot of what the X chromosome does is actually autosomal, meaning it doesn't have anything to do with sex. Many of the genes are directly related to adaptive immunity. If you have two or three extras lying around, your body might be waging an all out war against the mutagen."

Susan sighed. "And again, I'm merely speculating. This sounds less like science and more like science fiction. If I had an entire population to study, I could perhaps make some headway. But I have only you and your father."

Ryan sighed, knowing the time was at hand.

"And we are both ill."

CHAPTER 20

RYAN SAT IN HER FATHER'S underground chambers, awaiting the Grand Council meeting. The fever in her blood was high right now, leaving her exhausted as her immune system did fierce battle with the invader. She swam in and out of consciousness, at times almost enjoying the feeling. It reminded her of the lassitude of being fully bled. It would be a short time before her system overcame the pathogen, she could feel the microscopic forces assembling. But the battles were getting longer, and more frequent. It seemed almost as if the strain were ever-mutating, nearly as fast as her body could compensate.

What a brilliant plan, Ryan thought, appreciating any strategy so cleverly and brutally executed. To use her own unique anatomy against both her and her father was a stroke of genius, although, she thought with quiet fury, it would not save the one responsible.

The haze began to pass, and Ryan felt her strength returning. She stood and stretched, leaning her head to the side to crack her neck. She felt the heat in her body begin to dissipate, felt her skin begin to cool. It was a welcome relief, although she knew it would not last.

Edward was supposed to meet her, but apparently he had been delayed. He had not been in contact, but that did not concern Ryan as they often went for weeks in silence. She tilted her head to one side. The Grand Council was already assembling—she was late.

Eleven of the twelve witnesses were seated. Edward was not yet present, nor was his normally punctual liege. The five Old Ones were seated, nearly every expression completely impassive as all guarded their thoughts.

All except Aeron, who almost appeared to be enjoying himself, demonstrating an amazing and uncharacteristic amount of patience. For once, he didn't seem to mind waiting

The double doors were flung inward and Ryan strode in. Although not required by protocol, all eleven witnesses stood upon her entrance. When Ryan reached the center of their semi-circle, she turned to them.

"You are dismissed," she said abruptly, expecting no argument.

Nor did she receive any. Other than a few confused glances toward the Grand Council members, the witnesses reacted to her absolute authority with what she demanded: absolute obedience. They quickly filed out.

Ryan turned to the Council, calm and composed.

But Kusunoki saw the raging inferno in his pupil, the barely restrained fury tightly contained within the icy exterior. He saw it, and his concern for his pupil grew exponentially. He had to admit, though, as he felt an unfamiliar emotion that he could only identify as fear, perhaps not all of his concern was for the girl standing in front of him.

The dragon was here.

Ala saw it as well, saw the power and destruction flowing through the girl like the volcanic river of Nyiragongo. As Kusunoki, she was mesmerized and startled by the transformation in Victor's protégé. It was as if some prehistoric creature from the deepest, darkest part of the jungle stood before her.

Marilyn also noted the inferno within the girl, and was, against her better judgment, instantly aroused. She thought for once, however, she would express a degree of restraint. Better to not tempt fate, or perhaps in this case, the devil himself.

Ryan turned her hypnotic gaze on the raven-haired woman, reading her mind.

As if you had a choice, she said silently.

Marilyn smiled. The dragon had not come for her.

Ryan turned her gaze to Kusunoki, then to Ala.

You must not interfere, she said to them. What is in motion cannot be stopped.

Ryan then turned to Abigail, who gazed at her dispassionately with the unblinking stare of their Kind.

Ryan again spoke silently, with resignation but strangely without bitterness.

And I know that you will not.

Abigail slowly smiled, her eyes gleaming, confirming the betrayal Ryan had suspected.

Ryan looked down, but her attention was drawn to a set of perfect fingernails drumming lightly on the table in front of her. She finally turned her attention to the head of Grand Council, and was greeted by a pair of ice-blue eyes filled with a terrible amusement.

"So, my dear. How is your father?"

The voice was smooth, melodic, filled with a sensual malevolence that wrapped itself around Ryan as she stood there. If the other members of the Council thought she would explode in anger at the comment, they were again surprised.

"He's a bit under the weather these days," Ryan said, amused by her own comment. There was a dark sensuality underlying her own words. "There seems to be something going around."

Aeron merely smiled, still drumming his fingers. "If he is incapacitated, then as head of the Grand Council, I have no choice but to assume control of the hierarchy."

Both Ala and Kusunoki turned sharply to Aeron, both surprised and not. Marilyn also glanced at Aeron, then back at the girl. Only Abigail kept her eyes on Ryan, an enigmatic smile on her lips.

Ryan examined her fingernails, as if his statement were of no matter. She raised her eyes to him, her tone still casual, her words anything but. "Then I have no choice but to challenge you for that position."

Aeron smiled his shark's smile, pleased that all of the pieces were finally settling into place in this very protracted battle.

Ryan's tone was still casual, but the flames flickered in her eyes. "I personally care nothing for the position," she said with studied indifference. "I would just hate to disappoint my father."

This comment did not please Aeron, so he ignored it. "And will you choose a second?"

Ryan shook her head. "I do not need one."

Aeron smiled at the confidence. "Very well. Because you have made the challenge, it is my right to choose the venue."

Ryan nodded. "I know where to meet you."

Ryan made her way through the forest. It was remarkably unchanged in 400 years, still a dark and twisted place, remote from all life and living. It was hard to believe that such a place still existed in the 21st century, for it was as if she had stepped into the woods and stepped back in time.

And Ryan knew that was exactly Aeron's intent. Their battle was as psychological as it was physical. He wanted to remind her of a time when she had failed, a time when she had easily been defeated, a time when he probably would have slain her had Victor not appeared and rescued her.

Victor would not appear this time. Aeron had made certain of that. Ryan pushed thoughts of her father from her head. She could not carry him with her now.

Ryan felt the virus stir in her system, and cursed its timing. She did not wish to lie in the forest while it sent its fire through her veins. She was relieved to feel it settle, knowing it would not return for awhile. She pressed ahead.

It could have been days, but it did not seem long before she entered the clearing she had crossed so many years ago. She was not surprised to see the castle had been rebuilt, and appeared exactly as it had to the young boy's eyes centuries before.

She closed her eyes. What would have happened had she turned, so many years ago, and went back into the forest?

Aeron's thoughts came whispering out at her, confirming what she already knew.

It would not have mattered. I would have come after you.

She could sense Aeron waiting for her, as he had so many centuries before, drawing her in with his dark magnetism. He was waiting for her in the room where he had seduced her, when she had come upon him feasting on the remains of one of their Kind.

Ryan opened her eyes and stepped into the clearing, crossed the wooden bridge, then passed beneath the gate into the courtyard of the castle. The same torches flickered, welcoming her, and bringing unwelcome Memories of when she was here before.

She entered the castle, feeling strangely naked without a sword at her side even though she had given up wearing one centuries before. She fought the strength of her own Memories, wondering if Aeron knew how effective his strategy was.

She could feel him ahead of her in the darkness. He knew.

She entered the hallway leading to the great room, glancing to the alcove, knowing what she would find there. The chess board was set up, the same twisted, maniacal pieces in repose. Ryan noted that the bishop she had left for sacrifice had been replaced by the ivory queen. She glanced at the conquered piece for a moment, sitting quietly with the other pieces that had been removed from the board. With only a moment's thought, she moved the rook from her previous move another four spaces in another direction. She looked up.

"A most interesting strategy," Aeron said. "I would almost think you were throwing the game."

Ryan smiled. "I think you know me better than that."

"Not as well as I would like," he said, standing very near. "And not as well as I soon will."

Ryan put her hand on his chest, pushing him lightly away. The shock of the contact affected both, although perhaps Ryan more. She brushed past him into the great room.

It was much the same, although without a bloodied, dismembered corpse laying on the table. Aeron still preferred candlelight to electricity, and the room was so lit, with shadows flickering up the walls. There were a few modern touches, a newspaper, a few books, but the room was largely unchanged, perfectly recreated from four centuries earlier.

"I thought you would enjoy the familiar touch," Aeron said, reading her thoughts.

"Yes," Ryan said with a lightness she did not feel, "I appreciate your attention to detail."

Aeron smiled his shark's smile, his blue eyes examining her lithe form. "You could," he suggested mildly, "simply give up and spare yourself a defeat."

Ryan smiled at his arrogance. "And then what?"

Aeron's eyes gleamed. "You could become my Second."

"Hmm," Ryan said, "a most attractive offer," she said, indicating it was anything but. "But I think not."

Aeron shrugged. "I expected as much," he said without disappointment, "which is why I went to the trouble of having these made."

Ryan was curious in spite of herself. She moved to the case he held open before her. Two swords, both with a strange, gray-blue cast, lie on the bed of crushed velvet. She took one, wondering if she could decapitate him before he dropped the case. Instead she turned and swung the sword experimentally. It was heavy, but well-balanced. Its heft might favor Aeron, but its weight was not such that it would affect Ryan's speed.

"Tantalum carbide graphite," Aeron said, taking his own sword. "A composite material provided by the good scientists at Los Alamos Laboratory in New Mexico." As she looked askance at him, he elaborated.

"You are not the only one who poaches upon the US Department of Defense."

Ryan swung the sword again. "Yes, they do continually come up with new and innovative ways to destroy themselves." She swung the sword in an arc, then slashed downward. It split the huge oak table in two with ease.

"One of the hardest materials known to mankind," Aeron said, grinning wickedly. "I didn't want our little game to end too soon."

Ryan gazed at the deadly sharp edge of the blade. "Then let us not delay its commencement."

Aeron smiled with obvious pleasure, then struck with lightning speed, delivering a blow that should have sliced the girl in two.

But it did not, because Ryan was no longer standing there. She was already moving with her own preternatural speed, delivering a devastating, slashing counter.

Aeron brought his sword up, blocking what should have been a mortal blow. Ryan quickly disengaged, stepping rearward, analyzing her opponent.

She had fought endless battles, and her greatest opponent had been her own father. But she had a mental link with Victor that allowed her to anticipate almost every move. Victor was the stronger, but Ryan's skill had been equal, and her speed perhaps greater. It had created a balance between them that had resulted in battles of unmatched ferocity, with neither truly ever able to claim victory.

Ryan was far less certain of this outcome. She had never battled Aeron before, at least not with a sword. She knew that there was a streak of violent brutality in him that was unpredictable and dangerous. She found herself wishing for the deadly, quick beauty of the Katana.

But she had been born to the English broadsword, which quickly became evident when she launched a brilliant attack that Aeron barely deflected, backing six steps to do so.

He smiled, pleased, hefting the weight of his sword. "So, little one, you truly are the swordsman I have heard so much about."

Ryan felt his influence cloud her mind, felt the mocking endearment pull her into a world that existed centuries before. She shook her head, clearing the images from her mind.

"I think that killing has become so impersonal," Ryan said conversationally, shifting her footwork for his imminent attack, "I have always felt a sword delivered a much more intimate message."

Aeron smiled, then again struck like lightning. It was Ryan's turn to give ground, her sword flashing to meet the slashing arc of metal. When she had relinquished as much ground as she would, she locked swords with him, bringing him to an abrupt halt within inches of her face.

The two swords hovered between them, and Aeron took the opportunity to let his gaze linger on her lips. "So are intimacy and violence always so interrelated with you?"

Ryan stared back, amused. "That is your quality, not mine."

Aeron returned the smile, his teeth flashing in the shadows. "Don't be so sure, little one. You have quite a reputation yourself."

Ryan stepped sideways and disengaged, using Aeron's power against him as he was forced to step forward to maintain his balance. He still effortlessly blocked her next arcing attack, and she again danced out of the way of his slicing counter.

The two circled one another, mentally and physically testing the other. Neither appeared fatigued in any way, and it seemed that this contest could go on indefinitely.

Aeron struck again, delivering a devastating series of blows that Ryan countered with a dazzling defense. At the end of the series, Aeron sought to engage Ryan's sword, but she slipped away, dancing a few feet beyond the reach of his sword. She grabbed a tapestry, flinging it upon his weapon, but he sliced through it without effort, slashing back at her with immense force. She again was just beyond the flashing blade, but this time she tumbled backward onto a couch as it caught her at the back of the knees.

Aeron's sword was there and Ryan parried three times before the swords locked, and they were again face-to-face, this time with Ryan in a more vulnerable position on the settee.

"So do you remember this place, little one?" Aeron whispered through clenched teeth. "I believe you were sitting right there when you gave your life's blood to me."

This comment angered Ryan. "I did not give you anything," she said, her own teeth clenched. "You may have taken it by force, but I offered you nothing."

"Hmm," Aeron said, examining her golden eyelashes and the high color tracing the line of her cheekbones. "Surely you realize by now that those subtleties are meaningless amongst our Kind."

This comment infuriated Ryan and she found the strength to push him back, striking at him once more. He easily parried, amused by her fury. It did make her noticeably stronger, he noted. An interesting phenomenon.

Ryan stood, her sword extended to him in challenge. She was up to his psychological manipulation, and could return it in kind. "You offered me your blood," she reminded him, "you could simply allow my weapon to find its mark."

The tip of her sword hovered near the veins in his throat. Aeron was amused and aroused, but undeceived. "An interesting proposal. I somehow think the bloodletting would not be what I had in mind."

He smashed her sword away, again going on the attack, and Ryan yet again danced out of his reach, seeking an opening. She shifted her footwork, preparing to launch another flurry of blows, when a strange look passed over her features. The virus in her system stirred and a wave of dizziness overtook her.

Aeron smiled.

In an instant he lunged forward. Ryan brought her sword up with blinding speed, parrying the blow, as well as the multitude that followed it. She stepped backward with impossible grace, countering each slashing attack as she was pushed rearward.

But the outcome of the series was inevitable, and had not been in question from the very first strike. For in that momentary weakness, Aeron had gained a fraction of a second, and that was all he needed. In each subsequent paired move, the consequence of that lost instant was mirrored and magnified until culminating in the very last blow in which he drove his sword through her midsection.

Ryan stared into his ice-blue eyes which were filled with a malevolent amusement. She glanced down at the sword which was buried up to its hilt just beneath her ribs, impaling her in exactly the spot that had never healed, pinning her to the wall behind her. He had trapped the wrist of her sword hand against the wall with his free hand.

Aeron let his eyes drift downward to the blood that began to stream from the wound. He very slowly, excruciatingly, twisted the blade, inflicting even greater damage to the wounded area, increasing the blood flow.

Ryan closed her eyes, and when she opened them, she was again staring into ice blue eyes. She gathered her strength.

"That," she said evenly, "was cheating."

Aeron could no longer control himself. His desire for this one was all-consuming. He sliced into her neck with his perfect teeth, drawing her blood into his body even as it flowed downward from the wound he had inflicted.

The intensity of contact was agonizing, and Ryan's vision went white, then black. It was a torturous combination of pleasure and pain. The bond with Aeron was immediate and unbearably intense.

Aeron's heart staggered at the powerful onslaught, but even so it seemed he could not get enough of this girl, could not get close enough to her. He could take every fiery drop of her blood and he would still desire her in ways he could not fathom.

It took every ounce of his willpower to pull away. She looked at him, the deepening languor from his feeding and her injuries evident in her eyes. But even then, remarkably that spark of ever-present amusement was evident in their blue-green depths. He grasped the hilt of the sword and yanked it from her torso, causing her to fall forward onto him, grasping him for support. He lifted her into his arms, surprised at how light she was, and placed his lips on the wound from the sword.

He carried her to the sofa, the place he had seduced her so many centuries before, and was instantly upon her again. His teeth returned to the artery in her neck, taking the blood that flowed with such force. He was astonished at how powerful she had become in the few centuries that had passed, realizing that this 'boy' had become a magnificent creature.

She no longer fought him, relaxing against her will, and he held her less harshly, although no less tightly. Her hand actually curled onto his, and in her dazed state, she clutched his hand like a child. He gazed at the hand, feeling the oddest mixture of emotions.

He wanted to maim her, he wanted to consume her, he wanted to utterly destroy her.

He also wanted to own her, to protect her, to utterly possess her. And more than anything, he wanted her to want him.

He leaned away, and with his perfect fingernails gashed his own neck. The blood began to flow down his collarbone, then down his chest, seeping into his white shirt. The girl opened her eyes as he watched her intently.

Ryan took one look at the blood and moaned in anguish, turning away. She could not do this. She could not take this man's blood, knowing that if she did a part of her would be lost forever.

Aeron's eyes gleamed. The girl did want him. As desperately as he wanted her. He took her chin in his hand, forcing her to look at him.

"What's the matter, little one?" he whispered.

Ryan shook her head, trying to get him out of her mind. There was no hope for her if she allowed him into her body.

"Are you afraid of what you might find?"

Ryan felt utter hopelessness. She could not fight the desire that raged through her, did not even want to.

"I know what I will find," she said, inevitability in her tone.

She leaned upward and placed her lips on the stream of blood, following it to the open vein. Aeron shifted, helping her into position, and gasped when her lips touched his skin.

The pleasure was agonizing, her feeding a torment and dark gift. She drew the blood from his bursting veins, pulling it into her body with a hunger that matched his own. He could feel her heart drive his as the two organs fought for dominance and control.

As lost as he was to her in that moment, he was not going to allow her any advantage. As she fed from his neck, he turned her wrist and sliced into it, completing the union. The blood flowed from one to another, and then back again, finding its own dark rhythm and pulse.

And the mental bond was extraordinary. Aeron could see her entire life, laid before him in a manner that went far beyond mere intimacy. And she could see his, every nuance, every detail. There was no way to hide, no manner in which they could conceal themselves from the other. It was too much to process, a dizzying array of centuries flashing across the mental landscape in seconds.

Ryan was suddenly in the blood-red netherworld, as was Aeron. They stood face-to-face, Aeron holding her tightly in his arms lest she try to escape.

But she did not try to escape. Aeron looked down at her, then at the beckoning blackness beyond the edge.

"So what now?" Ryan asked, glancing at the blackness as if mildly entertained. "Do you intend to fling me off into the darkness?"

She seemed amused at this prospect, and he gazed down at her, remembering the intoxicating invitation she had given him centuries before, balancing playfully on the edge of death.

"Perhaps," he said, his eyes narrowing. It was such a tempting possibility, and would bring such immediate and immense physical gratification.

Ryan merely smiled. "Or perhaps you'd like to go there with me?"

Aeron's jaw clenched. She had no idea the power of her invitation. He looked into her eyes seeing the ever-present preternatural amusement.

Or perhaps she did.

She gazed into the darkness with a remarkable lack of concern, then up at the deepening red of the sky. "My wounds are great, you might actually be successful at tossing me into the great night."

She shrugged, as if it were of no consequence. "Perhaps not."

Aeron's struggle was great. She was taunting him with his greatest desire, appealing to the deepest, most predatory aspect within him. She was daring him to consummate their union as he had so many others over the centuries, to take her to the very brink of death and then fling her into its depths.

Ryan stared up at him curiously. She thought for certain he would have attempted to kill her by now. As always, in this world, that thought caused her no concern. And it wasn't even the certainty of outcome, whether she would live or she would die, that gave her such nonchalance.

It was simply that the edge of death was her playground.

She gazed off into the blackness, but then became aware of his intense scrutiny. She looked up at him, puzzled as to why he would merely stand there, staring at her. His blue eyes burned with a strange intensity, a look that Ryan had not seen before and did not understand. She looked at him, the question in her eyes.

And then he did the one thing that she least expected him to do, the one thing that she was completely unprepared for, the one thing for which she truly had no defense.

He kissed her.

It was passionate, brutal, filled with possession and longing. It was deep and prolonged, stunning on every level.

Aeron awoke with a start from the trance, lying atop the girl on the sofa. She was pale, obviously a result of her wounds and his feeding, as well as the virus that raged through her system. His blood was still on her lips. He knew that she had not withdrawn from him, but rather had ultimately succumbed to the combination of her injuries and her illness.

He gazed down at her, astonished that she could satisfy him even in her weakened condition, for he was truly sated. What astonished him even more was that he could feel a new hunger stirring even now; his desire undiminished by the physical gratification. The girl was like a drug to him, one that increased its potency upon every use.

She stirred, her golden eyelashes fluttering against her cheekbone, the heat rising from her cheeks. But she did not awaken, and he knew that she would not for some time.

He sat upright, his eyes narrowing, but unwilling to break physical contact with her. This had been a most unexpected outcome.

CHAPTER 21

RYAN SLOWLY OPENED HER EYES. For a moment she reveled in the sensation of her coverlet, the feeling of the silk against her skin. She closed her eyes again, breathing deeply the familiar smells. The air was fresh, scented of the deep ocean, with that peculiar, wonderful odor of ionization that surrounded waterfalls. She enjoyed the musicality of the water as it flowed downward to the ocean another thousand feet.

Ryan opened her eyes, her thoughts coalescing with frightening speed.

She sat up, her eyes seeking the open doors to the balcony and the figure that sat beyond.

Aeron was there, casually reading the newspaper while seated at the table. He was dressed in a billowing white shirt, open at the collar, and comfortable tan pants that were close-fitting but not tight. He was barefoot, his long legs crossed at the ankle, appearing for all the world like the lord of the manor relaxing at breakfast.

Ryan was furious. She threw the sheets back and left the bed, removing her bedclothes as she did so. She stalked to her closet and quickly pulled on a loose shirt and a pair of jeans, not bothering with shoes.

Aeron, sensing her presence behind him, looked up from his newspaper expectantly.

"Hello my dear, I trust you slept well."

Ryan moved in front of him, and he took the opportunity to admire her form.

"Where is my father?" she asked, a dangerous edge to her voice.

Aeron continued his perusal, then allowed his eyes to drift back to hers. "He's right where you left him, my dear." He continued his inventory, his arrogance pronounced. His eyes drifted to her throat, caressing the light bruise still evident on her neck. "As is Dr. Ryerson and her young son."

Ryan's jaw tightened further, and Aeron looked down at his paper once more, as if it were no matter. "Your staff, on the other hand, have all been replaced."

Ryan was livid. Without another word, she turned and was out the door.

Aeron sighed, folding his paper and getting to his feet. The girl had almost as bad a temper as he did.

Susan peered into a microscope. She was having a difficult time concentrating, and had been for quite some time. Without lifting her eyes, she looked to the guards at the door who watched her with unblinking eyes. They were frightening, with an insolence that was insulting. They also kept looking at her as if they wanted to eat her. Or worse.

Susan glanced over at Jason, who occupied himself by nervously playing with some test tubes. He, too, glanced over at the menacing figures by the door. He didn't want to be away from his mother right now, so he had to endure their presence.

Susan looked through the microscope, but was startled into nearly screaming as the laboratory door slammed open. She reached for Jason, but her fear moderated when she saw Ryan come through the door. It did not entirely diminish, however, because Ryan herself was in terrifying form.

Ryan took two steps and accosted the first guard.

"Get out," she said between clenched teeth.

Either the man was unable to process who was standing in front of him, or he was just genuinely slow. Ryan had patience for neither. She picked the man up by his belt and by his throat and threw him headfirst through the door, which, unfortunately for him, had just closed behind her.

Aeron was nearing the doorway when the man's head splintered through the door, followed by his entire body. He marveled at the force involved, which had been so perfectly concentrated it had not torn the door from the hinges, but rather exploded a hole right through it. He stepped over the prone figure and pushed through the material of the door that remained attached, just in time to see Ryan preparing a second missile.

He grabbed her roughly, trapping her wrists and pulling her away from the second guard. He thought he could restrain her for only a moment.

"Get out, you idiot," he snarled at the guard. The terrified man responded instantly, staggering toward the door and disappearing into the hallway.

"Ryan," Aeron said, struggling with the girl. "Stop it!"

He locked her into an embrace, picking her forcibly up off the ground. She struggled with him, face-to-face, but he would not release her. He concentrated all of his influence on her, and she felt and resisted the unwelcome soothing. But she was also keenly aware of his proximity, which was now having a different but just as immobilizing effect on her.

She stopped struggling, gazing into his eyes with fury. He took her measure for a moment, assessing her volatility, then set her on her feet. He did not release her.

Susan stared with eyes as wide as Jason's, but for different reasons. Jason was frightened by the fighting he had witnessed. The fighting frightened Susan as well, but it was the currents swirling between the two in front of her that dominated her attention.

The man was ruthlessly handsome, as fair as Ryan with startling blue eyes and a virility that was crushing. But it wasn't even his magnificent appearance that was so arresting.

It was the dark and violent sexual tension between he and Ryan that was astonishing, like some great beast that sat between them, ready to consume them both. The sensuality swirled between them, snaking outward with tendrils like smoke from a scarcely hidden fire.

"You can release me now," Ryan said sarcastically.

Aeron relaxed his hold, but still held her firmly against him, his hands about her waist. He glanced down at her with amusement "Aren't you going to introduce me?" he asked, nodding toward Susan.

Ryan's eyes flashed with anger and her jaw closed with an audible snap. Even so, she turned, and in her very compromising position, addressed Susan.

"Susan, this is Aeron," she said, biting her words off, "the one responsible for the attempt on my father's life."

"Hmm, yes," Aeron said without taking his eyes from Ryan, "it's not as if it was the first, my love." He finally raised his eyes to Susan. "I am pleased to meet you, Dr. Ryerson."

Susan gazed into the man's ice blue eyes and found him completely terrifying. Paradoxically, she also found him completely attractive, although it was difficult to reconcile the two.

Aeron turned back to Ryan, and with one final assessment of her stability, released her. Ryan quickly stepped back, pushing him away. Her actions seemed only to amuse him, increasing Ryan's irritation.

"We are on an island," she reminded him scathingly, "I hardly think Dr. Ryerson requires a guard."

Aeron examined the damaged door. "You are probably right," he said, surprising her. "Even so," he said, turning to her directly. "I do not want you to spend time with Dr. Ryerson alone."

Ryan's reply was immediate and caustic. "And at what point in time did you deceive yourself into thinking I care what you want?"

Aeron's reply was as icy as Ryan's was scorching. "Do not make me threaten the doctor in front of her son." He turned to face Ryan fully. "I trust the doctor to make intelligent decisions regarding her actions. I," he said with emphasis, "do not trust you at all."

He turned and stalked from the room, as did Ryan, who turned on her heel and left in the opposite direction.

The two human occupants stared wide-eyed as what was left of the door settled into a semi-closed position. As startling and violent as the entire confrontation had been, Susan had the oddest feeling she had just witnessed a lover's quarrel.

Ryan stood at her father's bedside, gazing down at him. He seemed serene, untouched, exactly as she had last seen him. He appeared no better, but no worse, than when she had been here before.

She sat down on the edge of the bed, taking his hand in hers. It was not warm, but neither was it cold and stiff like the dead. She held it quietly, her thoughts her own.

Aeron could strike at her father at any time. Ryan did not think she could escape with Victor, for Aeron knew where she was every second of the day. She could feel his presence loom over her even now. Although she thought it possible that she herself could escape, it would be quite impossible to take her comatose father.

And Susan Ryerson's presence complicated matters even more. The odds of her being able to rescue both Dr. Ryerson and her son, as well as her father, were minimal. And although Aeron surely knew her loyalty to her father was penultimate, he would not hesitate to use Susan and Jason as leverage.

Ryan glanced down at Victor once more. Aeron would not harm Victor, but not because he did not wish to. Victor's vulnerability was Aeron's greatest weapon against her. If he destroyed Victor, there would be nothing to hold Ryan in check.

Ryan again played all the options through her head. Of course, Aeron could try and kill her, leaving both her father and Susan helpless. But if that had been his objective, he could have easily struck at both of them prior to Ryan ever arriving back at the island. Apparently he had known where they were.

Ryan's eyes narrowed. No, he obviously wanted them as leverage, at least for the time being.

Ryan wandered back to her room. Aeron was not here, but he was not far. She walked out onto the balcony, unsurprised to see their eternal chess game sitting on the table. The rook that she had so aimlessly moved on her last turn was now in jeopardy from an ivory knight. She assessed the board, then turned away, declining to make a move at the moment.

She walked into the adjacent shower room, although "shower" and "room" were not really apt descriptions of the immense facilities.

The bath was a small indoor lake, complete with natural rock and hot springs. The lake had been part of the island prior to their arrival, as well as the hot springs that rose from a great underwater vent on the ocean floor. Victor built the castle around the water features, as well as the volcanic rock, creating a beautiful, prehistoric oasis.

The shower was part of the waterfall that fell adjacent to the castle, although this small portion pooled above, then flowed right through the structure. Ryan moved to it now, removing her clothing. The frigid water felt exhilarating against her skin, its gentle flow washing over her in small cascades. She reached for the bar of hand-made soap, enjoying its scent and frothy lather.

Ryan became aware of a presence, which did not surprise her, nor did it alter her behavior. She glanced over at Aeron, who leaned against a rock, watching her. She ignored him, continuing her ritual.

Aeron, for his part, was fascinated by the spectacle of the carelessly bathing creature. She was slender but powerfully built, no softness, nor hardness about her either, like some sinewy lioness, supple yet ready to strike with devastating strength. He watched the muscles ripple across her back as she bathed, saw the muscles in her thigh and calf flex as she leaned down, saw the perfection in her boyish hips and small backside. His eyes narrowed.

"Do you mind if I join you?" Aeron asked, his tone casual.

Ryan glanced over at him curiously, just the slightest irritation in her voice. "Suit yourself."

She turned away from him, not out of modesty, but because she had returned to her bar of soap. It never occurred to her to feel embarrassment, because nudity held no vulnerability for her, nor any relevance.

She did cast a sidelong glance at him as he undressed, more out of curiosity than anything else. The physical body was of interest to her aesthetically. She appreciated beauty and strength, as did all of their Kind. She rarely differentiated between male and female, enjoying the unique aspects of both.

In her sideways assessment, she realized that Aeron was probably the archetype of the perfect male physique. Broad shoulders and a muscular back tapered to a slender waist and slim hips, with powerful thighs and well-developed calves. He was leanly muscular with no thickness about him anywhere. When he turned, she noted his strong chest and ridged abdominal muscles. She turned back to her washing.

Aeron was aware of the scrutiny, and was amused by it. The girl really was an inhuman creature, possessing none of the normal cues that even their Kind retained after a few decades of humanity.

Ryan was trying to wash her back, which normally she had no difficulty doing. But the wound that had been twice opened beneath her ribs caused her pain, and she was having trouble reaching.

"Would you like me to help you with that?"

Aeron's smooth voice in her ear startled her, as did his proximity.

"I have been bathing myself quite competently for seven hundred years, now," she said, her slight irritation again on display, "I don't think I need your help."

Aeron merely smiled, taking the soap from her hands. He turned her by her shoulders and began lathering his hands. He began massaging the lather into her skin.

The sensation of his hands and the soapy lather against her exceptionally sensitive skin was electrifying. She had to will herself to stand still, wanting to pull away from him and the feelings it aroused. Instead, she stood staidly, patiently, like some great thoroughbred suffering the attention of a stable boy.

For Aeron, the sensations were exhilarating. The feel of her skin beneath his hands and the proximity of her body to his was breathtaking, had he any breath in him. The sight and feel and smell of her was intoxicating. Strangely enough, he felt something stirring within him, something that was quite impossible.

Aeron stopped, and Ryan became aware of his sudden stillness. She turned to look at him over her shoulder. He was looking down, his hands still on her shoulders.

Ryan glanced down curiously. She examined another part of his body, again noting his proportionality. She looked up at him, and he was gazing at her with an indeterminate expression in his blue eyes.

"Does that happen very often?" she asked, the question innocent without naïveté, just a trace amused, but more curious than anything else.

He gazed at her. "It hasn't happened in over 1500 years," he said mildly.

She glanced down again, then turned back to her washing. "It looks inconvenient."

Aeron gazed at the impossible creature in front of him. "Inconvenient" was both an understatement and incredibly accurate. Rhiannon Alexander was "inconvenient" in the same way. He grabbed her shoulders and forcibly turned her to face him.

There was a wicked mischief about her right now as her eyes lingered on the throbbing vein in his neck. Her eyes drifted to his mouth, then to his eyes.

"So are you going to kiss me again?" she asked, more amusement than bite in her words.

And Aeron did just that, biting his lip as his mouth covered hers.

The shock of his blood in her mouth was intensely pleasurable, and Ryan did not resist when the kiss deepened, unable to defy her most primitive instinct. The dark power flowed from his lips into her veins, and Ryan felt her control slipping away.

She turned her head, but he held it fast, gently but firmly guiding her to a new target. Her lips pressed against the throbbing vein in his neck. Although she knew she could not stop the inevitable, she could at least torture him by delay.

Aeron's frustration was immense as the girl lightly bit him, intentionally failing to break the skin. Her lips feathered the skin, cool against his burning flesh. He forcibly lifted her, carrying her three steps to the cushioned face of a smooth rock, where he pulled her down upon him.

"If you don't bite me," he whispered in fury, "I will take every ounce of blood in your body."

Ryan did not cease her torture of the blood vessel. "I get that a lot," she murmured.

He tensed and Ryan knew that she had pushed him as far as she could. It wouldn't have mattered, anyway, for her own hunger was overcoming any self-control she might have had left.

Her teeth sliced into his neck, hard and deep, her lips not letting a single drop of red fall from his skin. He arched and moaned from both pleasure and the sting of her bite. The girl was a monster, a beautiful, seductive, irresistible monster. She shifted her weight, and the feel of her body against his added a level of sensation that strained even his extraordinary senses.

He felt the languor begin to steal over him, felt the dark seduction of this One, the invitation to continue into that warm lethargy. It took every bit of his immense willpower to fight the dreamy torpor that was settling on him, the intoxication of the damned.

He wasn't even certain he could get the girl to stop, so physically powerful was she. But he was strong enough to roll her over, using his superior weight to restrain her beneath him. It took all of his strength, as well as all of his resolve, to pull away from her.

She looked up at him, the preternatural amusement evident.

I will get you sooner or later.

Aeron examined the girl's features, gathering his strength. "I don't think so," he said, lowering his head and violently piercing her neck.

And then he shifted his weight, pinning her, and pierced her again.

Ryan arched from the pain, clutching his back reflexively. It was difficult to determine which was the more painful, the first or second penetration.

For Aeron's part, he immediately froze. He slowly lifted his head, staring down at the girl in astonishment. It had never occurred to him that she was a virgin. He gazed down at her perfect features, searching both her eyes and mind.

There was no recrimination in her, no need, no want, no shame, no anger, no humiliation, truly, no recognizable human emotion associated with sex at all. The pain was natural to her, forever intertwined with desire. And to Aeron's growing understanding and wonder, she examined the act as a true innocent, responding as instinctively and unencumbered as a young wild animal passing into sexual maturity, curious and unafraid.

It was the most erotic thing he had ever come across in his entire, immortal life.

As Aeron examined her thoughts, she voiced one of her own.

"I now see how my mother was nearly killed in this act," she said through slightly clenched teeth.

The comment drove Aeron into madness. He again fell upon her neck, taking her life's blood into him. But instead of driving into her as he wanted, he moved more gently, methodically, with a gentle, painstaking consistency. If "all" of his anatomy was as altered as that which he knew, he could probably seriously injure the girl.

Ryan felt the pain in her neck increase, but the pain in her body decrease, replaced by a gentle but unrelenting rhythm that was in sharp contrast to the driving rhythm of their blood exchange.

Aeron fed on her, but would not allow the lethargy to take hold, demanding that she take his blood in turn. It was a demand that required little coercion, for her hunger was insatiable. The added level of sensation of the physical union was staggering, creating waves of pleasure and pain that threatened to crush them both.

Slowly, inexorably, the two rhythms began to merge, joining into a single driving force. Aeron felt the girl so perfectly joined with him that it seemed they were one, existing in a primordial union so old it would dwarf the history of this world. Their blood passed from one to the other in a continuous flow, surging through one heart and then the other, driven by the same insistent rhythm. The merging of their physical bodies became almost immaterial, simply one more strand of the web that wrapped about them so tightly it constricted time itself.

Aeron did not know if he would reach climax, having never experienced the act since his Change. He did not know if he could sustain the agonizing peak of pleasure that he and the girl had been at for what seemed days. He thought that if he did reach culmination, it would probably kill them both, for there couldn't be anything survivable beyond the ecstasy that they had already experienced.

He was wrong.

He and the girl were in the blood-red netherworld, as intertwined in this world as they were in the real one. But here there were waves of blood, flowing over them, lifting them upward, then crashing them downward, tumbling them about, dangerously close to the edge of blackness. The waves carried them back out to the red sea, but each set brought them inexorably closer to that edge.

Aeron knew that he should care, knew that he should release the girl, but he could not. He could not stop his passion, could not stop his rhythm, could not stop holding her. A wave pushed them to the black sand that edged the darkness, where licking flames cast deep shadows. The girl lay there for a moment, waiting languorously for the redness to wash over them again. She glanced into the blackness, unconcerned, then turned to him. He saw the devilish gleam in her eye, the demonic question she was posing to him

Are you sure you want to mate with the dragon?

Aeron was infuriated and inflamed; he did not relinquish his hold or slow his escalating rhythm in any way. He held her tightly, gazing down, a demonic light in his own eyes.

"My ancient name is Arawn," he said, his blue eyes gleaming.

The girl smiled, understanding the significance.

"And contrary to any foolish myths that state otherwise," he said through tightly clenched teeth, "the god and goddess of the underworld are one."

Rhiannon glanced up at the approaching wave, the face of which seemed to block out the sky. She turned to Aeron.

"I know."

And with one last great thrust, the wave carried them over the edge and into the blackness beyond.

Aeron semi-awoke, his mind clouded. He was exhausted and disoriented, but not so much that he didn't glance down to make certain the girl was still in his arms.

She was, completely unconscious, her features in perfect, angelic, androgynous repose.

He tried to concentrate, but his fatigue was too great. He could not process what had happened, why they were both not dead. He knew that they both had gone willingly into the blackness, but somehow had both survived.

The fatigue he felt was crushing, and he felt himself again drifting in and out of consciousness, listing toward the latter. He knew that the sun had crossed the sky several times during their fierce union. He pulled the girl close, knowing he would awaken if she stirred.

As he again fell asleep, he was disturbed by a flash, something less of a memory and more of an impression. He tried to raise his consciousness to analyze the meaning, but instead this last semi-coherent thought left him with uneasy dreams.

He turned in his sleep as the dreams took hold of him, dreams of something cold, something ancient, something prehistorically reptilian. Something that had reached out of the darkness with great hooked claws and arrested the girl's fall, stopping his descent only because he had been holding on to her.

CHAPTER 22

RYAN AWOKE. SHE WAS ONCE AGAIN in her bed, the feel of silk and the sound of the waterfall instantly familiar. She sat up. Familiar, and yet now completely alien, as was everything she had ever known.

She looked through the billowing curtains onto the balcony beyond. Aeron was seated there, as she knew he would be. She examined him, noting with a certain detachment how devastatingly handsome he was. She rose, leisurely dressed, and joined him on the balcony.

He glanced up as she sat down across from him. He tried to assess her mood, expecting anything from cold fury to complete indifference. He could not really get a fix on her frame of mind, however, as her demeanor seemed very enigmatic.

Ryan gazed down at the chess pieces. The ebony rook was still in jeopardy, but she declined to move it. Instead, she leaned forward, and moved a bishop that seemed quite out of play at the moment.

Aeron studied the move, realizing the rook had been a feint. The bishop was two moves away from placing his queen in an unrecoverable position. He studied the board for a moment longer, recognizing the very dangerous pattern developing. He placed his hand on the queen, preparing to move it, when there was a loud knock at the door.

"Come in," he said, irritation evident in his voice. He moved the queen, removing his hand from the piece. He looked up at the cowering servant who approached, while Ryan didn't bother. She leaned forward and now moved the rook. Aeron glanced quickly at the move, his attention divided, then back at the man.

"What?" he demanded, furious at the interruption.

"My lord," the man began, his voice shaking. He stopped, so great was his fear at delivering his message.

"If you don't spit it out, man," Aeron said, seething, "I will cut you into pieces where you stand."

"My lord," the man said, quaking, "Victor Alexander is gone."

Aeron glanced sharply at Ryan, who did not look up, the only indication that she had heard the slightest trace of a smile about her lips.

The man continued, his words tumbling out. "The doctor and her son are gone as well."

Aeron did not take his eyes from Ryan, who appeared immersed in the game board. "It's your move," she murmured.

"Where are they?" he asked, tightly controlled fury in his voice.

Ryan turned to look at him with her unblinking gaze. "It's your move," she said pointedly.

Aeron was furious, but knew he would not get a response without patronizing her. He reached down and moved the queen again, slamming the piece down.

"Where are they?" he again demanded, seething.

Ryan glanced up, amusement in her eyes. "I don't know," she said simply.

Aeron was about to explode, but then realized that the girl was telling the truth. There was no deception in her reply or in her mind.

Ryan casually lifted a knight, moving the piece its few spaces over and up. She spoke quietly, still amused, but with a subtle amazement in her words as well. "Whomever took them was powerful enough to come here unbeknownst to either you or I, someone powerful enough to move about completely unrevealed." She leaned back. "It's your move again."

Aeron looked down at the board, but his concentration was interrupted by the man who was still cowering nearby.

"My, my lord—," the man stammered.

"What?" Aeron said, biting off the syllable and fighting the urge to tear the man in two.

The man held a simple white envelope extended from his shaking hand.

"What is this?" Aeron demanded, snatching it from the man's grasp.

"I don't know, my lord." He nodded, indicating Ryan. "It's from the doctor, and it's addressed to her."

Aeron glared at Ryan, ripping the envelope open. He removed a single sheet of paper, staring at in incomprehension. He looked back up at her.

"What is this?" he demanded.

Ryan was still studiously ignoring the entire situation, her attention on the chess board. "I don't know," she said for the second time. "It's still your turn."

His fury was immense and growing. He wanted to tear the girl in two, but again he sensed that she was telling the truth. He leaned, down, slammed his queen into a new position, and thrust the piece of paper in front of her face.

Ryan took the paper, still engrossed in the board. She took her time, again moving her knight before turning her attention to the paper. She studied it for a long moment, noting a familiar, unique pattern, then lowered it as if it were no matter. "It's your turn again."

Aeron was seething at the implied blackmail. Her infernal sense of humor was going to get her killed, because he was out of patience with the entire situation. He again quickly examined the board, staying with his strategy. He moved his bishop into position to take out the knight that was aggravating his queen.

Ryan glanced up at the servant who was still quaking in the doorway. "You are dismissed," she said.

The servant turned on his heel, gladly obeying the absolute authority in that voice. This incensed Aeron further, and he snatched the letter from Ryan's hand.

"What is this?" he again demanded.

Ryan leaned back, thoughtful. "Do you know what mitochondrial DNA is?"

Aeron's reply was scathing. "No, my dear. I knew just enough of DNA to pay someone to create the pathogen that targeted your beloved father."

Ryan nodded, still thoughtful. "And me as well."

Aeron smiled. "And you as well, although it did not have quite the desired affect."

Ryan examined the chess board. "In theory, it shouldn't have affected me at all since mitochondrial is passed entirely down the mother's line." Ryan leaned forward, moving her knight. "But Victor and I are so genetically similar that I did inherit his."

"Obviously not enough," Aeron said.

"Not enough," Ryan agreed. "Not enough to affect me the way it did him."

Ryan was silent for a long moment. "It's your turn."

Aeron's irritation was lessening. He would find Victor, as well as the one who stood against his will. It was a short list. He looked back up at Ryan. And he would keep the girl with him, one way or another. He thought of their recent prolonged coupling. He could think of a few ways to restrain her right now. He moved the ivory bishop.

Ryan examined the move, continuing her conversation. "It was quite a brilliant plan though. Mitochondrial DNA can be quite common among people, and so specifically targeting it with a pathogen could be risky." Ryan moved a pawn. "Except when dealing with someone like Victor, who is so genetically unique that the target is precise."

He leaned forward, moving his castle. "So what is in that letter?" he said, still irked.

Ryan examined the move. "It's a DNA profile." She moved the pawn again, then looked up at him. "Yours."

Aeron felt time stop for him. The chess board seemed very far away, too far away for him to reach. Ryan conversationally asked a rhetorical question.

"Who knew that you and Victor were so close?"

Aeron felt the blood begin to pool in his extremities. "What are you saying?" he asked quietly.

"It's your move," Ryan said, gazing at him intently.

With a slight feeling of numbness, Aeron leaned forward and moved the bishop, knowing otherwise he would get no reply.

Ryan glanced at the board, then back up at him. "Apparently you and Victor had a common maternal ancestor," she said with some amusement, "not a mother, not a grandmother, but probably within three or four generations."

The numbness seeped into his lower extremities as the girl continued. "With that close of match, I am fairly certain the pathogen will affect you the same way it did Victor, since you have basically the same profile."

Then, very slowly and very deliberately, she leaned forward to move her rook for the very last time. She looked up at him, preternatural amusement in her unblinking eyes.

"Checkmate."

Aeron stared down at the board, stunned. It seemed impossible that it could have come to this. The pieces seemed to swim before him. He counted backward the moves that had transpired since the day she had so audaciously told him to surrender.

"Twenty," she confirmed for him.

He slowly raised his head, understanding but still disbelieving. He thought through every move that he had made, every contingency. He stared at the girl across from him. When he finally spoke, his words had a tinge of incredulity, a hint of resignation, but for the most part were amazingly matter-of-fact.

"You are in love with me," he stated.

Ryan said nothing, but did not deny it.

"—And yet," he continued, intrigued, "you would destroy me."

Ryan leaned forward, tipping the ivory king onto its side. She leaned back, steadily holding his gaze. "It seems to be my way," she said simply.

"And so what will you do with me," he asked, sarcasm creeping into his voice, "place me on a pedestal next to your corpse of a father?"

Ryan smiled a wicked smile. "Perhaps." She appeared to give the matter great thought. "Or maybe I will bury you at the bottom of the sea, in the chamber a mile beneath where we sit right now."

A dangerous glint appeared in Aeron's eyes. "Then perhaps you will go with me."

Ryan shook her head ruefully. "I'm afraid not. I have other engagements, including my coronation."

There was a lethal edge to Aeron right now. He was not going into the blackness alone. He would take the girl one way or another.

"The pathogen will not affect me that quickly," Aeron said. "I have more than enough time to settle with you."

Ryan again appeared regretful. "No, actually I'm afraid you only have," she paused, cocking her head to one side, "about four seconds."

It took two seconds for Aeron to process what she was saying, one second for her to get to the balcony's railing, and half a second for him to lunge and miss, feeling her slip through his grasp.

And then the world exploded.

CHAPTER 23

THE VESSEL EASED INTO THE SHALLOW WATERS. Several men jumped out, dragging the craft up onto the beach. One turned and politely helped a young, red-headed woman from the still rocking boat. She stepped onto the beach, her expression grim, as was that of the older, patrician gentleman who joined her.

"Dear God," Susan whispered under her breath. Although Edward was silent, he shared her assessment.

The island was destroyed. Where massive cliffs had once risen above the sea, there were now huge piles of rubble. Where there had been a waterfall, there was a great gaping black hole. There were no longer trees or plants or grass, or any type of stone edifices. Everything was flattened. The destruction was total.

A second vessel brushed into the sand, and there was a great deal of commotion as the men on the beach prepared for the next arrival, whom they greeted with great respect and reverence. The largest among them positioned themselves to help the beautiful older woman step onto the beach, who, despite her appearance, exited with effortless grace.

Susan turned to Abigail, wanting some type of reassurance, but Abigail, as always, was impossible to read. Her expression was unfathomable, tranquil but not encouraging, serene but not inspiring. The men quickly spread out in a search pattern.

In light of the fact that Susan was the only human occupant on the island, it was surprising that she found the object of their search before any of the others, and very quickly.

"Here, over here!" she yelled. She kneeled down to the severely-injured, unconscious figure, placing her hands on the artery in Ryan's throat. She couldn't feel a pulse, but that didn't mean anything. Edward came up behind her.

"Help me get these rocks off her."

Edward required no prompting, he was already hurling boulders from his master. He inwardly flinched when he saw what he uncovered. His master was grievously wounded. He did not see, or sense, any life signs from her. He was joined by several burly men, who also began flinging rocks from the prone figure.

Abigail approached on the arm of her consort, elegantly picking her way through the rubble.

"Here, stabilize her legs and spine so we can roll her over," Susan ordered. The men complied without hesitation. Susan took position at Ryan's head, stabilizing the neck.

"Ready. One, two, three."

The crew rolled the figure over with a gentleness that was astonishing, considering their rather fearsome appearance. Susan again felt for any life signs, frustrated because she didn't find any, frustrated because that didn't mean anything. She turned, looking up at Abigail, as did everyone who stood there.

Abigail stared down at the lifeless body, assessing.

"She lives," Abigail said at last.

Susan let out an audible sigh of relief, as did Edward, although his gesture was more from habit than need. Abigail nodded to her consort, who let loose several commands in a language that Susan had never heard. A troupe quickly assembled, two abreast and four deep. A platform was brought forward and set down next to Ryan's prone form. Then gently, with great deference and ceremony, the eight men lifted the girl and lay her on the platform. They then lifted the platform shoulder-high and began to slowly, solemnly carry it through the rubble, preceded by Abigail on the arm of her consort.

Susan followed the assembly, which seemed so filled with ritual and meaning, she felt she were following the funeral procession of a king.

EPILOGUE

JASON RAN THROUGH THE WELL-MANICURED gardens of the palatial estate. He particularly liked the maze in the ornamental gardens, because he could get lost in all the twists and turns. He could hear his mother calling him, her voice filled with exasperation. He giggled and sprinted into the maze.

He had rounded only the third hedge when he ran headlong into a man, tripping over his feet He would have fallen had the man not caught him.

"Hey there sport, better watch out."

Jason blushed. "I'm sorry, sir. I didn't see you there."

The man leaned down so that Jason didn't have to look up so high. He smiled a brilliant smile, his teeth white against his ebony skin. "That's okay." He cocked his head to one side. "I think I hear your mother coming, better be quiet."

Jason giggled, leaning against the hedge with his now fellow conspirator. He could hear his mom coming, too.

"Jason, if you don't get back here right this min—"

Jason jumped out at Susan just as she rounded the corner.

Susan gave out a little yelp, more to satisfy Jason than anything else. She could hear his giggling a mile away, and even if she hadn't, he was hardly enough to frighten her, considering what she had been through.

She was embarrassed, however, when she realized Jason wasn't alone.

"Oh, hi," she said, brushing her hair from her eyes. "I'm sorry. I hope Jason wasn't being too much of a nuisance."

The man stepped from the shadows, and Susan felt her heart miss a beat. The man was devilishly handsome with a gorgeous smile. He had beautiful, warm eyes and the knee-weakening charisma of all of Ryan's Kind.

He extended his hand.

"Dr. Ryerson, my name is Raphael."

"Like the turtle!" Jason yelled, running off.

"Or the painter," Raphael offered ruefully, his eyes on Susan.

Susan took his hand in hers. "Please call me Susan."

She held his hand for a moment, then blushed. "Oh, I'm sorry." She backed away nervously. "I guess I should find Jason."

"Let me help you," Raphael offered, and Susan felt an unfamiliar leap of joy at the prospect.

They exited the maze, and Jason again jumped out at them.

"Boo!" he yelled with more enthusiasm than success.

Raphael caught him, swinging him effortlessly up onto his shoulders. He smiled down at Susan, offering his arm.

Susan hesitated only the briefest moment, just enough to suggest some sort of decorum, then settled comfortably on his arm. They walked arm-in-arm across the courtyard.

Marilyn moved into the courtyard and began walking toward Edward, having already sensed his presence. Dr. Ryerson was in her path, and quite surprisingly, on the arm of one of her Kind, a handsome young black man. They were talking intimately, as if old friends.

As she neared, she had the subtlest sense of familiarity. The man was of her lineage.

Raphael looked up, amazed at the One coming toward him. The woman was ravishingly beautiful, with power beyond reason. Every step, every tilt of her hip, every flick of her eyelashes, every smoldering glance bespoke seduction. As she stalked by, she flicked that smoldering gaze

Susan's way, amusement in her voice.

"Enjoy yourself, Dr. Ryerson."

The raven-haired woman did not alter her stride, and did not look back. Raphael glanced down at Susan, who had turned bright red.

For whatever reason, he felt like hugging her.

And so he did.

Ryan stood at the window, watching.

"You have chosen well."

Ryan knew Abigail was there, even before she had spoken.

"He seems an appropriate match."

Ryan looked down at her hands on the windowsill. There was a long moment of silence before she spoke again.

"I should not have doubted you."

Abigail smiled.

"I told you," she said serenely, "I live to serve your father." She moved to Ryan's side, staring out the window. "As I live to serve you."

Ryan continued to look out the window, but was staring at nothing. Abigail extended her influence to the girl, sensing her mood. It was subdued, filled with a strange uncertainty. Ryan made no attempt to hide her mind from the matriarch.

Abigail found the girl's mood fascinating, because the girl was now more powerful than she had ever been, perhaps even more powerful than her father. Having recovered from her wounds and nearly defeated the virus in her system, Ryan had risen like a phoenix from the ashes of the world she had destroyed.

But as always, Ryan seemed oblivious to this fact.

Ryan felt Abigail's gentle, insistent probing, felt her influence settle on her like some great mantle, soothing and seductive. She closed her eyes, offering no resistance.

Abigail smiled. It was time.

"Come rest with me awhile, my dear," she said gently.

Ryan knew that it was not a request. And with the peculiar obedience that only Abigail inspired in her, she took the hand that the matriarch offered, allowing her to lead her from the room.

Abigail leaned against a pile of cushions, settling into the bed, smoothing her skirt. Ryan lay down beside her, her head upon the cushions and upon Abigail's lap.

Abigail stroked her hair, and Ryan closed her eyes at the sensation. She could feel Abigail's presence settle on her, its comforting warmth spreading throughout her extremities, ensnaring her, entangling her, binding her.

Ryan did not resist in any way, opening her eyes only when she felt Abigail's silent command. She looked up.

Abigail held the girl's gaze, then slowly pulled the neckline of her gown to the side, revealing the smooth, perfect skin below. Ryan eyes dropped to the hand's resting place, below the collarbone, just above the breast. She saw the blood that flowed through the vein, just beneath the cream-colored skin.

And she saw clearly, Abigail's control over her, saw that to take her blood was to subjugate herself in ways she little understood, perhaps forever. Ryan saw that not all dominance came by physical power, and realized that she was facing One who was master of that alternate domain.

Ryan no longer cared. She leaned forward, slicing the perfect skin, and felt the blood flow into her mouth.

For once, Abigail was unable to maintain her perfect poise. It seemed impossible that the hunger of another could bring her such pleasure. She held the girl in her arms, cradling her head, feeling the warmth of the girl's need spread throughout her body.

In the instant Abigail's blood touched her lips, Ryan grasped an astonishing fact: Abigail had concealed herself from all of them. She was startled at the enormous power residing in the woman she fed upon, sensing the immense force coiled inside Abigail like a colossal, primeval serpent. She tried to process this information, to comprehend the motive, to understand the implications. But it was too late.

The serpent was unwinding.

Ryan laid her head back on the cushion, a trace of blood on her lips. She gazed up at Abigail, whose eyes were filled with amusement, an enigmatic smile on her lips.

"It is time, little one."

Ryan could not resist her, could not withstand her gentle, indomitable, controlling seduction. She turned her head, laying her fevered cheek against the cool, silky softness, leaving the throbbing veins in her neck exposed.

Abigail lowered her head, and Ryan felt the coolness of her lips just before she felt the sting of her teeth. The ache did not subside, but rather swelled to keep pace with the accompanying pleasure. Ryan felt the blood drain from her system, felt the dangerous lassitude begin to steal over her, felt her limbs grow heavy, and conversely, her body grow unbearably light. She could not fight, did not want to fight, the languor that stole her will.

Abigail's pleasure was intense, the dark power she was consuming at times threatening to consume her. But she was in complete control, reveling in the sights and sensations the girl provided, forcing the girl gently but firmly into complete submission. She savored the culmination of her six hundred year seduction, enjoying it the more for its intricate, convoluted path. She pushed the girl's heart, demanding obedience from that organ as well, treating it with the same tender and torturous domination she did the girl.

Ryan was in the blood-red netherworld, unsurprised that she was there by herself. Abigail had deceived them all, disguising her immense power with her cool poise and demeanor, her matronly elegance, her aloof refinement. Ryan stood on the very edge of the blackness, looking into the void. She wondered what it would feel like when she fell into the darkness, and felt curiously detached at the prospect.

The world swayed, and she teetered on the edge. Her balance was such that it would take merely a push to pitch her headfirst into the void. She was not surprised when she felt that pressure at her back, nor when she felt her weight began to shift inexorably forward.

She was surprised, however, when that momentum was arrested, and her fall halted by a powerful grasp. She was pulled rearward into an all-encompassing embrace.

"I will not allow that, little one," came the seductive whisper in her ear.

Ryan gazed into the blackness, then closed her eyes. And as she had so many times in the physical world, she took Abigail's hand and pressed it to her chest.

Edward escorted Marilyn to Victor's side.

"Would you like to be alone, my lady?"

Marilyn shook her head. "No. I simply wanted to pay my respects."

Edward stared down at the prone man. "Dr. Ryerson believes that Ryan's blood will provide a cure for her father."

Marilyn did not look up. "That is not surprising. The girl has many gifts."

"As does the One who holds her now."

Marilyn glanced over at Edward sharply. "And what gift do you believe Abigail has?"

Edward did not lower his eyes, and although his words were circumspect, there was an underlying edge to them. "I believe she has a gift that no one else has."

"And what might that be?" Marilyn asked, sarcasm in her voice.

Edward still did not yield. "The ability to hide from Ryan."

Marilyn's eyes narrowed. This little man had more insight than she gave him credit for. She was intrigued by his speculation. "Go on."

Edward began his list. "Victor is 'indisposed.' Aeron is missing and possibly destroyed. Kusunoki and Ala have sworn allegiance to Ryan, and you yourself are loyal to my master."

Marilyn did not speak, waiting for him to continue.

"It seems that out of everyone in this protracted, tragic situation, Abigail has emerged unscathed."

Edward gazed at her with unblinking eyes.

"And now she has Ryan," Marilyn finished for him.

"Yes," Edward said, "now she has Ryan."

Marilyn stared at the patrician gentleman. "It would be best for you to keep your thoughts to yourself on this matter," she said, her warning apparent.

Edward nodded politely, bowing as the dark-haired woman brushed by him. He noted that she had not disagreed with him.

Marilyn entered Abigail's chambers, noting that they were decorated in Abigail's ever-present white. In fact, this room was decorated overwhelmingly in white, with no color in it anywhere. The carpets were white, the drapes were white, the comforter was white. Even Abigail was dressed in white, leaning against white cushions, holding the girl, dressed in white, in her arms.

The only color in the entire room was a touch of red upon Abigail's décolleté, and a trace of the same color upon Ryan's lips. Ryan slept like a child in Abigail's arms.

"I am surprised you do not feed her from your breast," Marilyn said scathingly.

Abigail merely smiled at the barb, stroking the girl's hair. "That is always a possibility, my dear."

Marilyn's eyes narrowed at the thought. Ryan shifted feverishly, and Abigail stroked her soothingly, calming her. She again turned her attention to the dark-haired woman in front of her. She continued casually.

"You see, Marilyn, that was your mistake, as was everyone else's."

Marilyn could not control her sarcasm. "And what might that be?"

Abigail again stroked the girl's hair, reveling in the dormant power present in the prone figure even now. Her words were calm, matter-of-fact.

"Ryan does not need friends, companions, or lovers," she said simply. "She does not need servants, or subjects, or acquaintances of any Kind." Abigail looked up a Marilyn. "She could have those without measure." She returned to stroking the girl. "There is only one thing that Ryan has lacked in her entire, eternal, immortal life."

"And what is that?" Marilyn asked, her sarcasm barely contained.

Abigail gazed at her, a gleam in her eye.

"A mother."

And Marilyn understood. Understood how great the orchestration, how complex the manipulation, how deep the hooks were that now pierced Ryan's skin. She now understood Abigail's game, from start to finish.

"And so now you will fill that role for her," Marilyn said, putting the final pieces together.

Abigail did not respond, the triumph in her eyes speaking for her.

Marilyn thought through all of the implications, thought about the man lying in the next room comatose, thought about the thousands who had died in this diversion, thought about the girl lying exhausted before her. She placed the final piece.

"And now you are Queen Mother," Marilyn said.

Abigail could have offered any number of responses, any number of excuses, any number of clarifications. She could have offered any number of explanations, objections, or elucidations. She could have agreed or disagreed, confirmed or denied.

Instead, she simply sat there, stroking the girl's feverish brow, gazing up at Marilyn with the unblinking gaze of their Kind.

And she smiled.